Once Upon a *Drunken* Angel

A Novel by

Robert Remail

Once Upon a Drunken Angel by Robert Remail.

© 2023 by Robert Remail

ISBN 9798856372662

Cover Design by 100Covers.com

To everyone who has loved before…

each giving a piece of their heart
and taking a piece of someone else's in return,
for the things taught to one another and the things learned,
for the gentle words spoken and the promises made,
for the hands held when they needed holding
and the hugs given and received when wanted most,
and lastly, for the tenderness of the gift we call love!

Once Upon a *Drunken* Angel

Book One

Model

The first time I ever saw him, he was sitting alone at a small table trying to return a glass of wine, which was not to his liking. I had just walked into the Mediterra Beach Club, which was located a stone's throw away from where I lived, a place called—you guessed it—Mediterra. The club sat on the Gulf of Mexico, on a beautiful beach called Bonita. Mediterra was a gated community for the slightly snobby and above crowd. I was the former of the two, I suppose, because I resided in a rather nice but small townhouse, not one of the large single-family homes abundant in Mediterra.

I had a date that afternoon with a model. Yes, you heard me correctly—I had a date with a model. I arrived early to get a good spot near the boats. Location was important when trying to impress, and I was definitely trying to impress. Models don't come around that often for me, and I wanted this one to count. Truth be told—something I have a big problem with—she was my first and only model.

I should mention that she was also a blind date, compliments of my sister, Lucy, who works in Miami as a photographer with the occasional model or two for clients. Lucy stayed on the vague side when I asked her how she had convinced this woman to go out with me; it certainly wasn't from showing her a picture, that's for sure. I'm not a bad-looking guy; it's just that I'm not a handsome one either. I seem to slide right down the middle in the looks and body department. I work out at the gym as often as I hit the lottery, so this being June, I'd say I hit the weights zero times this year.

The Grill, which is the club's best restaurant, was always crowded and always fun. I knew at least a dozen people here, and that was just in the outdoor section. I hadn't been inside yet, but the bar's patrons were spilling through both doors and onto the terrace. Definitely a happening day here, and I was hoping the view and atmosphere would have a hypnotic effect on my date. Maybe, just maybe, I would get lucky later.

But first, I had to convince her I was not a loser. Believe me, at forty-two years old, never married, and only middle-of-the-road successful, that can be hard to do. So what was my plan? Same one I always go with: fabrication. That's right, I fib a little or, depending on the situation, I fib a lot. I don't think fibbing is such a bad thing; I find it a helpful tool in dealing with the opposite sex. I tried that truth thing a few times in the past, but it was so dull, and I always regretted the choice, so now I go with slight fabrication, and sometimes it actually works. The downside? It never works for long. Sooner or later, people see through my cock-and-bull, and that's the end of that.

But today I felt lucky. I had this hunch ever since getting out of bed this morning that today was my day. Let's call it a premonition that I, Michael Holland, was about to come into some good luck.

As I looked for a table with an exceptional water view, I passed a man dressed all in white, including a button-down shirt with the long sleeves rolled up to give it that three-quarter look and white shorts that reached his knees. He had risen from his seat and was insisting to the waiter that he'd been brought the wrong wine.

The Truth

I was caught off guard when this same white-clad man called out to me. "Michael!" he said. "Please come here and tell this good man that this is not Stag's Leap Cabernet."

I don't know what compelled me—maybe the fact that I was only a couple feet away or the way Whitey had called me by name—but I turned and approached his table with an affable expression at the ready. I hadn't a clue who the guy was or how he knew me, but who was I to question another man questioning a Stag's Leap Cabernet?

I approached the table and realized that Whitey dwarfed me by at least four inches. He had silvery white hair, too long and too gray for a man his age, which I'd guess to be mid-forties. A pair of black sunglasses sat on his table beside a book that had no title or picture on its cover. It was just a leather-bound book, the same size as any other book you'd carry to the beach or pool. On his head was a straw hat, straight out of a Panama Jack advertisement except that it was white. Which seemed odd because I couldn't recall ever seeing a white one before.

"Be the judge and tell us please, Michael, Stag's Leap or bottom-of-the-barrel sludge?"

I didn't know squat about wine because I'm a diehard beer drinker, but what the hell? I lifted the glass and gave the contents a quick sniff. Then I took a sip, swirled it around in my mouth, swallowed, and declared it sludge.

The waiter, who didn't look old enough to drink, made a quiet apology and said he'd return with another glass. Whitey raised his hand and his voice to get the waiter's attention. "And please bring my friend here a bottle of Stella. He'll be joining me, thank you."

The waiter disappeared and I found myself a little confused.

Whitey grinned. "You look like you're going to burst, Michael. I bet you're just bubbling inside with questions, yes?"

I sure was, but I didn't know where to start. "Have we met?" I asked.

"Never. But I know all about you, Michael."

"Let's start with that. How do you know my name?"

"Like I said, I know all about you, from the cradle to this morning, when you climbed out of bed and felt like today was your lucky day."

Okay, that floored me. Creepy, to say the least. "All right, buddy, joke's over. I've got a date, and it's time I said goodbye."

"Oh, she's not coming. I believe the term is, 'you've been stood up.'"

I stared at him, my mouth agape, wondering who the hell this character really was and what he wanted from me.

"Your model, Michael—Domino, I believe her name is—well, she's had a change of heart. It appears that the favor she was doing for your sister, Lucy, wasn't worth it. You see, your sister did indeed show her your picture, and Domino realized that her time could be better spent elsewhere."

"How the hell—"

"I feel terrible for you, truly I do, but there is a bright side. There's always a bright side, remember that."

The waiter returned and placed our drinks on the table. My new friend sat down and enjoyed a satisfying sip from his glass. "Ah, now that's Stag's Leap." He nodded at the waiter. "My compliments to you, my young friend."

The waiter smiled as he departed. I then dropped into the chair beside my omniscient acquaintance and gave him a good hard look. "What's this all about? How do you know so much

4

about me?"

"Let me start by introducing myself. I am the archangel Gabriel. And it is such a pleasure to finally meet you."

I picked up my Stella and took a long pull. Then I gazed into the eyes of my drinking companion, which were the brightest blue I'd ever seen. And his smile was so quick and contagious. If I had to pick one word to describe him? Happy, dammit. Utterly friggin' happy.

Please Be Understanding

"Am I being filmed?" I said. "Is this like a *Punk'd* reality show?"

Then I took another swig of my beer and a quick peek at my watch. Hm, my date did seem to be running late.

"Michael, I told you, Domino isn't coming. You're being stood up."

Okay, nice eyes, great smile, but this guy was pushing the envelope and getting on my nerves now. Still, I didn't want to cause a scene and have Domino's first impression of me be of the confrontational type.

Whitey/Gabriel sighed. "What shall I do to convince you that I'm speaking the truth, Michael? Tell me what to say or do to convince you that I'm here to help, not hurt."

"Why would I need help?" I asked, trying not to sound as annoyed as I was. "And what could you do, anyway?"

"I'm the answer to your prayers, Michael. Listen, you've been skipping church every Sunday for the last ten years, am I right?"

I nodded.

"You attended Catholic school all the way through college, correct?"

Again, I nodded.

"And you've been praying every day for as long as you can remember for a woman to fall in love with you. A woman who would love you unconditionally and make you happy and content. A woman who would fill in the missing parts of your life."

I spit out the beer in my mouth, giving everyone in the vicinity something to laugh at. Then I stood up and wiped away the liquid running down my shirt. Enough of this!

"Who the hell are you?" I shouted.

"Oh, sit back down. You're making a dreary spectacle of yourself. Besides, I already told you who I am. I'm the archangel Gabriel."

"Okay, Gabe, you said you're here to help me, right?"

"Yes, I'm here in answer to your prayers."

"And for the record, how does that work?"

"I've already told you things no one else could possibly know. Who else knows about your secret prayers? Have you ever mentioned them to anyone?"

He had me there. I'd never spoken to a soul about my prayers—ever. I took a closer look-see at the guy. Something was amiss, but I couldn't get a grip on it. "Okay, let's see a miracle."

Gabe just stared at me, expressionless for a full minute.

"If you are who you say you are," I continued, "then prove it. Any run-of-the-mill miracle will do."

"Given that you're such a good Catholic boy, I'm sure you're familiar with the scriptures. Thou shall not put thy God to the test. Ring a bell?"

"Something like that, sure, but you're not God, remember? You're an archangel, completely different thing."

"I hadn't thought about it that way. You're quite right. Okay, I'll do it. I'm sure the boss will be perturbed with me, but I'll deal with it later. What would you have me do? Uh, no, there will be none of that. No mountain of gold or endless supply of supermodels."

"Wait. You read my mind?"

"A dog could read your mind, Michael. So what's it going to be? Wait. I've got one, and I've done it before. Quite simple, really. I'll stop time. Will that be satisfactory?"

"The floor is all yours, Nostradamus. Take it away."

"All right, I'm going to need a little help with this. Repeat after me, if you will: Alakazam."

I snorted. "Are you serious?"

"Please, just do as I ask."

Gabe raised his hands off the table and gave them a shake, then peered into my eyes. "Abracadabra," he said. "Alakazam. Hocus-pocus. And... presto-change-o!" Then he clapped once and waved his hands again through the air. "Boom!" He yelled the last word so loudly that everyone around us turned to stare at the two oddballs.

Gabe was laughing quietly. "You should have seen your face, Michael. Priceless! Got you, didn't I?" Still chuckling, he leaned in closer. "I said I was an archangel, not a magician. But seeing your face, it was worth the trip down here just for that."

"Are you through? Can I go home now?"

"No, I told you I would stop time for you. But just for one minute, not a second more. And I'm an angel of my word."

"Fine, stop it then, Mr. Archangel."

"I already did."

Vicky Verky

The first thing that hit me was the sound, or should I say the lack of sound? It was dead-friggin' silent, like I'd never heard before. You could hear a frog farting fifty miles away. Slowly, I turned my head. Everything and everyone was frozen, like in some crazy-ass dream where I was the only one who could get up and move around, able to do whatever I wanted. Immediately, I rose from my chair and explored my surroundings.

"How did you… What did you…"

"Well, as Jimmy likes to say, it's simply complicated."

"Who's Jimmy? Is that you-know-who's first name?" I asked, pointing skyward.

"Don't be silly. I'm quoting Jimmy Buffett, my go-to, my man. I simply adore him. So much wisdom and talent for such a tiny man. Keep hoping I'll get to meet him. Could you imagine me meeting the one and only Jimmy Buffett?"

"Can't you just go *poof* and go see him?" I said, snapping my fingers.

"Boss wouldn't allow it. We're here to serve Him, not ourselves." Gabe gestured to the statue-like figures in our midst. "Take a good look around, Michael. Just ten seconds left."

I approached a cute female bar patron. What the heck, she'll never know. So I reached out and—

"Don't even think about it," Gabe said. "Now sit yourself back down."

With a sigh, I took one last look around. I still couldn't believe what I was seeing. And then with no magic incantations, no waving of the arms or hands, everything and everyone started moving again.

"Another round, gentlemen?" Our young waiter hovered over

us.

Gabriel spoke right up. "Wonderful idea. We'll both have the same, please."

And before I could process what had transpired, the waiter was off, then back again with our drinks, and I was still waking up from what felt like a crazy dream.

"It takes a couple of minutes to readjust after the time jumps," Gabe said. "You'll be fine in a moment."

"You really are an archangel?"

"That's what I've been trying to tell you, my friend."

"What are you doing here? What do you want from me?"

"Ah, glad you finally asked. I don't want a thing from you. I'm here for you as the answer to your prayers."

"You mean the woman who will allow me to live happily ever after?"

"You've been searching for a soul mate, Michael, and I'm here to give that to you. To introduce you to Michael Holland's one and only soul mate."

I glanced around, then back at Gabe. "Awesome. Where is she? Is she here? When do I get to meet her?"

"It doesn't quite work like that."

"How does it work then, Gabe?"

"I prefer Gabriel, if you don't mind. And we'll start at the beginning. With God. God has heard all of your prayers, and He wants to help. He truly does, but—"

"But what? Is there a problem?"

"The problem is you. You have a small habit of stretching the truth at times. Or should I say, you have a problem navigating through honesty?"

"Huh? What does that mean?"

"It means you're quite the fibber. You have always had a

problem with telling the whole truth. You are a good person, you treat your fellow man correctly, and you're not a thief, but you have left a trail of deceit—a road paved with bullshit—for your entire life."

"Excuse me, Gabriel, but are you allowed to use that kind of language? Just wondering, you know."

"I'm allowed an allotment each calendar year."

"And if you go over it?"

"Required meeting with the boss."

"That a bad thing?"

"Depends on what kind of day He's having."

"And how often does He have a bad day, if I may ask?"

"Let's stick with your problems, shall we, Michael? God has graciously agreed to grant your prayers."

"When?"

"Immediately."

"Holy crap. Can I thank Him?"

"I'm glad you brought that up because there is one teeny weeny tiny bit of a condition that goes along with the big guy answering your prayer."

"Oh, geez."

"God wants you to stop fibbing."

"That's it? Done. No problem."

"There you go again. You just did it."

"What?"

"Told another fib."

"But how——"

"Don't ask; I just know, and we'll leave it at that."

"Then how do we do this? If God doesn't want to take me at my word, then what?"

"That's part of the problem; we both know your word is

worth goose poop, don't we?"

"Does that count as part of your allotment?"

"'Poop' is a freebie."

"Thank God."

"Now you've got the picture." Gabriel laughed while I just stared and awaited further explanation. "Don't you think that was funny, Michael? Come now. Like Jimmy says, if we all couldn't laugh, then we'd all go insane."

"Gabriel, please just tell me where we stand with this truth-telling thing."

"Sorry, I've a tendency to get off-track every now and again. Back to business. All God wants from you is a demonstration. He would like you to tell the truth and nothing but the truth—so help you, you-know-who—for one week, starting right now."

"So I can't tell a lie for one week? That's it? Easy-peasy. I can totally do that!"

Revue

I sat back in my chair, thinking I really had won the lottery. "Just to be clear, if I, Michael, can tell the truth for one straight week, starting today, God will answer my prayer and find me true love? Does that about sum it up?"

"Yes."

"Is God going to watch me for the next week?"

"God is always watching you, but more to your point, no. That's why I'm here. I'll be by your side, day and night, for one week."

"But how will you know if I'm lying?"

Gabriel sighed and seemed bored. "Really? I mean, an angel

11

knows what an angel knows."

"Then that settles it. I'll do it, no problem."

"I like your confidence, not to mention your spunk. Let's begin."

A strange feeling enveloped me. I believed that Gabriel was indeed who he said, but I had this sneaking suspicion that I was being watched—by someone other than Gabriel. My body shivered, but I couldn't shake the paranoid feeling.

"Oh, and Michael, one more small thing I forgot to mention."

"Here we go."

"It's just that you can't tell anyone who I really am, and you can't lie about it either."

"Well, that's certainly a pickle."

"I'm sure you'll come up with something. Just don't lie, and don't tell anyone that I am the archangel Gabriel. Okay, the clock is running."

"What should I do first?"

"You might want to start by paying your tab."

"Right, yes, good idea. Can I get your tab for you?"

"You already have. I charged it to your account when I arrived."

"Nice. But I mean, where should we go from here?"

"Where would you normally go from here?"

"Home."

"Then home it is."

"Tell me, Michael, how are you fixed for fine wine back at your place?"

"Nil. Does that about sum it up for you?"

"Indeed. We will have to remedy that. What say we stop on the way home at an establishment that prides itself on the selling of fine wines?"

Remember What

"Some people say there is a little bit of heaven right here on earth, and I agree," Gabriel spouted. "It's right here, under our own feet. We surely have arrived." Then we walked through the doors of Total Wine, the largest wine purveyor in the state. Gabriel was drawing looks everywhere we went. The stares and reactions varied from individual to individual. Some looked at him as though he were an eccentric like Mark Twain, a strange codger who'd stepped out of the past. Others seemed curious, as if they might know the white-clad gentleman. Still others gazed at him wantonly, if that makes any sense.

Gabriel strolled the aisles like a child at an amusement park for the first time. His smile and joy reverberated throughout the store, and he seemed in no rush to leave. He lingered near the red selections, seeming utterly dismissive of the whites. I made a mental note to ask him about the difference between red and white. Maybe I could learn a little something during our week together.

As Gabriel wandered to another section, I stretched to my full height of 5 feet, 11 and 3/4 inches, and grabbed a bottle from the upper shelf. Silver Oak Cabernet, the label said, for 174 dollars! What? How could a bottle of wine cost that much? Crazy! As I stepped back to check out additional overpriced bottles, she hit me with her cart.

"I'm terribly sorry," the beautiful stranger said. "Are you okay?"

"I'm fine, really, no worries, all good," I said, sounding like an idiot.

"I really need to pay more attention. I've been told I'm a terror with shopping carts." She pointed at the bottle in my hand.

"Mm, you've got great taste. That's a personal favorite of mine."
Her sunny smile lit up the place.

Out of nowhere, Gabriel appeared. He grabbed the bottle
from my hands and placed it in his already-full cart. "Great taste
indeed, Michael," he said before continuing on with his
shopping.

"He a friend of yours?" the pretty lady asked.

"Remember, Michael," Gabriel yelled from afar, "I can hear
you."

The woman stared at me, awaiting an answer. She was close
to my height with lovely long chestnut hair parted right down
the center. Her eyes were disproportionately large, which gave
her a striking, mesmerizing appearance. She wore tight jeans,
but not too tight, and a light-gray shirt that let her belly button
play peek-a-boo with the world. She had an hourglass figure and
a heart-shaped ass. Very rare to come across these days, but
happily, still in existence. Oddly, though, she was barefooted—
in a public store, no less.

"Well?" she asked.

"Well what now?"

"Is that gentlemen a friend of yours?"

"Oh, of course."

"Then you both have extraordinary taste in wine. Must be for
a special occasion. What are you celebrating?"

For the first time in my life, I had nothing to say, or rather, I
had nothing I could say without fibbing. Hm, this challenge
might be tougher than I'd thought. I waved away her question.
"Enough about me and my friend. What are you doing here?"

She shrugged. "Shopping for wine."

"Right, no, I see, wine, I got it." I nodded dumbly.

With a slight expression of concern, she smiled and continued

14

down the aisle. "Well, enjoy your wine."

Great, here I go again. Same old pattern. Meet a beautiful girl, scare a beautiful girl—a disheartening cycle.

"I can see why you need the help of God," Gabriel said with a chuckle. "That was... well, simply pathetic."

Again, it was as if he'd appeared out of nowhere. I hadn't even heard the shopping cart, and here he was standing next to me. His cart contents had increased significantly in the short time it took for Miss Hourglass to write me off. I pointed to the bottles. "Uh, dude, that's a couple hundred dollars' worth of wine, no?"

He gave me a pitiful smile. "Not even close. I passed the thousand-dollar mark in the first aisle."

"But how can you pay if you don't carry money? You got a credit card hidden in your pocket?"

"Don't try to be funny, Michael. It doesn't become you."

"I'm not being funny. Seriously, how do you intend to pay for all that?"

"I've no intention of paying. We're going to steal it."

"What? But you work for you-know-who. What would He say?"

"Oh, Michael, you make things too easy for me. Gotcha again!" He followed up with a celebratory chuckle. "Archangels don't steal. Try and keep up; otherwise, I'll grow bored with you, and that's never a good thing."

"What's that supposed to mean?"

"Never you mind. Just go pay for my wine."

"Pay for your wine? Are you nuts?"

Messed Around

We were less than a mile from Total Wine when flashing lights filled my rearview mirror. Damn, a motorcycle policeman. Not only had I drunk two beers, but I was chauffeuring an angel around, which I believe would make anybody nervous.

"Problem?" Gabriel asked.

"I'm being pulled over by the five-oh."

"The who?"

"The five-oh. The police."

"Oh, were you speeding?"

"Probably." I pulled over to the side of the road. "Okay, Gabriel, let me do the talking."

"My pleasure."

A young officer got off his bike and approached my window. He looked from me to Gabriel a couple times, then asked for my license, registration, and insurance card. As he checked them, he asked me if I knew why I'd been stopped. "Well, I'm not positive, Officer," I said, avoiding eye contact.

Gabriel cleared his throat.

"If I had to guess," I continued, "I would say speeding."

"Oh, so you knew you were speeding then?"

"I guess."

"You guess or you know?"

"I know. I know I was speeding, okay?"

"Have you been drinking today, sir?"

I took a deep breath and blurted, "I had two beers at the marina during lunch."

Gabriel then leaned over me to speak to the officer. "Afternoon, Officer. I had a whole bottle of wine."

"And who are you?" the cop asked.

16

"Tell him who I am, Michael."

"I can't," I muttered.

"Why?" said Gabriel at full volume.

I tried to speak without moving my lips. "Because you told me I wasn't allowed to, remember?"

"Oh, yes. Well, I give you permission, just this one time."

"Sir," the officer said to Gabriel, "who are you?"

"I'm the guy who is going to drink all that wine in the back seat, Officer. We've just come from a delightful place called Total Wine, and we've really stocked up. May I offer you a bottle? You look like a red wine kind of chap."

The officer glanced at the wine in the back and gave me a look I'll never forget. "Let me get this straight. You both admit you've been drinking, and you admit you've just come from a wine store where you purchased a ton of wine, and—never mind. Please step out of the car."

He slowly put his right hand on the butt of his pistol and stepped back, giving me room to exit my car.

"There is no need to get out of the car, Michael," Gabriel said. "This will be over in a moment. Tell him who I am."

"Officer," I said, preparing for the cuffs, "This is the archangel Gabriel, and I'm bringing him home with me."

The officer frowned—hard. "Step out of the car. Now."

Gabriel leaned over again. "Officer Harper, correct?"

"That's what it says here." He pointed to his name tag.

"First name Jim, yes? You live over on Mulberry, just across from Vine Street, isn't that correct?"

"What's going on here?" Officer Harper's voice shook.

"I told you," I said. "He's archangel Gabriel."

"This some sort of video thing? For TV? Huh? You filming me right now?"

"I can assure you we are not filming you," Gabriel said.

"Then how do you know who I am?"

"Same way I know that you were sitting on your motorcycle a few minutes ago feeling guilty about all the time you spend flirting with your dispatcher, Yolanda Charles. Yolanda is seven years younger than you and she laughs at your jokes, which makes you feel younger too. And that's okay because you haven't taken it any further than that. But you want to. You think about it all the time. You wonder what it would be like to kiss her with her mouth open so your tongues can dance in each other's mouths. But what stops you are your son—he turns two tomorrow, and he's your whole life—and your wife, a very becoming woman who stays home and cares for your son. Naturally, you feel tremendous guilt over your flirting and fantasizing. It even keeps you up at night."

Officer Harper's mouth hung open. He handed me back my credentials, returned to his motorcycle, and drove off.

"That was fun," Gabriel said with a soft giggle.

Get Smart

"Tell me, Michael, do you know the address of any good strip clubs?" Gabriel asked as we drove back to my place.

"Excuse me?"

"Do you know the address of any good strip clubs around here?"

"Dude, you're an angel."

Gabriel sounded bored. "Just because I'm an angel doesn't mean I'm an angel."

"But why a strip club?"

"Why does anyone go to a strip club?"

"To see half-naked women shaking their stuff."

"Precisely. And it's exactly what you need."

"What *I* need? I don't need no strip club."

"Sure you do. You're a virgin, are you not?"

I slammed on the brake, causing the Jeep behind me to swerve and lay on his horn. "How do you know that?" I said, shaking a finger at my passenger as I got back up to speed. "That's private stuff, mister. You can't go around saying that out loud! What if someone heard you?"

"Michael, Michael, just relax, I'm not here to embarrass you. Just the opposite. That's why I recommended the strip club. I'm trying to get you—how do I put this?—in the mood."

"Jesus! I mean, geez. I mean, what the hell!"

"I thought that maybe when the time did come for you to lose your"—he lowered his voice to a whisper—"virginity, it would be best handled by a pro. Someone to guide you through the nuances that come with making love to a woman."

"You're beginning to creep me out, Gabriel."

"Let's start over, shall we? At the end of our week, if all goes well, you will be introduced to the woman of your dreams. After the two of you fall head-over-heels in love—*boom*! It will be time to consummate the relationship. And you don't want to flounder, do you?"

"Of course not. But I've read up on it. I've seen a few movies."

"Surely you've heard that practice makes perfect. That's where the strip club comes in. What do you think? We head to a club, talk up one of the cuties, tell her about your predicament, and *boom*, Bob's your uncle! What do you say?"

"Absolutely not. And who the hell is Bob?"

19

"Okay, I understand." He tented his hands and rested his chin atop them. "I'm on the same page as you now, and I won't make the same mistake twice. In fact, now that I think about it, the strip club idea was off base. I should have given it more thought before throwing it out there. We all good?"

"No worries."

"Good. Now let me ask you this. Do you know the name of any good escort services?"

I slammed my fist against the steering wheel. "Come on!"

"What? You've never heard of an escort service? This may be why you have such trouble getting your noodle wet."

"I'm not hiring a prostitute!"

"Why not? It's an honorable profession that hearkens back to Biblical times."

"Might be old, but it ain't honorable."

"Not for us to judge, is it, Michael? Let he who is without sin cast the first stone."

Hourglass

On what turned out to be a very long drive home, Mr. Archangel made me play Jimmy Buffett the whole way. As if that weren't bad enough, he sang along with Jimmy—loudly. When we finally arrived, I had to carry in all the wine due to Gabriel's bad back. Go figure. But he explained it was from supporting his wings for so long. *Yeah, right.*

While I found places to stow the wine, Gabriel checked out my place. "Nice digs, Michael. You've done wonders, considering the square footage you have to work with."

I looked over to see if he was kidding, but he was busy

making a selection from our—or rather, *my*—recent wine purchase. "Ah, this will do," he said, proceeding to open a bottle of Kamen Cabernet. "Pour you a glass?"

"No, thank you. I'll stick with beer." I grabbed one from the fridge but then changed my mind. I needed to keep my wits about me. So I put it back and turned around to find Gabriel gone. Damn, he was one fast angel.

"Join me," he said from my small balcony, which was on the second floor of my townhouse, connected to my bedroom.

I snatched a bottle of water and went to find my guest.

His shoes were off, a wineglass next to him on a small table as he lounged in a chair that looked small against his six-foot-four frame.

"Have a seat," he said, pointing to the chair opposite him. Then he sipped his wine. "Ooh, this is spectacular! You have no idea what you're missing."

"Do they have wine in heaven?" I asked.

"Of course."

"How do you pay for it?"

He laughed. "It's free, my dear boy. Everything in heaven is free."

"I'll bet you've got a lot of drunk angels running around up there."

He waggled a long finger in my direction. "The stories I could tell, oh, the stories I could tell." Then he reached inside his shirt pocket—a pocket I hadn't noticed earlier—and took out that leather-bound book I'd seen at the marina. He placed it down and retrieved something else from the same pocket. It looked like an old-fashioned hourglass with sand running from the top to the bottom. But the sand was barely moving, only a few grains at a time. And there were digital numbers on the hourglass's

base, running backward. The display currently read 166.25, and
the last number on the right ticked down once per minute or so.

Gabriel must have noticed my interest. "Curious about my
hourglass? Let me explain. Both the sand and the numbers
represent the time left on our contract. With this device, there
can be no disputing when the time expires and our contractual
agreement ends. When we started, the display read 168.00,
which is the number of hours in an earthly week. Any
questions?"

"About a thousand, but I'll hold off for now."

Footprint

"We need a game plan, Michael," Gabriel declared as he
emptied his wine glass. "No good will come from, as they say,
winging it. Give it some thought as I refresh my beverage. Back
in a jiffy."

With Gabriel gone, I glanced down at the neighborhood pool,
which was below and to the left of my place. It was a top selling
point when I bought the place—excellent view of the pool,
which meant excellent view of bikinis. The pool was packed, as
usual. Just another sunny day on Florida's west coast.

"Michael," Gabriel said upon returning with a full glass, "I
checked out your guest bedroom. It will do nicely."

"Glad you like it."

"But do you perchance have extra pillows. I simply adore
extra pillows."

"I'm sure I can come up with some for you."

"Splendid! You given any thought to a game plan while I was
gone?"

"No, sorry, my mind wandered."

"No worries. I took the liberty of forming the beginnings of a footprint."

"What's a footprint?

"Like a blueprint for our future endeavors."

"We can do anything you like today, but tomorrow I've got to work."

"Actually, you don't. I forgot to tell you that you've taken the week off."

"No way. I've got a full schedule."

"I took the liberty of sending your office an e-mail from you. You requested an emergency week off for mental health reasons. They replied, 'No surprise there.'" Then Gabriel took a beat. "Ah, got you again! They just replied, 'Okay.' Nothing else. So you're good to go."

"Mental health reasons? Are you crazy?"

"No, but your office thinks *you* are." And there it was—that quiet Gabriel laugh that I was coming to know all too well.

Innocence in Paradise

Apparently, Gabriel had no problem metabolizing alcohol because he was sipping on his third glass while lying back on one of my recliners. And let's not forget that he'd polished off quite a bit at the marina. Perhaps he'd even forgotten that I was around because he kept letting loose the occasional fart. "Michael," he said after a soft toot, "I am a firm believer in doing what's natural and what the body needs to do, so mind your own garden and stop worrying about my gas attacks, okay?"

"So you can—"

"I know everything about you. I've read your file twice."

"I have a file?"

"Of course. Why wouldn't you?"

"Does everyone have a file?"

"No, just you because you're so special," he said, the sarcasm dripping. "Of course everyone has a file."

"So God really is keeping tabs on me?" The thought made me nervous.

"God keeps tabs on everyone, including me."

"You? Why? You prone to trouble?"

"God keeps tabs on us all because he loves us and cares for us. He's not trying to catch us doing something bad. Too easy, right? I mean, we are human. And by 'we,' I mean 'you,' of course. I'm no longer human."

"So, uh, what's in my file?"

"The good and the bad."

"What about the ugly?"

"Ho. Ho."

"So does everyone have a file from the second they're conceived?"

"Inside each person's file is every word they've ever uttered and every thought they've ever had. The good and the bad."

"Can God see what we're doing while we're doing it?"

"Yes and no."

"A bit vague there."

"Well, God can see you, and yes, He is watching, but not every second of every minute of every hour, understand? Because He's very busy, very busy indeed. He can't watch everyone all the time. There are almost eight billion people on the planet, and that's a lot of souls. And let's state the obvious: God isn't interested in some of the things that you do. For

24

example, He doesn't care to watch you drop a deuce."

I grimaced.

"Oh, Michael, don't get all embarrassed on me now. Everyone poops. And that's not all. Lovemaking, mowing lawns, pulling weeds—you get the picture. These are all things that God doesn't need to watch over."

I raised my hand like a grade-schooler.

"Yes, Michael?"

"Tell me about heaven."

"Now that's a sticky wicket. I'm not here to write a book on paradise. I'd love to, but certain topics are off limits."

"How about one thing that sticks out—that won't get you in hot water with your boss?"

"You mean *our* boss, Michael." Gabriel stayed quiet for a long moment. "All right, one word, okay? You ready? Innocence. Innocence in paradise, a splendid welcoming innocence."

Pretty One

Later, Gabriel pointed down at the pool. "What, may I ask, is going on down there?"

"Happy Hour. It's a meet-and-greet, get-drunk kind of deal."

Gabriel clapped his hands together. "Oh, we must go. Let's grab some wine and head on down. Jimmy always says that women and water are in short supply, but not here at your place."

As stated earlier, I live in a gated community with many types of dwellings: condos, townhouses, single-family homes, and the ever-popular McMansions. There are two golf courses, each with their own clubhouse, restaurant, and bar. Plus four pools, one in each corner of the development. My pool is the largest and craziest because the condos and townhouses are mostly occupied by single adults trying to merge with one another.

So we joined the myriad of people frolicking about in various forms of undress. Most were probably two drinks in already. Gabriel quickly laid claim to a four-top and poured himself a glass of wine, tossing me a bottle of water from the bag he'd carried down.

"At some point, Michael, you have to start fishing."

I cocked my head at him questioningly.

He glanced skyward, as if looking for guidance and patience. "What I mean is, you bait the hook and cast your line in the water. Then you wait."

"For?"

"Oh dear. You wait until you get a nibble, Michael. Then you slowly reel it in. How difficult does that sound?"

"You mean—"

"Girls, Michael! You meet girls!"

"Oh, gotcha. You were doing a metaphor, so to speak."

"And they say you don't catch on quick."

"Who says that? Does my file say that?"

"Doesn't matter."

"It matters to me."

"Do you want to debate or do you want to meet women?"

I harrumphed, and somehow it made me feel better. "Okay, Mister Smarty Angel, why do I have to learn how to meet girls if, in a week, God is going to reward me with the girl of my dreams?"

"He will, but I can assure you she will not come inside of a box. You'll need to add a little effort of your own."

"Here we go. Another condition."

"Think of it this way. Have you ever heard the old joke about a man praying every day of his life—same prayer over and over? 'Dear God, please let me win the lottery.' Over and over, ad infinitum. Until one day, the sky opens, and the face of an angry man appears. The man looks up and realizes that God is about to speak to him. God looks down on the man and says, 'So you wish to hit the lottery?' The man nods. And God says, 'Then go buy a damn ticket already!' And the skies close up."

"Does God really use the word 'damn'?"

"That's what you got out of that?" Gabriel shook his head. "But yes, God swears, especially when He gets angry. Now what else did you get from that story?"

"God is willing to help the man win the lottery, but the man has to help himself first by getting a lottery ticket."

"May wonders never cease! There's hope for you yet, my friend."

Gabriel refilled his wine glass while I checked out the bathing suit styles the girls were wearing this year. Well, that was a lie. I guess I was really checking out what was inside the bathing suit styles. Then it hit me. I was glad I had only thought that thought because if I'd said it aloud, it would have been a lie and I'd be screwed. Damn! I had to be careful. I had to think about what I was thinking about before I opened my mouth. Guess it was time to get my mind off this crazy stuff, so I came up with a question for Gabriel. I was about to ask him if he ever considered giving up wine for Lent, but then I saw Miss Hourglass getting out of the pool. I knew it was her right away, even though her hair was wet and she was barely dressed.

"Hey, Gabriel, oh geez, it's the pretty one. Look!"

Gabriel followed my inelegant point. "Oh my, yes," he said. "It's the girl from Total Wine. What's she doing here?"

"I'm gonna ask her."

"Ooh, probably not a good idea. Striking out twice on the same day with the same woman? Not exactly a morale booster, is it?"

Rose, I Said

In less than three minutes, I had the young lady sitting at our table in the shade.

"Michael, I'm impressed," Gabriel said as I approached with the pretty one in tow.

"Don't give him too much credit," she said. "He lured me over here with the promise of fantastic wine."

"I should have thought of that myself, my dear," Gabriel said. "Please have a seat and I will indeed pour you a glass of a fine Cabernet."

I could have sworn that when I left the table to pursue Miss Hourglass, there had been only a bottle of water and a single glass of wine, but now there was another glass on the table. Gabriel reached into his bag, retrieved his bottle of Cabernet, and filled it for our guest.

"Gabriel," I said, "meet Annie. Annie, this is Gabriel."

"The pleasure is one hundred percent mine," Gabriel said, leaning forward to kiss the back of Annie's hand. She blushed.

"Annie works in the library downtown, and she recently moved here from Cincinnati."

"Wonderful," Gabriel said, practically falling out of his seat. Then he followed up with a serenade. "She came down from Cincinnati, it took her three days on the bus." When he finished, a huge smile ran across his face. "Jimmy Buffett, you know."

"Yes, I know," Annie said.

"You're a Parrot Head?" he said.

"Isn't everyone?"

Gabriel gestured in my direction. "Not this nobody from nowhere. He never even heard of Jimmy Buffett before today."

I shook my head to let her know he was kidding.

Annie sipped her wine, making abundantly clear she was enjoying it. "What is this nectar of the gods that I'm sipping on?"

"Kamen, with a K," Gabriel said, "a wonderful Cabernet from California. Michael bought it."

She raised her glass in my direction. "It's wonderful. So how do you two know each other again?"

"I'll let Michael tell you. He has such a gift with words."

"We're friends," I blurted. "We have this wonderful arrangement too. I buy the wine and Gabriel drinks it. Why don't you ask Gabriel where he does all of his shopping, Annie? As you can see, he does enjoy the color white. I think it rather works for him, gives him a relaxed Mark Twain kind of vibe."

"All-white suits you just fine, Gabe."

"Oh, he doesn't like to be called—"

"Thank you, Annie. You're too kind."

Out of nowhere, Rose Williscroft appeared at my side. "Michael, I thought that was you."

Just great. Rose was the girl I wanted to forget more than any other. Another blind date gone bad, compliments of my sister again. But it wasn't just a blind date gone bad; it had been the blind date from hell.

Gabriel stood and extended his hand to Rose. "I'm Gabriel. So pleased to meet you."

Rose shook his hand and introduced herself to both Gabriel and Annie.

"Please," Gabriel said, "have a seat and join us."

"Wow, manners," she said. "So unlike your friend here." She pointed to me. "Maybe you could teach him, Gabriel?"

"I shall try," Gabriel said, gesturing to Annie. "Annie here is a new friend of ours. She recently moved here from Cincinnati." He sang his song again, much to my dismay.

"Oh, Jimmy Buffett, right?" Rose said.

Gabriel smiled. "A good ear and a pretty face. You must have them banging down your door."

"You'd think," Rose said with a self-deprecating smile.

"How is it that you know Michael, Rose?" Gabriel asked with a twinkle in his eye.

"We dated a bit."

"Didn't end well?" Annie asked, jumping in.

"Okay, okay, let's talk about something else," I said. "Who remembers the past anyway? The future, that's where we need to be looking."

"I remember the past very well," Rose said. "We'd been dating for about two weeks, then one day, poof!"

Gabriel leaned forward. "Poof?"

"Yeah, poof, he was gone. Just like that. No goodbye, no *I'm sorry*. He just stopped calling."

Three pairs of accusing eyes settled on me as I sank deeper into my chair.

Gabriel finally spoke. "Did you ever learn the reason for his inexcusable behavior?"

"No, but I'd love to know what I did wrong." She raised a brow in my direction.

"Tell her, Michael," Gabriel said. "She has a right to know, and as I often say, honesty is the best policy." Gabriel seemed to be bursting with joy. "And I, for one, am on pins and needles."

"Okay, okay," I said, "it was just a little case of…"

"Yes, Michael? Please continue."

"I'm all ears," Rose said, tapping her feet now.

"A case of body odor," I said quietly.

"Body odor?" Rose shouted, incredulous.

"And bad breath," I added in a near-whisper.

"Oh my God," Rose said.

"Sorry, my dear," Gabriel chimed in, "but God doesn't have anything to do with body odor or bad breath."

"How dare you?" she said, her dagger-like eyes tearing into my soul. "I knew you were a shithead, but this takes the cake."

"Is there anything else that you didn't like about Rose?" Gabriel prodded. His damn smile couldn't have been any bigger or brighter, while I wanted nothing more than to bury my head in the sand.

I mumbled an answer.

"What's that?" Gabriel said. "I didn't quite hear you."

"Farting," I said louder than necessary. "She farts a lot, okay?"

Annie's jaw fell open, and Rose gasped.

"Asshole!" Rose shouted. "You are a complete asshole!"

Those were her last words before she departed, and I realized I hadn't asked what she was doing here at Mediterra; she didn't live here, after all. Could she possibly have been hoping to bump into me?

"I think I'll be leaving also," Annie said, downing her last sip of wine. "Thank you both for such an entertaining happy hour. And Michael, good luck with all your future ex-girlfriends. You're going to need it." She leaned down and spoke close to Gabriel's ear. "You need to find better friends."

Then she walked out of my life for the second time.

"Looks like she forgot her purse," Gabriel said, and he was off, pocketbook in hand, chasing after Annie. I should have been the one to do it. It would have given me an opportunity to explain myself, but then again, how could I explain away what had indeed been the truth?

Go

As we returned to my townhouse. Gabriel announced that he needed a nap, and before I could even complain about what he'd done in front of the ladies, he took off ahead of me and did whatever angels do at nap time. I grabbed a beer and went to the balcony to reflect. Man, I'd been so excited about my prospects with that supermodel, but in retrospect, of course she was a no-show. And as for bumping into Rose, well, she was like a bad penny that kept turning up, but today had marked the first time I'd actually spoken to her since the breakup. At least she didn't bring up the birthday story; that would have been a tough one to get through in front of Gabriel and Annie.

It was fun, in a weird sort of way, meeting Annie. Too bad we didn't meet under different circumstances. I would like to have gotten to know her. But that ship had sailed, like so many others. Sure, she was a little tall, and her teeth kinda stuck out, but I found those qualities endearing. And what about the way she stuck her right thumb in the top part of her hair, then gently brought it all the way to the back. Sometimes, I noticed, she even repeated the process two times in a row.

Would I ever see her again? And if I did, what could I say to convince her I wasn't a lunatic? Wait a minute—is that snoring? Geez, a snoring angel, just what I needed. Part of me felt certain that if I fell asleep, there'd be no angel when I woke up. I'd be all alone and it would have all been a crazy dream.

I finished my beer, closed my eyes, and listened to the snoring of a lanky angel who was here to grant my prayers—if I behaved and refrained from telling a lie for the next seven days. If Vegas were giving odds, let's just say they wouldn't be in my favor.

"Wake up, sleepy head! Time is of the essence."

I was still on the balcony, and I only had one eye half open, but it was enough to see that Gabriel was still here. He appeared to have taken a shower and changed his clothes—despite having brought no luggage. He was still dressed in white, but the shorts were now pants, and his shirt was an untucked short-sleeve golf shirt. And his hat was somehow… different.

"Come on, come on, Michael, time to hop in the shower. We've a big night ahead."

I rose from the chair, my back aching. "Why all the urgency?"

"We have a date tonight, and tardiness is not an option, so do what you must to make yourself presentable to the world, and lets be off, shall we?"

"*We* have a date? Since when and with who?"

"*Whom*, Michael. And it's with the enchanting Annie."

"Whoa, seriously?"

"When I returned her purse, I convinced her to allow us to buy her dinner tonight. And by 'us,' I mean 'you' because angels—"

"I know, I know. No money. That's getting a little old, by the way."

"Not as old as me."

"How old are you, anyway?"

"Hm, if you can guess my age anytime during the next seven days, all bets are off, and you head directly to GO. Which means no more telling the truth, and you still get the girl of your dreams; how does that sound?"

"Four hundred," I spit out immediately.

"Not even close. Now go get ready."

"How'd you convince Annie to have dinner with us?"

"Told her we'd be taking her to Ocean Prime down on 5th."

"Ocean Prime! Are you nuts? They only take reservations, and they're booked at least a month out."

"Will you please go shower?"

Reluctantly, I obeyed, wondering if Ocean Prime would allow Gabriel to keep his hat on. Guess I'd find out. As the hot water gave me my first relaxed moment of the day, my mind went straight to Annie. Would I be 0 for 3 or—if I ran into a little luck—might I go 1 for 3? After the shower, I sprinkled on extra cologne. You can never go with too much cologne, I always say.

Pulling Mussels from a Shell

I drove and Jimmy B. sang. So did Gabriel, hitting every lyric perfectly. I wondered why we weren't picking Annie up, but then I figured she wanted a clean getaway if things went badly.

I'd worn my best beige slacks and my lucky pink shirt. Not sure why I called it my lucky shirt—I'd never gotten lucky in it—but what the heck?

Annie had arrived before us and watched as we came strolling down the sidewalk, both of us with our eyes glued to her outfit. It was a peach dress, which went perfectly with her brown puppy dog eyes. The hem hit a few inches below her knees and swayed in the mild breeze. Her heels looked great and put her a few inches over six feet, which drew attention—in a good way—

34

from other passersby.

I was apprehensive about getting in, but Gabriel reassured me. Annie gave Gabriel a big kiss on the cheek, while I received a brief handshake. What was up with that?

At the hostess stand, we were asked what name the reservation was under. Gabriel stepped forward. "Angel. Gabriel Angel, party of three."

"Wow," Annie said, "what a pretty name." She smiled. "It suits you, Gabe, it really does."

And then, lo and behold, I heard, "Yes, Mr. Angel, right this way."

We were led to a table by the window with a bay view—easily one of the best in the place. The delight on Annie's face was a joy to behold.

"You must have connections, Gabe."

"Let's just say that I know the man upstairs."

The waiter announced the specials. Gabriel made a fuss over the inclusion of mussels fresh from Prince Edward Island, though I was wondering where the mozzarella sticks were on the menu.

Gabriel insisted we start with the mussels. I hated mussels, but I kept my mouth shut because I was learning that my mouth might be the main cause of my troubles. As I perused the menu, I stole glances at Annie. She was so attractive. I hoped Gabriel didn't notice my sneaky glimpses, but he always seemed to know what was rattling around in my head, even before I did.

I thought it odd that the waiter had not started off by taking our drink order, but then he suddenly appeared with two bottles off Crown Point Cabernet and three large wine glasses. "Compliments of the house, Mr. Angel. We do hope it meets with your approval."

A glass was set in front of each of us, and a small bit of wine was poured into Gabriel's glass. He did what I refer to as the sniff-and-twirl, then took it all into his mouth with one quick movement.

Our appetizers came and went, and dinner soon followed. All seemed to be going well. No foot in mouth disease for me; nor did I find myself tripping over my own two feet. There was even a minute or two where I felt I shined. And Gabriel seemed to be in my court for once. Best of all, Annie actually laughed at one of my jokes. Things were going very well indeed.

And then dessert came.

Another Nail in My Heart

Gabriel took his coffee black, and Annie took hers with extra cream and sugar. Not being a coffee lover, I declined. For dessert, Gabriel ordered crème Brûlée, Annie went with tiramisu, and I opted for the brownie topped with vanilla ice cream. Before taking his first bite, Gabriel reached into his pocket and retrieved that same leather book. He placed it on the table, then pulled out the hourglass from earlier. It seemed like the sand hadn't dropped much since the last time I saw it, but the number had. The display read 162.50.

"What's that?" Annie asked.

"My favorite book, the greatest ever written. I take it everywhere I go."

"And that?" she asked, pointing to the hourglass.

"That? I'm sure Michael could explain it better than I, right, Michael?"

And there it was, another nail in my heart, another pill to

swallow, a glass of poison offered.

"May I touch it?" Annie asked.

"Of course," Gabriel said, "but don't turn it upside down. That would be very bad indeed."

Annie picked it up and examined it. Then she set it down and looked toward me for an explanation.

"It's an hourglass," I said. "How's your dessert?"

"Fine, thanks. So what's the story behind the hourglass?"

I turned to Gabriel. "Tell me, Gabriel, in a position like this, what would Jimmy Buffett do?"

"Why, he'd say, 'Pour me something tall and strong.'" Of course, Gabriel had sung the answer.

"Good idea," I said, raising my hand toward the waiter to order stronger drinks, but Annie grabbed my arm and lowered it.

"Okay, you two, I get it." She gazed straight at me. "Let's play with the new girl, but you really need to get a better routine."

The waiter sidled up, placed the bill dead in the center of the table, then thanked us for coming.

Gabriel patted his stomach and let out a small but distinct yawn. "Thank you, Michael, for a glorious dinner. Your generosity knows no bounds."

"Yes, Michael, it was a wonderful dinner. Thank you."

When I looked down, the bill was sitting right in front of me. I dreaded looking at it. I mean, damn, if this spending didn't slow down soon, my bank account was going to cry murder!

I reached for my wallet, which is when the fun began. Or rather, when the shit hit the fan.

In Quintessence

Nothing in my back pocket. Not even a piece of lint. No wallet. Nada. I checked the other pocket. Nope. Then I noticed the enormous smile on Gabriel's face. "I'm thinking a nightcap," he said. "Perhaps at that new place over on Broad. Any takers?"

Annie smiled. "Great idea, but only one. I've got work in the morning. Maybe we could walk over?"

"But of course, my sweet Annie," Gabriel said. "Marvelous idea."

"Uh, Gabriel," I said, "I seem to have left my wallet at home. Could you, uh—"

"But Michael, you told me this was a treat for my birthday, so I left my wallet at home as well."

Annie looked from Gabriel to me, then at the bill, then back to me. "Really?" she said. "Really?"

Gabriel stood abruptly and smiled. "Well, I'll leave you two to sort this out, Don't need my blood pressure spiking on my birthday." And off he went.

"Tell me the truth," Annie said. "You guys set me up. Great restaurant, expensive wine, roped me in, and now you're leaving me with the bill—and humiliated, to boot."

The waiter came over and asked if everything was all right.

"No!" Annie said. "Everything is not all right." She set her eyes on me. "I knew there was something up with you right from the start. I'll bet you don't even live at Mediterra. I'm such a fool."

"Annie, I swear, I did not do this intentionally."

"What about your friend, the birthday boy? Look me in the eye and tell me he had nothing to do with your wallet not being in your pocket. Go on, tell me that old Gabe isn't in on this."

She grabbed the bill and took a look at the number on the bottom. "Four hundred dollars? Motherfu—"

"It was the wine, I think."

"I know it was the wine. I'm not stupid."

"Listen, I'll go get the money from a cash machine."

"How? You don't have a wallet."

"I'm trying to think."

"You have five seconds to get your ass out of this restaurant before I start screaming."

"But Annie, I—"

"Two seconds!"

"I'll pay you back, I promise."

"One second."

As I turned to leave, I saw tears well up in her eyes. Then the waiter shot me a look of pure disgust, so I did what anyone would do: I left—quickly.

Gabriel was waiting outside. "Magnificent job of not telling a lie, Michael, just magnificent."

"I thought angels weren't allowed to lie."

"I didn't tell a lie."

"Oh, really, birthday boy? Look me in the eye and tell me it just happens to be your birthday today."

"Well, it could be. Angels don't know their actual birthdays, so technically, today could be my birthday."

"Now I've heard it all. What an in-quintessence explanation."

When the Hangover Strikes

The next morning was as bright and sunny as the day before. Not too hot and the humidity was staying at bay. It felt strange getting up on a Monday morning and not going to work. But sure enough, I got an email from work telling me that all was well and to enjoy myself. It was written by my boss, Chris Tilbrook, who was generally terse and unsentimental, but this email contained underlying innuendoes: *I'm not sure if you know, but my wife has had some problems of her own, emotionally speaking. She has found amazing results with Dr. Keith Wilkinson.* Chris included contact info for the good doctor, with three words spelled out in all caps: *JUST IN CASE.*

I worked for the *Miami Herald*, in the entertainment arena. My job was incredibly easy, not to mention fun. I was a critic. I reviewed movies, television shows, books, plays, and music. I usually got to see movies before they came out, though some producers didn't want their movies to be reviewed before they came out, for obvious reasons. Same with books and plays, but as for music, I just filled in when our music guy was busy.

I'd been infatuated with films and books for as long as I could remember, so I couldn't believe I got paid to do what I loved most. Besides, I was a sucker for a great love story. Who wasn't? Given my job, I spent a lot of time at theaters and libraries. The library I frequented most was Headquarters Regional Library at 2385 Orange Blossom Road in North Naples. It was the biggest of all the local libraries—only one story, but it stretched for well over a block. It had the look and feel of an old Spanish fort, complete with a tower on its left-hand side, and its main entrance boasted a splendid fountain, which welcomed each day's visitors.

Anyway, no work today, so I dragged Gabriel out of bed and went straight to the bank to get some cash. I didn't want Annie thinking I was a dirtbag. I withdrew the exact amount that I owed her, then thought better of it. I tripled the amount. Heck, I had six more days with the tightest angel on earth, so I was sure I would need more. Gabriel, adorned in white sweatpants, white sneakers, and a white sweatshirt, seemed sluggish. I couldn't help but wonder if all the drinking was catching up with him.

After the bank, it was time to repay Annie at the library. Gabriel insisted that he wanted to go with me to help smooth things over, but then he let me know that he needed breakfast first. So off we went.

We stopped at a bakery I'd never noticed before: Angelic Desserts, I kid you not. It was on Vanderbilt Beach Road, and it turned out to be fabulous. We were at a small table by the window eating our croissants when I hit Gabriel with a question. "Can angels get drunk?"

He assessed me with hungover eyes. "Why do you ask?"

"Just curious. And if they can, is it frowned upon by the boss?"

"Very funny, Michael. You get an A-plus for effort. Now tell me, how do you propose to fix this mess you've gotten yourself into with Annie?"

"That *I've* gotten *myself* into?"

"Exactly."

"Were you even there last night?"

"Let's not quibble, Michael. We need a plan." Then, without blinking an eye, he put out his hand. "Can I have some money? I'd give anything for another one of these wonderful croissants."

The Knack

"Oh my God," said Rose's voice from behind me. "What are you doing here? Are you stalking me now? Wasn't yesterday's public humiliation enough?"

I turned my head and gave her a weak smile.

"Good morning, Rose, care to join us?" Gabriel said.

"Yes, I'd just love to be heckled some more."

Rose the Malodorous was wearing raggedy old sweats, the type you might reluctantly wear around the house but not to a bakery in downtown Naples. Guess she hadn't planned to run into anyone. But as Gabriel might say, We make plans and God laughs. In Rose's case, He was no doubt laughing.

"Please," Gabriel said, "allow me to make up for Michael's rude behavior. Let me buy you a cup of coffee and anything else you desire on this fine morning."

Rose looked hesitant but joined us nonetheless. She ordered a large this-and-that-and-this coffee with a name longer than the national anthem, plus a half-dozen jelly donuts. I decided not to ask about the strange order.

After some friendly banter, Gabriel must have gotten bored and decided to rile things up. A part of me was tempted to lie about something so I could be rid of this Jimmy-Buffett-quoting, half-in-the-bag, white-clad, money-grubbing excuse for an angel. Maybe there was some type of complaint box? Or an 800 number I could call to discuss my dissatisfaction with my assigned angel?

"Michael," Gabriel was saying, "I was just telling Rose how wonderful she looked this morning. Don't you agree?"

Bastard.

"Rose," I said confidently, "I have always been an advocate of wearing sweats anytime, day or night. You definitely pull it off."

In a low voice, Gabriel muttered, "Safe at first."

"Furthermore, Rose, I should never have mentioned all that

body odor stuff in public."

"He's going for second, ladies and gentlemen."

"One should never discuss another's personal hygiene in mixed company," I said.

"Thank you, Michael," Rose said. "I appreciate you saying that."

"Safe at second."

"One more thing, Rose," I said. "I was an absolute cad yesterday and for that I'd like to sincerely apologize. I only hope you can forgive me."

"Holy cow, a stolen base, safe at third."

When Rose and I both stared questioningly at Gabriel, he looked away and began to play with his coffee cup. Rose then leaned in, kissed me on the cheek, and thanked me for the coffee and donuts.

On our walk over to the library, I asked Gabriel if he was a baseball fan.

"Yes. How'd you know?"

Library Girl

"Do you know what Jimmy Buffett says about libraries?" Gabriel asked after we'd entered. "He says they're filled with useless but important information."

He looked at me for a response, and it was my pleasure not to give him one. Instead, I asked an older librarian if Annie was working. She pointed to a large wall-mounted ladder, the type that can slide around. You don't see them as often now, probably for insurance reasons, but this place was old, and the rolling ladder added to its charm.

Annie was near the top rung, reshelving books in the nosebleeds. She wore a light floral sundress, perfect for showing off exactly what needed showing off. Oh, and she was barefoot. You couldn't tell from my current vantage point, but I'd peeked yesterday and I must say, as far as feet go, not half bad.

She noticed the two of us, then turned her head away, giving it a visible shake of disappointment as she began her descent. "Way too early in the day for you two buffoons," she said quietly. "Please go away." She jumped off the bottom rung and headed for the front desk.

"Annie, please, you've got us all wrong," I said.

She whipped around. "Okay, what? What the hell do you want from me? Need me to buy you breakfast?"

I approached her slowly, not wanting to scare her and have her start screaming in a public library. I pulled out an envelope. "Please take this, and please accept my apologies for last night. It's all the money you laid out for dinner and the tip too."

"Fine, apology accepted. Now if you don't mind, I've got work to do."

"We feel terrible about Michael forgetting his wallet," Gabriel said. "Perhaps we can do something to make it up to you?"

"No, thanks. Let's just go our separate ways and pretend we don't know each other when our paths cross at Mediterra, okay?"

"If that's the way you want it," I said, "fine with me. But next time someone makes a small mistake, an honest mistake, try getting over yourself and giving the poor fellow a break. Have a nice day with your books."

I tapped Gabriel on the arm and motioned him to the door. As I put my first foot through the exit, I looked back one last time.

Annie was staring right at me, her eyes wide and surprised.

"How do you think that went?" I said when we were outside.

"Depends how you look at it."

"Well, how do you look at it?"

"You'll understand better if I use baseball terminology."

"No, please. Just give it to me. Five words or less."

"Fine. You pooped the bed, Michael."

Misadventure

"Let's get changed for golf," Gabriel said. "Proper attire is as important as what your score card reads."

"Angels play golf?"

"What did you think—that we just fly around all day waiting to get assigned to saps like you?"

"I'm no sap. Come on, that's offensive."

"How else would you explain 0 for 3 with the lovely Annie?"

"That's because of you."

"Is that what you tell yourself so you can sleep at night? And be careful, Michael, there's no such thing as being offended. It's just a word propagated by the guy who lives below." He pointed straight down. "Being offended is just another way of complaining and whining about the world. People make fusses about things because it gives them something to consume their otherwise dull and boring lives. For some, complaining becomes a fine art, even though it gets them nowhere and does nothing to move them ahead in life."

"Interesting perspective."

"Here's more. What if every time some group or individual was offended by something or someone, that thing or that person gets removed? For example, let's say a statue offends a group of people, so it's taken away. Next, a group of people gather together to pray in the park each morning, but a handful of people complain. So the praying people are removed. But what if I'm offended by the people who got offended? Will they be removed, and if so, who's left? Something to think about."

While Gabriel finished changing into his golf outfit, I made a cup of tea. I could hear him through the bedroom door, singing something about a lone palm tree. Finally, he emerged, dressed in—you guessed it—all white: slacks, shirt, and brand-new, unscuffed shoes that bore a hint of gold.

The outfit didn't surprise me, but the all-white golf bag did. It had his name printed in black along its side: Gabriel Angel.

We headed to the car, and I asked if he wanted to play the north or south course. He chose neither.

"You're not that good, huh?" I said. "Would you rather play an easy public course? Maybe some mini-golf?"

"We're playing at Tiburon, Michael, the course Greg Norman designed."

"Sorry, Gabriel, but you need to be a member there and have a tee time in advance."

"I am and I do. Now give this car of yours a little gas or we'll be late—and angels dislike being late."

As we went over to drop our clubs off, Gabriel leaned toward me. "Don't embarrass me, Michael. Just try to hit the ball straight and keep it on the fairway."

"I'm a 15 handicap, Gabriel. You even know what that is?"

"As I've told you, I know everything there is to know about you. For instance, up until recently, you were a high handicap just coming down to a mid-handicap. When you were a high handicap, you were basically a bogey golfer, shooting around

46

90. To sum up your current game, you're good at making par but struggle to make birdies to make up for your bogeys. Now let's get on with it."

I was dying to see what happened when Gabriel went to check in, but that all fizzled when the two gentlemen at the desk jumped to attention upon seeing Gabriel.

"Mr. Angel, so good to see you again. Anything we can do for you today before you tee off?"

Gabriel leaned toward them. "Is Jimmy playing today?"

"No, I'm sorry, sir. Mr. Buffet played yesterday."

"Just my luck, then. Guess I'm stuck with this mid-handicapper all day."

They both smiled on cue.

Within a few minutes, it was time for us to tee off. "So what's your handicap?" I asked.

"You have to understand Michael, I've been very busy of late, leaving me with little time for golf."

"Just tell me."

"Seven handicap cloud."

"Meaning?"

"I'm a seven handicap, but up in heaven, we add the word 'cloud' at the end because that's where we play: in the clouds."

"Wow, so there's golf in heaven. Does you-know-who play?"

"He sure does. Bit of a temper when he hits a bad shot, in fact. But keep that to yourself. I don't want to be reading that somewhere next week."

Hits of the Year

At the 18th hole. Gabriel led by two strokes, and I could see that he was a tad nervous. I was enjoying the game of my life, having just hit the ball straight down the 18th fairway, roughly two hundred and seventy-five yards, my best of the day. "Hit of the year!" I exclaimed.

"*Drive*, Michael. It was your best drive of the year."

"Tomato, to-mah-to."

Gabriel then stepped up and hit his ball so long and straight that it seemed to take on a will of its own, wanting nothing more than to reach the green.

"How long you been playing again?" I asked.

"Since the game was invented."

Gabriel ended up birdying the hole, and I ended with a double bogey. So close, so close.

"Come now, Michael, I'll buy you a drink at Sydney's and we can discuss the who, what, and when of this evening."

Sydney's lived up to its reputation—one of the nicest clubhouse bars I'd ever been in. I ordered a Stella and Gabriel settled on a bottle of Silver Oak Cabernet from Napa.

"Michael, you passed with flying colors today."

"What's that supposed to mean?"

"The two of us playing golf was a test. Because if anyone is going to lie or cheat, it's going to be on a golf course. But shockingly, you didn't cheat or lie about your game once. Commendable, very commendable."

Gabriel then pulled out his leather-bound book and hourglass. The number read 142.00 even.

"Gabriel, you said that in the big scope of things, you know all about me. So I'm curious—how do I compare to others?"

"That's a hard one to tackle. You're better than some, worse than others. In all, you're not a bad man. You've just lost your way, and I'm here to help you find your way back."

48

"You mean back to church?"

"No, back to God. You've prayed for something all your life but because it hasn't happened, you blame God for not giving it to you."

"Wait a minute. I don't blame God for anything."

"Subconsciously, you do. And it's okay to question God, to have doubts. But it's not okay to give up on him. Think about it. You haven't been to church in ten years, but you've never stopped praying for a soul mate to share your life." He sipped his wine. "But here's the thing. You don't need God's help to find a partner. You can do it on your own. Why do you think that God hasn't already intervened on your behalf? Because he doesn't need to. In essence, Michael, you are your own worst enemy. You use any excuse you can to find fault in everyone you meet, then you use your quote-unquote humor and your fibbing to drive away the ones you like most."

"I don't know, Gabriel, that—"

"Just open your eyes if you want to see the truth. It's right in front of you. It's always been there for your viewing pleasure."

Talk about a cold slap in the face. And when he reached over to refill his glass, he added the final insult. "God's not to blame, Michael. You are."

F-Hole

"How often do you help out someone like me, Gabriel?"

"Hard to say. It's not my job to do this exact sort of thing."

"Then what is your exact sort of thing?"

"I am an angel announcer, the Herald of Visions, a Messenger of God. I make God's message understandable to people and help them accept it with a pure heart. I'm also a saint. And a patron saint."

"Of what?"

"I am the Patron Saint of Communication and Telecommunication. And one last thing. I help eliminate dark thoughts and help bring clarity and purity to people's lives."

"Heck of a resume. So where do I fit into all of that?"

"You are what we refer to as an F-HOLE."

I almost spit out the last sips of my Stella. "A what?"

"An F-HOLE. F for 'Forsaken' and HOLE for 'Heaven Onsite Life Evaluation.' Try saying that five times fast."

"No, thanks."

"It means you're a tough case, handle with care, use kid gloves. Which is where I come in. I handle the hard ones, and you are a hard one. But don't worry, I'll have you back and running on all eight cylinders soon, as long as you keep up your end of the bargain."

"Doesn't everyone fib, though, to a certain degree?"

"Of course, but you're the one who wants something from God. Show some sacrifice, show him that you deserve his help."

The bartender brought me another Stella and poured what was left of the wine into Gabriel's glass.

"Here's to you, Michael," Gabriel said by manner of a toast. "In your quest to find the perfect mate, I salute you."

We clinked, bottle to glass, and drank.

"Are you really a member here?" I asked.

"They think I am, so I am. It's hard to explain. Best to just go with it."

"And the bill for the round of golf and these cocktails? How does that work out?"

"I was just about to bring that to your attention. As you may know, most clubs are cashless, but I convinced them to bend the rules and let you pay for the entire day." He rose from the bar. "Don't be stingy with the tip now., Michael. It's a reflection on you, you know."

With perfect timing, the bartender placed a bill in front of me. How convenient.

Hop, Skip, and Jump

Back at my place, I found a note taped to my door from Annie, inviting us to dinner at her place at 7:00 p.m. sharp.

"Wow," Gabriel said, "I guess your good looks, charm, and enthralling personality won the day. Either that or it's the three dozen white roses you sent her today."

"Are you serious?"

"Of course. So when you see a charge from Harry's House of Flowers on your next statement, it's legit."

After Gabriel went to shower, I heard him singing about cheeseburgers. Then we both got spiffy. Gabriel dressed in all white again: white Levi jeans and a simple white tee shirt with a white dinner jacket over it, all of which somehow worked.

I offered to take my car, but Gabriel insisted that since it was just a hop, skip, and jump away, we should walk. So we did, and we were rewarded with a nice surprise after ringing Annie's doorbell.

The surprise's name was Daphne. She answered the door wearing a cute sundress—mostly pink, with a pattern of white lilies running throughout. She invited us in and led the way to the kitchen, where Annie was hard at work. To Annie's right was a table set for four with three vases in its center, each containing a dozen white roses.

Gabriel presented the bottle of red wine he'd brought from the stock in my kitchen, a selection called Jarvis, a Cab Franc, whatever that meant. Annie came over and gave me a kiss on the cheek and a small hug. Gabriel received no kiss and a hug that was only half the length of mine. That was an encouraging sign.

"I see you've met my friend, Daphne," Annie said. "She works with me at the library. I told her about you two characters and she didn't believe a word. So I invited her to see for herself."

Annie took off her apron and announced that dinner was ready. "A quick drink first?" she said.

Gabriel poured wine for everyone. Daphne took a sip and turned to Annie. "You were right about the wine. It's stunning." She shifted her attention to Gabriel. "You know a lot about wines, Gabriel?"

"They're of a hobby of mine," he said. "Wine and I go so far back that I sometimes have trouble remembering when and where I first discovered my fondness for it."

"What do you do, Gabriel, that you can afford such fine wines every day?"

"Excellent question, Daphne," I said, jumping in. "Tell her what you do, Gabriel. I'm sure we'd all find it fascinating."

"These days, I'm busy being Michael's best friend, and I've come from afar to help him put his life back together."

"Well, that makes total sense," Annie said, laughing. "He needs help more than anybody I've ever met." Then she smiled and clapped her hands together. "Okay, you guys, let's eat!"

Daphne

"How long are you here for, Gabriel?" Daphne asked between mouthfuls of baked ziti.

"Just a week, then it's off to another adventure."

"And Michael, what do you do for a living?"

"I work for the *Miami Herald* as a critic."

"Movies? Things like that?"

"Do you do book reviews, Michael?" Annie said, jumping in before I could answer Daphne.

"I do movies, books, plays and television shows."

"Sounds like a cool job," Annie said.

"Have you ever pissed off someone famous by giving them a bad review?" Daphne said.

"There was this one time in New York. I was there to review a new play opening on Broadway. It starred a major movie star who'd never done theater before—for good reason, as it turned out."

"You have to tell us who it is," Daphne said.

"Since it's public record anyway, it was Glenn Difford."

"No way!"

"Yes, and let's just say he wasn't too pleased with my review."

"What was the play?" Annie asked.

"It was an adaptation of an old Stephen King novel, the one where the main character has to chew off his hand to free himself from the evil clutches of a stalker holding him prisoner at a beach house in Bermuda."

"I saw the movie; it sucked big time," Daphne said.

"So did the book and the play," I said, "with the play being the worst of the three, I might add."

"Get to the good stuff, Michael," Gabriel said. "Tell them what you wrote and what happened next."

I gave Gabriel a disparaging look but did as requested. "I stated in the review that Glenn Difford should stick to his fan base and only do action movies because anything else seems to cause great pain to the eyes of the viewing public."

"You didn't," Daphne said.

"And what else, Michael?" Gabriel prompted.

"I wrote that I'd seen better acting by the guy at the Dunkin' Donuts takeout window when he gets your order wrong."

The ladies gasped.

"And then I might have said something about leaving the real acting to the professionals, and perhaps he might want to consider working as a performer at the zoo, if and when his film career takes a shit. Which it most certainly will."

Annie shook her head disapprovingly, while Daphne seemed not only giddy but genuinely impressed.

Gabriel just smiled that smile of his. "He still hasn't gotten to the good part."

I sighed and continued. "Difford came looking for me. Wanted to kick my ass."

"Did he find you?" Daphne asked.

"Yep, while I was dining with a friend in the city. Came in with his entourage, about six of them, and you should have seen the look on his face when he spotted me."

Daphne was hanging on every syllable, but Annie seemed like she couldn't care less.

"He beelined it straight for my table, his crew in tow. Gave me the old stare-down—didn't say a word for a full minute. Then came the famous Glenn Difford smile, and he said, 'Hello, Michael, how's your meal so far?' Before I could answer, he spoke again. 'Seen any good shows lately? I'm a big fan of your reviews. You really have a flair for the narrative.' Then the stare returned, and the big question came next. 'You a good swimmer, Michael? 'Cause I've got a big boat, and me and the guys would love to take you out fishing sometime. You like to fish, Michael?' This time, he waited for answer, but when I didn't respond, he leaned down and got in my face and said, 'People who can, do. People who can't become critics. Remember that next time you're writing. And one more thing, your job is to review, not attack. Making it personal is not nice.' Then he stood back up for all to hear and said he'd have his guys call my guys to set up that fishing trip."

Bonkers

With dinner over and the night winding down, I was on Annie's balcony sharing a nightcap with her. Gabriel was inside being peppered by Daphne.

"That was a wonderful dinner, Annie. Thank you so much, and thanks for giving me a second chance."

"More like fourth chance."

We were standing just a few feet apart, and for the first time, I found myself thinking about kissing her. "Yeah, I don't have a way with words when I talk to pretty women, and sometimes the words I do use are not chosen wisely."

"But you're a critic. You find the words then, don't you?"

"Some people would disagree with you on that, but yes, I do try."

"Then try now. Tell me in the best way what Michael is thinking and feeling right now."

She took a step closer to me and gazed into my eyes. A few minutes ago, when we had first come out here, she'd pulled her hair back behind her ears. She looked so pretty that way.

"Annie, I've never been married before."

"I have. Trust me, it's not all it's cracked up to be." She took another step closer.

"But as a guy in his forties, I should probably have more experience in talking to a beautiful woman, but sadly I don't."

"Any beautiful woman in particular you're referring to?"

I took a step closer to her, leaving us mere inches apart. Something stirred in my gut and told me to close the gap.

As if reading my mind, Annie moved in even closer. "You were saying?" she whispered.

"You're the beautiful woman, Annie, and you make me so nervous."

"Why?"

"Because I'm afraid I'm going to say something stupid and spoil this moment happening between us." Our lips were millimeters apart.

"What's happening between us?"

I could feel her breath on my face. It smelled of wine, and it smelled inviting. Then we both leaned forward, and any space left between us disappeared. Our lips met for the very first time, and it felt perfect. It felt right. After a moment, we stopped, then started again. Her hands and arms were all over me, exploring, mapping, marking a territory they seemed to be claiming. So I followed suit. We both breathed in long heavy strides, in harmony, as one.

Her lips were soft and wet, eager and giving. Most importantly, they were on mine. After a few minutes, we stopped and gathered our breath. Then we heard a noise from inside.

"What was that?" I asked.

Another sound rang out, like furniture being moved.

"Think they're going at it?" Annie said with a grin.

"I don't think so. In fact I'd bet against it."

"What does that mean? Is Gabriel married?"

"Nope, not married."

"Is he gay? I mean, given the outfits he wears, I could see it."

"Uh, nope, not gay."

"Does he have a girlfriend somewhere? Because if he does, I don't think that would stop Daphne."

"No, he's just, um—"

"What?"

"Not interested," I blurted. "He's not interested."

"What do you mean?"

"Annie, it's not my place to discuss Gabriel behind his back."

She walked over to her wine and downed a sip. "Come on, what's the big secret? Obviously, something's not right, and something is not jelling here. Just when I thought we were moving forward, you revert to the old Michael."

She opened the door and went inside. I followed a foot or so behind, nearly colliding with her because she'd frozen in place. There, in front of us, Gabriel and Daphne were in various forms of undress, playing Naked Twister. Bonkers.

Lost for Words

"Well, hello you two," Gabriel said, trying to put his hand on a yellow circle. "Did you have fun on the balcony?"

A topless Daphne, who at least had the decency to seem a tad embarrassed, glared at Gabriel. "You said they'd be out there for an hour!"

"Seems I guessed wrong, my dear Daphne."

She got up, gathered her garments, and went off to the bathroom, giggling. Gabriel still had on white boxer shorts but nothing else.

"What were you two doing?" I asked.

"What does it look like?"

"Uh, Naked Twister?"

"Exactly, so why ask?"

"I don't know. I'm at a total loss for words."

"Try this. Breathe in, breathe out, move on. It's Jimmy's answer to almost every off-kilter situation."

"Has Jimmy ever seen you playing Naked Twister?"

"He has not."

"If he did, he might have a little more to say."

Annie had gone to check on Daphne, giving me a minute alone with Gabriel. "Rumor has it that Daphne has the hots for you, Gabriel."

"Really? Do tell."

"What the fuck? This isn't ninth grade here. And you're an angel. Shouldn't you act like it?"

"How does an angel act, may I ask?"

"How about angelic? Besides, I told Annie you wouldn't have any interest in Daphne."

"I know, and may I say, very commendable on your part."

"But then we find you two doing... this!"

"Michael, you tend your garden and I'll tend mine, seem fair? Now, let's talk about tomorrow?"

"What's going on tomorrow?"

"We're taking the girls to the beach."

"But I thought—"

"Try not to think too much. It's part of your problem. Just go with the flow once in a while."

The ladies returned, both giggling now. Annie gave me the eye, but I didn't know if it was the good eye or the bad eye. "I hear we're going to the beach tomorrow," she said.

"Unless you two have to work," I said.

"We're going to take a half-day and meet you guys at Naples Grande at noon. They say it's the best beach in town."

Slightly Drunk

As Gabriel and I walked home that night, the skies opened up. We were soaking wet by the time we returned. Gabriel disappeared into his room, emerging a moment later dry and wearing white boxers decorated with winged angels playing horn instruments.

"Nice shorts," I said.

"Gift from my mother," he said.

I slipped into some boxers of my own. They were red with a picture of Santa Claus on the front.

"Nice shorts," Gabriel said. "Gift from your sister who passed away a few years ago?"

"How do you remember every little detail of my file?"

"That's no little detail. It was actually a very big deal to you, wasn't it? Those shorts were the last gift your sister ever gave you, and you treasure them. You can't put them on without thinking about her."

I wiped a tear away, then looked at Gabriel, who'd somehow managed to open a bottle of wine and pour himself a glass. "It seems unfair that you know every detail about me, but I know nothing about you."

"What would you have me do to help even up the score?"

"Let me ask you some questions."

"Maybe, but I have what you folks down here would call a Non-Disclosure Agreement, and my penalty for breaking is substantial."

"So what can you tell me?"

"You ask, and I'll either answer or pass, okay?"

"All right. Is there really a heaven?"

"Come on, you can do better than that. Aren't I proof enough of heaven?"

"Okay, what's heaven like?"

"It would take me a hundred years to describe it, and that still wouldn't do it justice. Let's just say it's Some Fantastic Place."

"Do angels really fly around heaven?"

"Only the ones who have their wings. Angels must earn their wings."

"Do you have wings?"

"I've had wings for almost forever."

"Can I see them?"

"No."

"Does everyone go to heaven?"

"No."

"Is there really a second place?" I pointed downward.

"Yes, but I won't answer questions about down south. The fact that it exists is bad enough."

"You said there's wine in heaven. Is there food?"

"Yes. Is there you-know-what?"

"You mean bumping uglies?"

"Yes."

"No comment."

"When you die, do you go straight to heaven?"

"Yes and no. Can you be more... let's say no."

"Have you met God?"

"We play golf every Thursday if I'm not down here helping schleps like you."

"Have you ever come down to help one of us schleps and failed?"

"No comment." Gabriel poured himself more wine and started looking on the sleepy side. "Are we done?"

"Just a few more. Do angels have powers, like can you move things without touching them?"

"Some do, some don't. Depends on ranking."

"You ever been married?"

"No comment."

"Last question. Is there dating in heaven?"

I waited for a response, but then I heard Gabriel snoring and noticed the empty wine bottle.

The Call

I'd only been in bed for about thirty minutes when my cellphone went off. There was no name, and I didn't recognize the number. I was about to shut it off when I felt a small itch on my back. What that had to do with taking the call, I don't know, except somehow I knew the two were related.

"Did I wake you?"

As soon as I heard the voice, I bolted upright. "Annie, hey, no, I was—" Oops, I caught myself; I'd almost lied to make her feel better. "I mean, yes, I was sleeping, but if I'm going to be awakened in the middle of the night, I'm glad it's you.

Everything okay?"

"Yeah. I just wanted to apologize for earlier. I was hard on you, especially after you were trying so hard to be nice to me."

"No worries. You were fine. If anything, I should be apologizing to you for stealing those kisses."

"You weren't stealing them; I was giving them away."

"Is that a fact?"

"It's also one of the reasons I'm calling. Those kisses... I can't stop thinking about them. And... and I want more."

My first urge was to stand on my bed and jump up and down, but I repressed it. "Is that so?"

"Do you think we might find some time tomorrow at the beach to be alone, or will we have to wait?"

"Oh, we'll find the time, I promise you that."

"By the way, did you like the ziti?"

"I loved it."

"Do you like the person who made the ziti?"

"I sure do."

"I like you too."

"So Annie, why are you asking me all these questions right now?"

"Because I didn't want to wait until tomorrow for my review. I mean, you're a critic, right? So I decided to go right to the source and find out early what the results were."

"So it was a date, huh? How did I do?"

"Flying colors."

"One more question. How did you get my cell number?"

"Gabriel gave it to me; he said it might come in handy."

Robert Remail

The Prisoner

As we sipped coffee and drove to the beach the next day, Gabriel asked, "Do you think I had too much to drink yesterday?"

"Dude, you're a grown-ass angel. Who am I to tell you when you've had too much to drink?"

"Excellent answer to a hard question. I salute you, sir. And by the way, keep last night's answers to yourself."

"Hey, what happens on earth, stays on earth."

"Oh, that's rich. How did your phone call with Annie go last night?"

"Fabulous."

"Let's thank the girls by taking them out to dinner tonight. I know just the place."

"What's up with you and Daphne?"

Gabriel pretended to be busy drinking his coffee and avoided the question.

"Gabriel, I asked—"

"I know what you asked me, but that is a fine line I do not feel like crossing at this time. As Jimmy always says, 'There's a fine line between Saturday night and Sunday morning.'"

We arrived at Naples Grand Beach about an hour before the ladies were due. I've always had a hard time picking the right spot to set up on a beach, but Gabriel told me he had everything already in place, so I trusted him. In front of a beautiful corner cabana was a sign that read: Angel—Party of 4.

"Ah, we've arrived," he said. Inside were four lounge chairs, four small tables, a refrigerator, an outdoor couch, and a hot tub for four.

"Good morning, Mr. Angel," said our cabana boy. "I hope

you've found everything in order?"

"Oh yes, it's just fine, many thanks."

The cabana boy dressed more like a butler, not like you would expect on a beach but in full black-on-black attire. "My name is Francis, but everyone calls me Frank. If there is anything I can do for you, please let me know. You'll find full menus inside, and remember that we are all-inclusive, so everything is already paid for. Enjoy!" And off went our new best friend, Frank.

The cabanas faced the ocean, and we had the most perfect view of the ocean. I couldn't wait for the girls to arrive! I was wearing a white button-down long-sleeve shirt with the sleeves rolled up, and dark pink shorts. I pulled off the shorts to reveal my bathing suit—baby blue with pink pinstripes. Gabriel had on a large white tee that said, *I Love Angels*. On the back it said, *Angels Kick Butt*. He was already in his trunks—white, of course, with images of winged angels in bathing suits and surfing on red boards across blue waves. Couldn't top that. Not in Naples anyway.

I immediately recognized Annie's voice when she said, "Wow!"

"This has to be the coolest thing I've ever seen," Daphne said.

"Not too shabby," Annie added.

Gabriel and I each received a quick kiss hello from both girls. And once they caught a clear glimpse of what Gabriel was wearing, their faces broke out into smiles.

"You rock that outfit, Gabriel," Daphne said.

The ladies then revealed their bikinis. Daphne's look-at-me coral suit highlighted all that would normally need highlighting. Annie wore a simple white bikini that looked custom-made for her. Absolute perfection.

It was only a little after one in the afternoon, and Frank

brought us our second round of drinks. I stuck with Stella's, but the girls were enjoying "boat drinks," as Jimmy would say. Gabriel, of course, sipped wine—very slowly, I might add, as if nursing a hangover.

Frank suggested we let him make our food decisions for the day, so we did. And that was all it took to put us in foodie heaven, a smidge of paradise and a whopping portion of deliciousness. From shrimp cocktail to coconut shrimp to shrimp salad, we covered all the shrimp bases and then went down an endless highway of hors d'oeuvres. When we decided to give the hot tub a whirl, an endless river of chocolates arrived.

The jokes and the laughter that a hot tub can bring out between virtual strangers is amazing. I learned more about my three companions in that hot tub than I learned the during the rest of our time together. The looks we received from the people walking by and peeking at us were just as precious as the looks on our own faces.

I looked around and realized that although I was having a tremendous amount of fun, I still felt trapped. Like I was some type of prisoner. But if it weren't for my agreement with Gabriel, I wouldn't be here, and I wouldn't have enjoyed a lovely late-night conversation with a sexy, interesting woman. So there was more than one way to look at things, I had to remember.

Up the Junction

Mid-afternoon, we took a swim, told stupid jokes to each other, and ordered a huge amount of ice cream and a few more drinks. All in all, not a bad day. Gabriel turned out to be one hell of a body surfer. Who knew? The crazy thing was that whenever

Gabriel spoke, no matter the topic, you found yourself listening intently. And not just me. He seemed to affect everyone that way.

Drying off after a second swim, a commotion broke out at the far end of the beach. People were headed in that direction, and I finally asked a woman what all the fuss was about.

"It's Glenn Difford," she said. "He's shooting a commercial down there."

"For what?"

"His new Broadway show. They're premiering it here on Thursday night at the Adrienne Arsht Center before taking it to New York."

"What's it called?"

"*Up the Junction*," she said before scampering away to join the throng.

I plopped down into my lounge chair and took the final sip of beer from my bottle, which is when I noticed Gabriel's leather book and hourglass on one of the small tables. The digital numbers now read 119.0. Man, could I take 119 more hours of this? Could I afford it?

Gabriel's voice broke into my thoughts. "I've a wonderful idea for dinner tonight, ladies, and of course it's on us. Let's go to Trattoria Angela over on Vanderbilt Rd."

"But Gabriel—"

Gabriel shook his finger at me. "Michael, please, no working your brain during drinking hours. And yes, that's from my main man, Jimmy. Anyway, Trattoria's owners, Enrico and his beautiful wife, Angela, are old friends of mine. We go way back. They had another restaurant with the same name in Naples, Italy, but Angela convinced Enrico to move here. They'll be delighted to see me!"

"I'm in," Annie said, and Daphne said she'd go only if she could sit next to Gabriel. He readily agreed.

I knew one thing for sure—if they started talking baby talk to each other, I'd need a break, so I invited Annie for a walk on the beach.

Woman's World

We strolled along the ocean's edge, enjoying the breeze.

"Would you mind if I held your hand, Annie?"

"You don't have to ask. Just take it. A woman will let you know right away if it's okay.

"I see, said the blind man." Then I took her hand, and to my relief, no objection! "I enjoyed our talk last night. In fact, I've enjoyed all our talks so far."

"Even the ones where you were being yelled at?"

"Kinda, yeah."

"You don't have much experience with women, do you?"

"How could you tell?"

"Lack of confidence, for one. You get nervous, you occasionally say the wrong thing, well more than occasionally, actually."

"I know."

"You know, you're very good-looking, I'm surprised you've never been married."

"Ha! I've hardly had a girlfriend before! Shit, fuck. Did I just say that out loud?"

"You did. And I don't believe you for one single minute. You were dating that Rose lady."

"We went out three or four times, and each date, I was

painfully troubled. She's pretty attractive, and my head kept playing games with me."

"Like what?"

"Like the ones that mess with your head."

We stopped walking long enough for me to take her face into my hands and slowly kiss her. Then I stopped and stared at her for a second before kissing her again.

No way! What are the odds?

I knew the voice and couldn't have been more annoyed at its sound. "Well, hello again, Michael."

Standing in front of Annie and me was the one and only Rose.

"You won't believe this," I blurted, "but we were just talking about you, Rose."

She grinned. "Oh, I believe it."

She was wearing an all-white one-piece that clung to her body.

"I'm part of the group shooting the Glenn Difford commercial," she explained.

"Did you get to see him?" Annie asked.

"Yes, but it's no big deal. You've seen one movie star, you've seen them all. So you two are together, I see. Shall I mark a date on my calendar?"

Sweat formed on my forehead, especially as Annie also seemed to be waiting for my answer. Then she linked her arm in mine and turned me toward her before planting a soft kiss on my lips. She kissed me for a full minute before pulling away! Then, looking at Rose, she said, "We're just fuck buddies for now, right, Michael?"

Stumbling for something to say, I asked Rose if she was seeing anyone.

"I am, but that's none of your business. I've been seeing him for a while, and he hasn't got any hangups. Nice to know that they're not all assholes out there."

After we parted ways, Annie turned to me. "What did you put her through, Michael? She's one bitter chick."

I tried to protest, but Annie persisted. Before I started the story—the one that I was sure would make Annie take off running or at least take out a restraining order—I had a thought. Why was I allowing myself to be told what to do by Annie? What kind of power did she hold over me that made me want to do everything she asked? Then it dawned on me, something I'd heard since childhood that struck me as so true: It's a woman's world.

Sex Master

My fourth date with Rose happened to fall on Rose's birthday, so I wanted to make it special. One that she would never forget. But "never" is a very long time, and I inadvertently hit the nail on the head, because she'll never forget that particular birthday.

"I'm not sure where to start, but here goes," I said. "Try not to interrupt because I'd rather tell it quickly and then move on. Deal?

"Deal."

"So, Rose invited me over for a quiet dinner at her place, a one-story ranch in a small neighborhood a stone's throw away from a manmade lake. I picked up a bottle of wine and a twelve-pack of beer and headed over for what I thought might be a consummating night. Rose answered the door and, judging by her outfit, she had the same thing on her mind. She ushered me in, poured me a beer, and told me she needed a minute to finish getting ready. So, I relaxed and started snooping around her place. Nothing too intrusive, but I did open a drawer or two.

"I noticed she had a thing for candles. At least a dozen were burning throughout her house. I also opened a door on the left side of her kitchen. It was her garage, and the door was up, which I thought was kinda strange but hey, not my house. Then Rose called for me.

"At the time, I didn't realize it, but I accidently left the door open that led to her garage. So Rose was calling from her bedroom, and I joined her. Turns out, she was naked, but that wasn't the surprising part. The surprising part was that she had somehow handcuffed both her feet and her hands to the bed."

"How did she—"

"No idea. I wasn't there for that part. And not only that, but she had covered herself in oil—a lot of oil. And I kid you not, she had a huge bowl of whipped cream sitting next to the bed. And Jell-O. Three different kinds, or should I say flavors? And let's not forget the fruit. A banana and a—Christ, this is embarrassing—a cucumber."

"Technically, a cucumber isn't a fruit," Annie said. "It's a vegetable."

"Do you want to hear the rest of the story or don't you? Okay, so now I'm standing in her bedroom, and Rose is, well, squirming around on the bed, which I really didn't find to be a turn-on. In fact, I wasn't finding any of it a turn-on. And then she literally asked me, 'Are you turned on, baby? Because I am. I'm so turned on, and I'm all yours, all yours! Do whatever you like, just don't hurt me, okay?' Then she goes into hostess mode and tells me there's a blindfold on the nightstand and a few more toys if I'm interested. I looked to where she was referring and, sure enough, she wasn't exaggerating.

"I had never been in a position like this before, and I was in a state of shock. I didn't know what to say, let alone what to do. And that's when the big crash came."

"What big crash?"

"Are you going to let me tell it or not?"

"Tell it."

"There was a crash in the living room, like something had fallen over. Rose went from all hot and bothered to 'get me the fuck out of these cuffs' in a heartbeat. Before I could ask her where the keys to the cuffs were, there came another noise, but this time it was louder and closer, followed a weird-sounding noise. So I decide I've gotta see what's going on, and Rose screams, 'Don't leave me here!'

"I told her I'd be right back, and I just kinda peeked out of into the hall. At which point I screamed, tore back into the room, and jumped onto her bed. Which scared the bejeezus out of her, but I'm sort of a big baby at times, so I couldn't help it.

"Rose is screaming and asking what it was, so I look down at her and say as calmly as I can, "'It's a gator. There's an actual alligator in your house.'

"'You're shitting me!' she screams. And as if on cue, the gator pokes its head into Rose's room, lets out a snorting sound, and takes a tour. At which point I asked Rose if she smelled something burning."

Trust Me to Open My mouth

"That's when the smoke alarms went off,' I continued. "And they were loud. Smoke was finding its way into her bedroom, and our alligator friend didn't seem to be going anywhere. Between the gator, the smoke, and the naked and oily screaming woman, I was finding it hard to make a decision. But from a distance, I could hear what sounded like a fire truck. And while all this was happening, I didn't realize that I was bouncing."

"Excuse me?"

"Bouncing. On the bed. Going up and down. Some kind of self-comfort thing going on, I guess. Not like a trampoline, just a nice steady up and down. 'Michael,' Rose said, 'stop bouncing or I'm going to be sick!'

"And then she was. I'm telling ya, it was like *The Exorcist*. It went everywhere, but mostly on her since she was lying on her back and all. And even though she had pleaded with me to stop the bouncing, I didn't realize I was still doing it until I saw the throw-up also bouncing up and down. And then things took a definite turn for the worse."

"How in the hell could it get worse?"

"Well, with all the bouncing and the smell of Rose's puke, I succumbed. I fell down right on top of her and vomited, well, everywhere. If you thought Rose was screaming before—nope! She really let it rip then. And then the cavalry arrived, and we both saw a fireman running down Rose's hallway chasing an alligator.

"Water was being sprayed everywhere, and that same fireman ran past the bedroom door again, but this time the gator was chasing him. Which is when the firecrackers went off."

"Firecrackers? Who was lighting off firecrackers?"

"No one. Turns out that it wasn't firecrackers. It was bullets. The police had arrived, and they shot the gator. Which was a good thing because the gator thing was getting old. And then, lo and behold, two cops and several firemen made their way into the bedroom. First thing they did was bust out a window with an axe to let the smoke escape. Then they all turned to me as if I were responsible for the chaos. 'Don't look at me,' I said to them. 'She did this to herself.'

"The closest policeman asked Rose if this was true. It took her a while, but then she admitted that she did indeed cuff and tie herself. The cop just shook his head and muttered, 'Weirdos.'

"As a couple officers tried to help Rose get uncuffed, I heard a sneeze through the shattered window. So I turned to see a half-dozen neighbors peeking into the bedroom. Rose asked the police to get rid of them, and they told her to chill because they were busy trying to uncuff her. Which led to the next problem. Rose's cuffs were hardly official, which meant the keys the police used for their cuffs wouldn't work.

"By then, the gawkers were filming and snapping away with their phones. At which point I announced that I needed to leave because the stench was going to make me sick again. The cop looked at me and said, 'Hey, buddy, next time just bring flowers.' Which made everyone chuckle. And then a bike horn honked twice. It was the clown."

"The what, now?"

"I'd ordered a clown, which I'd completely forgotten about."

"Why?"

"It was her birthday surprise. I thought it would be cool to have a clown present her with flowers and sing happy birthday."

"You've got to be kidding."

"Nope, I got a clown. And he'd just arrived, squeezing his bike horn to beat the band. Then he stuck his head in the window and asked Rose, whose hands were still bound, if she was the birthday girl. When she nodded, he climbed in, placed the flowers on her stomach—which, don't forget, was covered in vomit—and proceeded to sing 'Happy Birthday.' For good measure, everyone joined in.

"And that, Annie, is why I don't think Rose will ever forget the birthday she spent with me."

Who Are You?

Later that night, the four of us entered Trattoria Angela. Gabriel was dressed in white, and the ladies looked great, both dressed to impress in shades of navy, Annie with the longer of the two dresses, leaving Daphne with the shorter. We were greeted by Angela herself. Immediately upon seeing Gabriel, she bear-hugged him and kissed him on both cheeks. Then she went on about how it had been too long since she had seen him, and she promised him the best meal of his life.

Then Enrico appeared, delivered his kisses, and repeated everything Angela had said. The ladies and I may as well have been invisible, but Gabriel finally introduced us.

"We have saved the best table for you and your guests," Enrico said. "Come, we will show you."

And show us they did. The table was exquisite, providing the illusion that we were off on our own little island even though we were only a few feet away from the next table. The restaurant's décor was Southern Italy, and with a drink in your system and one eye shut, you could imagine you were actually there.

"Tonight, you no pay," Enrico said. "Everything on us. We insist."

"And we will select for you," Angela said. "No need for menus." Not needing an answer, she said a waiter would be right over to take our drink order.

Our butts were barely in the chairs when the waiter appeared with two bottles of wine. "Good evening, everyone. Angela has sent over this wine to start you off." Then he approached Gabriel with the bottles.

"Ah, Leonetti Cabernet," Gabriel said, "from the Walla Walla Valley. Superb choice. Please thank Angela for me."

Glasses were poured for all of us, so when Gabriel raised his glass to make a toast, I figured why not and took a sip. It wasn't bad. By my third sip, I really enjoyed it, so much so that when the waiter came back, I didn't even order a beer.

Daphne took a sip of wine, then leaned in toward Annie and said, "I've had more fun in the last couple days than I've had in the last couple months."

Annie nodded in agreement as Daphne raised her glass toward Gabriel. "I'd like to propose a toast to our host. The man who constantly brings sunshine into our lives."

Gabriel raised his glass and spoke. "I must say, I've met a tremendous amount of people, and you three are amongst my very favorites. So, I return the salute and toast my new friends. Salud!" And we all clanged glasses.

"Michael," Gabriel said, "I can't believe you told Annie the unabridged version of Rose's best birthday story."

"I want to hear it too," Daphne whined.

"Maybe one day Michael will share it with you as well," Gabriel said.

"Or Annie can fill you in during a slow day at work," I said.

Gabriel seemed familiar with each and every dish brought out to our table. He took great pleasure in describing each item, its origins, its history, and its place in the world of Italian food. I don't usually like having my food chosen for me, but that feeling subsided after the first course arrived. It was a bewilderingly good focaccia and antipasto platter, and Gabriel acted as though he had gone back into the kitchen and made it himself.

Then came linguini and clams in portions that were too big to comprehend for appetizers. That was followed by gnocchi molisani, which is tomato in basil sauce. Finally, the main dish came out—Vitello Saltimbocca. I wasn't hungry at all, but I had to make a little room after taking just a single look. When I couldn't eat another bite, I suggested to the table that we decline dessert.

"Absolutely not," Daphne said. "Are you crazy? I can't wait to see what they bring out next!"

She didn't have to wait long before grappe and espressos were placed in front us, along with a single cannoli each. In the center of our table, a Torta Della Nonna—a simple lemon cake—was placed. As I raised the cannoli to my lips, I heard my name being called out from behind me.

Tongue Like a Knife

"Well, what do we have here?" said Glenn Difford, the dipshit of all dipshits. "Mr. Film Critic at large. I didn't know they let asswipes in here."

The hostess was seating Glenn and his companion right next to us. Just my luck. But at least we were getting ready to leave, so maybe this could be over quickly.

Glenn hovered over our table and asked if I would like to introduce him to my friends.

"No, not really," I was forced to say because of the no-lying rule.

Glenn seemed taken aback, then introduced himself. When

he went to shake hands with Gabriel, he paused and gave Gabriel a strange look. "Have we met?"

"I'm sure that we haven't, Mr. Difford," Gabriel said. "I would remember meeting such a famous movie star."

"Nice outfit, by the way. Takes guts to wear all white when we all live in such a colorful world."

It was meant to be a dig, which seemed to register with Gabriel. "Why, thank you, sir," Gabriel said. "A compliment is always a welcome bit of treasure."

Glenn was about to introduce his guest when Gabriel interrupted. "Sorry, Glenn, just a quick question if you don't mind. I'm wondering who dresses who?" He pointed at Glenn and his date. They wore matching outfits, and if I had to describe them, I'd say they looked like matching pinball machines. And that was being kind.

"This is my girlfriend, Lola, a lovely and talented fashion designer from New York, who has a show in Miami the day after tomorrow. And to answer your question, Lola designed and chose our outfits."

"Ah, I see" Gabriel said with a subtle smirk.

"Lola is in charge of my entire wardrobe, and the feedback has been nothing but positive."

"Michael," Gabriel said, "what are your thoughts on these incredibly colorful outfits, and please don't hold back. Tell the lovely Lola how talented she is."

I readied myself and gave it a go. "They're interesting," I said. Then I took a long sip of wine.

"Interesting how, Michael?"

"Well, they're colorful, to say the least. And…"

"Eye-catching," Annie added.

"Please, Michael, finish what you were going to say," Gabriel said.

"Honestly, they make you two look like a couple of pinball machines."

Daphne, who was sipping her wine, spit it back into her glass, which seemed to please Gabriel greatly.

"What the fuck?" were the first words any of us heard from Lola's mouth. "How dare you? Obviously, you have no idea about fashion."

"Nor do you, it seems," I said.

She grabbed Glenn's arm. "I've never been so humiliated."

"Oh, sure you have," I said. "In fact, I bet more times than not, you've bared the wrong end of a tongue like a knife."

"What the hell is that supposed to mean?"

Glenn broke in. "He's insulting you, babe."

"I know that!" she screamed. "What are you going to do about it?"

"Yes, Glenn," Gabriel said. "What are you going to do about it?"

"Let's just stop this now," Annie said. "Maybe we could all take a minute to gather our thoughts. Glenn and Lola, why don't you have a seat at your table, and we'll be out of here before you know it."

"Who the fuck are you, anyway?" Glenn said to Annie.

"Hey, no need for that," I said.

"Go fuck yourself, shithead," Glenn said. "Why don't you go review a Little League game or something. Oh wait, you don't comprehend sports. You just pretend to know about fine arts while you ridicule the rest of us for a living."

"I know one thing," I said. "Those outfits you're wearing are definitely not fine art. Fine garbage would be more accurate."

"Mr. Difford," Daphne said, "could I have an autograph

please? I was thinking maybe you could sign my napkin."

Lola picked up a glass of water and threw it at Daphne. "Here's your autograph. Hope you fucking treasure it."

Enrico and Angela came out from the kitchen and hurried over. "What are you doing to my favorite customers, you angry, nasty man?" Angela shouted at Glenn.

In turn, Glenn spit on his table, then flipped the whole thing over, causing quite a loud crash. "I wouldn't eat here if the food was fucking free!" Then he took Lola by the hand and stomped out past the crowd of rubberneckers and gawkers.

Wrong Side of the Moon

We were too wired to go home, so Gabriel suggested a nightcap at Off The Hook Comedy Club. By day, it was a restaurant called Captain Brian's Seafood, but at night, it became a popular comedy club. It attracted some pretty big names, but the big draw was that in between acts, they let audience members take a crack at stand-up.

We got a table near the stage, but Gabriel seemed disappointed with the wine list. After much huffing and puffing, he decided on two bottles of Justin Isosceles. I was quickly informed that I was about to try my first Bordeaux.

Gabriel then took out his leather book and hourglass, which read 110.5, although the sand seemed to have moved only a tad.

The wine turned out to be pretty good, and by my second sip, the emcee came out and introduced the upcoming comedian. The emcee was a short guy with a goatee and a waiter's jacket from the fifties. His shoes were patent leather and shined like they were on military display. "So now, ladies and gentlemen, without further ado, let's give a warm Off The Hook welcome to Gabriel Angel."

The crowd clapped. *What?* Did I just hear right? Gabriel was instantly on his feet and heading to the stage.

"What's going on, Michael?" Annie asked. "Did you know about this?"

"I'm not surprised in the least," Daphne said. "Gabriel is a man of many talents."

Annie and I just gave her a look.

Gabriel grabbed the mike. "So glad to be here with all of you! By show of hands, how many of you were born on the wrong side of the moon?"

Two people raised their hands; both looked confused and drunk.

"Always one or two in the crowd," Gabriel said. "One day I would like to meet someone born on the right side of the moon, but everyone's always from the wrong side. How can that be? So I played golf yesterday, had one heck of a game, shot an 86. Then right after that, I shot a 94 on the back nine." The crowd chuckled.

"I play other sports as well. I'm a big bowler, but if I play golf and bowl in the same day, I have trouble keeping the scores right. At the bar last night, I was telling the guys I shot 128, then quickly realized that was my bowling score, but it was too late. My handicap just went to heaven, but not in a good way.

"You all know the old adage, Why do they call golf, golf? Because 'fuck' was taken. But did you know that the game was originally intended as a torture device? That's right—it was invented by the poor to keep the rich occupied while the poor slept with their women. I'm serious, I'm not making any of this up. Google it if you don't believe me. Just type in the word 'loser' and up it will come. Wait—that's not it. 'Loser' just brings up a picture of you playing golf. Try typing in 'big loser'—no, wait, that just brings up a picture of you getting home from golf and finding all your clothes on the front lawn because you promised your wife you weren't going to play golf. Okay, try typing in 'the corner of Done and Where Did It All Go?' No, wait, that just brings up your new address.

"How many women do we have here that like to play golf? Wow, that's a lot of hands. Now drop your hands if you're referring to mini-golf. Wow, look at those hands drop. Ladies, seriously, mini-golf isn't something that you should be ashamed of. After all, it was specifically invented to keep women off the real courses. Men play golf, woman play mini-golf. It's a known fact, nothing to be ashamed of. But then one day, the inevitable happened. A woman found her way onto a real golf course. And this woman, she liked what she was seeing. This was a BIG course, and yes, she sure did like BIG. And it was a LONG course, and she sure did like LONG. And finally, it was a HARD course, and she certainly liked it HARD. So she decided she would stay and play, even if she had to play with herself. She wasn't leaving, ever. Then she decided to tell all her friends about this course and how it was big and long and hard, and that was all it took. The women came in droves. They came and they came and they came. Good night, ladies and gentlemen, it's been a pleasure. Thank you."

That SOB got a standing ovation. He took three bows before coming back down and taking a sip of his wine. Both Annie and Daphne got up from their seats and gave him big hugs and told him how wonderful he was.

What's Wrong With This Picture?

Gabriel celebrated by ordering two more bottles of wine, one for him and one for the three of us to split. Daphne was practically sitting in his lap and making it obvious that she was drunk and horny.

Annie got up to use the ladies' room, and Daphne went with her, so I turned to Gabriel. "What's wrong with this picture?"

"Haven't a clue."

"Quit it. You know damn well what I'm talking about. You're leading that poor girl on. And I'm dying to know what you're going to do if the hole you're digging gets too deep?"

"Again, Michael, I'm not sure—"

"You're flirting your ass off with Daphne, and she's doing it right back. Is this even allowed or permitted by the big guy?

"I've got it all under control."

"You think you have this under control, but you were playing Naked Twister with her the other night."

"Just relax and have a good time, Michael. Hey, I've a wonderful idea. Why don't you give stand-up a whirl?"

"That's a big no. Not part of our contract and just, well, no."

Annie and Daphne had returned and must have heard part of the conversation because Annie blurted out, "I think you're funny, Michael. You'd be great. Give it a try."

"Let me think on that," I said. "Okay, no."

"So, Gabriel," Annie said, "you said you're only going to be in town until noon on Sunday. Where are you off to next?"

"I've got a couple of logs in the fire, as they say," he answered. "I'm just not sure which to tackle next."

"Can you at least share your plans for the rest of the week?"

"And do they include us?" Daphne added.

"They'll always include you, my dear," Gabriel said as he poured the last bit of wine from his bottle and into his glass.

"What are you girls doing tomorrow?" I asked.

"Working," they said simultaneously.

"Well, that won't do," Gabriel said. "You're both calling in sick tomorrow. I insist."

"We can't just call in sick."

"But you look terribly sick to me, even as we speak. I can see you're both fading right in front of my eyes. Don't you think, Michael?"

"No, they look fine."

"Take a closer look. They both need a little R&R."

Daphne took her last sip of wine, then looked at Annie. "Come to think of it, I am feeling a little under the weather. How about you, Annie?"

"It depends on what Mr. Angel has in mind," Annie said.

"Simply this," Gabriel said. "Adventure."

Separate Beds

Just after midnight, my cell rang. It was Annie, the one and only midnight caller.

"Why am I not surprised by this call?" I said upon answering.

"Come on, you were waiting for me to call, admit it."

"Well, there's a difference between waiting for someone to call and hoping someone will call, see what I mean?"

"So, you were hoping I'd call?"

"And waiting," I threw in with a quiet laugh.

"Where should we start tonight?"

"How about this? We didn't spend enough time kissing

today."

"Did you sneak a peek into my diary? Because that's what I wrote down for biggest regret of the day."

"Maybe we can remedy that tomorrow, now that you're spending the day with Gabriel and me. Which reminds me, why did you let him talk you into calling in sick?"

"He didn't talk me into anything. I'm a big girl, and I wear big-girl pants, and I can make big-girl decisions. Plus, I've got some vacation days to burn."

"When you say 'some,' you mean?"

"The rest of the week."

"Wow."

"Good wow or bad wow?"

"Great wow. But may I ask why you're doing it?"

"This has been a really cool and, dare I say, *interesting* week so far, and if my instincts are correct, it will only get better."

"Anything else? Like maybe you're having certain feelings?"

"Nope."

"Okay, fine. What about Daphne? Also taking vacation days?"

"No, she has the flu. Out for the rest of the week."

"I see."

"Tell me what you see, Michael."

"I see a very pretty girl, too pretty for the guy she's currently hanging around with, for sure. I see her as not just a woman but as someone who could become a friend, a very close friend. I see her with a smile that radiates through the clouds on a miserable day. I see this pretty girl for more than she sees herself, which is just ordinary. I want to scream at her and to the world that she is anything but ordinary. In fact, she's extraordinary.

"And if anyone asked me why I thought this, I would simply say that this girl knows how to listen. She listens intently and caringly. She looks into your soul, not to judge but to see who you really are. I can see her lighting up a room just by walking into it. And then I see those same lights dim when she leaves. But this girl also saddens me because I know in my heart that this girl will never see me the way I see her. She is too good for me."

Annie stayed quiet for a minute, then finally said, "I'll see you tomorrow, Michael."

I put my cell down and stared at my ceiling. I thought about her in her bed, and me here in my bed, and I wondered if we'd ever have late-night conversations without being in separate beds.

First Thing Wrong

The four of us met at Joe's Diner on Tamiami Trail for a hearty breakfast. Gabriel had said that for what he had planned, we'd need full stomachs. Breakfast was wonderful, and I had a sneaking suspicion that when Gabriel was finally gone and out of my life, my bank account would be smaller, but my waist would be larger.

To my surprise, Annie tried to pay for breakfast, but Gabriel wouldn't hear of it. "Never forget to pay when a woman's involved. Jimmy always says," he explained.

"How about Jimmy pays for breakfast?" I said, hoping to get a smile from the table, but none were forthcoming.

Gabriel was wearing a white cowboy hat, white jeans, and a white golf shirt. I'd been tempted to wear all black just to see if anyone would notice, but I changed my mind and went with jeans, sneakers, and a tee-shirt. The girls did the same.

After breakfast, Gabriel informed us that he'd be driving my car. Can angels drive? I mean, I had a fairly new Ford Explorer, and I wanted to keep it that way, so I was hesitant to hand the keys over. "I don't suppose you have a license?" I asked.

"A license to fly," he said.

I gave him the keys and prayed. The girls hopped in the back, excited for whatever lay ahead.

Gabriel turned out to be a pro, so I set my mind on trying to figure out what he had up his sleeve. If I knew him at all, the day's adventure would surely cost me some money.

"How far are we going?"

"Not far."

"How long will we be gone?"

"Not long."

"This going to cost me money?"

"Yes, lots."

Then he took a right where the sign on the road said: Welcome to Flexjet Airport.

"Wow," Annie said. "Where are we going?"

"On an adventure, my dear. We are in pursuit of Jimmy."

He pulled up to a small jet. It looked brand-new and was painted a shiny white with blue lettering on the side: *Angel On Board*. On the back of the plane was a giant bumper sticker: *Angels Never Drink and Fly*.

Great Escape

"I don't know about this, Gabriel," I said once we'd exited

86

the car.

"But I told you, I have a license to fly."

"I thought you meant with your own wings. For this, don't you have to file a flight plan?"

"Done."

"What about inspecting the plane, like a prefight check list or something?"

"Done. Everything's done."

We joined the girls inside the plane. Damn, it was narrow and claustrophobic inside. Eight-seater. The girls had already made themselves mimosas and acting giddy, not seeming to care where we were headed.

I was left in the back of the plane with them while Gabriel sat up front in the cockpit. The engines turned over, and before I knew it, we started to move. Seconds later, we were on the runway and picking up speed. And then—boom—we all had wings.

"Whoo-hoo!" Gabriel exclaimed. "Nothing like flying."

The plane took a solid right and made my stomach flip.

"Hey Michael, you want to copilot for a while?"

"Not really."

"Come on. I'll tell you where we're going and what we're going to do when we get there."

I clambered into the copilot's seat, seeing nothing but clouds and blue sky rushing past. Not as bad as I thought it would be!

"You like it, don't you Michael?"

"I do. Well, I kind of do."

"So we're headed to Key West. We'll be there in about forty-five minutes. You're going to love it, and so will the girls."

The flight went fast, and Gabriel seemed to know what he was doing, so I chilled out and tried to have a good time. A car awaited us in Key West, a white Cadillac SUV, to be precise. The bumper sticker on the back read: *Angels Do It Wearing Wings*.

To my surprise, we had a driver named Jimmy. And as Jimmy pulled out onto the main highway, I only had one thought running through my brain: How much does a fucking private jet cost?

Gone to the Dogs

Our driver Jimmy didn't speak much English. He was fine with yes and no, but not much else. And we soon found out that he didn't actually know the difference between yes and no. The answer seemed to depend on his mood. Welcome to Key West.

Our first stop was Margaritaville itself. Home to food fun and everything Jimmy Buffett. You could eat a cheeseburger in paradise and then buy a Jimmy Buffett potholder. It was just past noon and the girls wanted to have a drink and a small bite, so we asked for a table and sat our asses down. The waiter came over to take our order, and Gabriel waggled his finger at him, motioning him to come closer. "Is Jimmy here?"

"Jimmy who?"

"Buffett, your boss."

"Oh, no, sir, he's not here."

"Was he here earlier?

"No sir, Mr. Jimmy has not been here today."

"Do you expect him today?"

"No sir, he is not expected, as far as I know."

"But he could pop in, right? I mean, it's not like he has to call ahead for a table. He could just pop through the door any second if he wanted to, right?"

"I guess so, sir."

"Okay, I'll have a tall glass of ice water and some volcano nachos for the table, and I'll take a cheeseburger in paradise, medium please. And I'll have it Jimmy's way, please."

"Jimmy's way, sir?"

"Yes."

At this point, my six-foot-four friend stood up and sang loudly: "Jimmy likes his with lettuce and tomato!" Then he sang the entire chorus of the song before taking a bow or three. Scant applause followed because we kinda had the place to ourselves. The girls and I also ordered cheeseburgers in paradise. As soon as the girls finished, they jumped up and went shopping in the merchandise part of Margaritaville.

"I was really hoping we'd bump into Jimmy here," Gabriel said as I paid the bill.

"Come on," I said, "let's go see what kind of trouble the girls are getting into."

We found Daphne in a shop trying on bikinis, while Annie was in the knickknack section looking at all things angel. She was holding a small book titled *Finding Your Guardian Angel*. I glanced at Gabriel, who looked back at me and shrugged.

Gabriel then picked up a small cherub playing guitar. It couldn't have been more than four inches tall. Of course, it was white, although the guitar was blue. At the bottom was inscribed the word "Margaritaville."

He seemed mesmerized by it, and the longer he held it, the more convinced I was that he was going to buy it. But I was wrong. After what seemed like a small eternity, he put it back on the shelf, and the enormous smile that had been on his face traded itself in for a large frown.

I picked out a coffee mug with "Why Don't We Get Drunk and Screw?" written across the front. Annie loved it, which was surprising, and Gabriel just shook his head. We all walked out with some type of souvenir, except for Gabriel.

"Where to next?" I asked our frowning tour guide.

Gabriel pointed up the street. "Time for a Scorpion Shot," he said.

The place was called Lucy's Retired Surfers Bar. I would have personally called it Gone To The Dogs Bar. It was a shabby little dive down the back of some alley. Gabriel had needed to ask for directions three times before we finally stumbled across it. And when we got there, none of us wanted to go in except for our mighty tour guide.

Once inside, we learned that feet could stick to a floor in real life. The girls kept asking Gabriel if they had to stay, and he responded that once the shots were done, we could all leave, but not a second sooner. A waitress named Baby Jane came over to take our drink order. It was hard to understand her because when she spoke, she made a whistling sound through her teeth. And that was only because all the front ones were missing—top and bottom—but who the hell was I to judge?

Gabriel pulled his usual Gabriel crap; he leaned in close to our waitress and whispered in her ear.

"Jimmy *who*?" she responded.

"Jimmy Buffett," Gabriel said in his regular voice.

"Here's the deal. Order or get the fuck out."

Gabriel obeyed. "One water, large and cold, and three Scorpion Shots please. And don't forget the tee shirts. That's why we're here, we want the tee shirts."

Annie was not having fun. I could tell by the look on her face. Daphne, on the other hand, was checking the place out with mild interest. At the same time, the men at the bar were checking her out. Not one of them looked like an ex-surfer—more like a bunch of ex-cons.

Baby Jane came back and dropped our drinks on the table, and I do mean dropped. Under her arm she was carrying what looked like new tee shirts. "Rule is I gotta watch you do the shots," she whistled.

On the table were three shot glasses, each filled with some type of liquid, and at the bottom lay something that resembled a dead bug.

"What is that?" I asked, pointing.

"These are Scorpion Shots, house specialty. It's tequila and a dead scorpion. You do the shot without spilling, gagging, or any other stupid thing, and you get the tee-shirt. You got sixty seconds from when I say go. Any questions?"

Before we could respond, Baby Jane exclaimed, "Good." Then she sat her own hourglass on the table and flipped it, the sand started moving fast.

"Cheers," Gabriel said, picking up his glass of water and chugging.

Annie spoke first. "No way in hell I'm touching that thing. Dead, alive, I don't care."

Daphne chimed in. "I'll give it a try if everyone else does."

"Look," Gabriel said, "you've only got thirty seconds left. Do it or you'll regret it for the rest of your lives, trust me. DO IT. NOW."

Baby Jane chimed in with her own advice. "Forget your blind ambition and trust your intuition. Now chug!"

I don't know what came over me, but I picked up the shot glass, looked at Annie and said. "This is for Annie, the coolest girl I've ever met." Then bam! I popped that sucker down, scorpion and all. Daphne followed suit and popped hers down as well. Annie just kept shaking her head no.

"Ten seconds," Gabriel announced.

Annie grabbed her shot glass and popped that sucker down, then slammed that sucker back down on the table all in a single motion.

"Time!" yelled Baby Jane. Then she added an uncaring "Congratulations" as she threw the check and three tee-shirts on the table in front of me. "By the way, Jimmy does come in once in a while, and my advice to you all earlier was actually a Jimmy quote. God, I just love that boy." Then she was off, never to return.

There's a Voice

Our next destination was The Green Parrot on Duval Street. It was only one rung up the ladder from last place. As we made our way through the door, Gabriel said, "I'll bet this is the place we find Jimmy. I hear he's always here, sipping on a cold beer."

So, we entered place number three and dump number two, and yes, the ladies and I were all wearing our new tee-shirts. Gabriel asked his usual question of the bartender, then ordered a large water for himself and told us to get whatever we wanted. We all settled for water.

We had only been there a minute before some guy straight out of the sixties came over and asked Annie to dance. She demurred.

"But this is my favorite song," he persisted. "You can't say no when my favorite song is playing."

"There's no music on," she said.

"So?"

"Never mind. Just go away, please."

"What if I don't want to? What if I want to dance with you?"

Despite the Scorpion Shot moving around in my stomach and the fact that the sixties dude looked strong, I decided I had to say something because if I didn't, I was sure I'd regret it later.

"I'll dance with you, hippie dude," I said.

"What?"

"I'll dance with you. I think you're kinda cute."

He stared at me in surprise.

"Actually, I'm just kidding," I said. "I find you repulsive."

"In what way?"

"Well, your unwashed hair for starters. A close second would be your breath. And finally, it looks like your clothes haven't been washed once this year."

"You can't talk to me that way," he slurred.

"I just did. Now go back and sit down before I embarrass your sorry ass in front of all your friends here."

He leaned in close to me and took a hard look. Then he simply said, "Okay."

Next establishment was Captain Tony's, Jimmy's favorite place in the whole world, according to Gabriel. I actually liked Captain Tony's; from the short time we were there, it spoke to me in a way that said welcome and take off your bra if you're wearing one. There were bras nailed all over the walls, the ceilings, and everywhere else imaginable.

"We can skip this place," Gabriel said after taking a peek inside.

Then we headed to Sloppy Joe's, my personal favorite. We ordered beers, then sat back and enjoyed the crowd. It turned out that this place not only hosted Jimmy but was Ernest

Hemingway's main hangout when he lived in Key West. After one uneventful round, the girls wanted more time to shop. Gabriel whispered into my ear, so I took out my wallet and handed over my credit card. In turn, he handed it to the girls and told them everything was on him.

Rough Ride

Back at the airport, Gabriel seemed a little down that we hadn't run into Jimmy. It had let air out of his wings, so to speak. We said goodbye to Jimmy, our driver, whom I tipped. Then we were off.

Within minutes, the sky grew dark, then we heard our first rumble of thunder, followed by a roar of thunder. Next came the onslaught of rain. When it started hitting us sideways, the tension onboard became noticeable. Even Gabriel had some sweat on his brow.

Three times, the plane suddenly dropped, then just as suddenly stopped dropping, giving us a hard jolt. We also got violently pushed left and then right. The girls were no longer smiling as they gripped their armrests, and I tried my best not to vomit.

"Bit of a bumpy ride, eh?" Gabriel said, sounding unconcerned.

"Are we okay?" I asked as the plane took another sudden drop.

"Oh yes, no worries here."

And that's when the lights went out, along with the control panel. The plane started to lose altitude, making my stomach turn, but it was the nosedive that came right after that made me throw up all over the control panel and the front window.

"Okay let's see," Gabriel said. "What to do, what to do."

Annie screamed in an "We're all going to die!" kind of way, and Daphne had her eyes squeezed shut and seemed to be praying.

"This ever happened before?" I asked Gabriel.

"Nope."

"Can you tell me what's happening?"

"I'm trying to restart our engines."

Of course, he could afford to be calm. He had nothing to lose because angels can't exactly get killed in plane crashes, can they?

We were violently thrashed about as we soared toward the ground, and I'd swear I could taste that damn scorpion again, which only made me feel more nauseated.

"Everything okay there, Michael? Not going to toss your cookies again, are you?"

I closed my eyes and prayed.

Then the rain halted, just like that. A moment later, the plane's engines coughed and came back to life. In the distance, the sun shone through the breaking clouds and the howling of the wind ceased.

Gabriel took a wide sharp turn to the right, bringing dread to my stomach.

"Don't worry," Gabriel said. "Just lining us up for our final approach."

"Really? We're almost there?"

"Yes, really."

The girls were now smiling and breathing easier. A few minutes later, Gabriel set us down on a sunny runway at Flexjet Airport, where our adventure had started a few short hours ago.

Book Two

Good Times Bring Me Down

"I hope a good time was had by all," Gabriel said as we all climbed into my Explorer, Gabriel at the wheel.

"If that was good times," I said, "I would just like to say that good times bring me down. There's a quote for you Gabriel. Sorry it's not from Jimmy, but it will have to do."

"I like it, Michael," he said. "Now I've got one for you. 'With a little love and luck, we'll all get by.'"

Annie and Daphne declared it a good one as Gabriel pondered our next stop. "What say we go have ourselves a tasty, fun, laid-back dinner?"

We all agreed, and Celebration Park—a well-known food truck on Becca Avenue—became our destination. You could say Becca Avenue was Food Truck Heaven, with hundreds of trucks that served anything from hot dogs to lobster tails cooked by gourmet chefs. Daphne volunteered to stay with the table, telling Gabriel to pick out something for her, anything at all as long as the portion was big.

Gabriel handed my credit card to Annie and asked her to grab drinks for us all while suggesting that I would pick out her food, which she surprisingly she agreed to. Gabriel then disappeared and left me on my own, but before I got far, Annie tapped me on the shoulder.

"Michael, your card was declined."

"You're kidding."

"Why are you surprised, given the way you've been spending. Do you have another card?"

"Yes, but I gave it to Gabriel. Wait, I might have one for emergencies." I fished through my wallet. "Here you go." I reluctantly handed her a card and wondered why she didn't offer to buy the drinks, but I figured it out later. Gabriel had sent her to a very expensive wine truck, and she had purchased two bottles of Caymus Cabernet.

Meanwhile, Gabriel was showing off all the food he had gotten with my other card, receiving oohs and aahs from the girls. Just as I was about to bite into my crabcake sandwich, the inevitable happened.

"Son of a bitch. Is that you, Michael?" Rose was standing behind us with a man I had never seen before.

"Why is it everywhere I go, you turn up like a bad penny?" she continued.

Then Gabriel invited Rose and her friend to join us, which they did. The six of us fit snugly at the table, and Gabriel immediately poured them some wine. Rose seemed impressed, but her friend, whose name turned out to be Jools, couldn't have cared less. In fact, he didn't seem to be interested in anything, including his date.

Slap and Tickle

"Rose," Annie said, "I've heard so much about you from Michael. How you ever lasted four dates with him, I'd say it was a small miracle!"

"Did he tell you about my birthday?" Rose asked, clearly hoping the answer would be no.

"He did, and I 'd like to say that I think you handled the whole situation very well."

"I haven't heard the story yet," Daphne said.

"And you're not going to hear it," I said.

"If you two won't tell me, I'm sure I can get Gabriel to tell me later." She gave Gabriel a little tickle.

"We'll see, Daphne," Gabriel said. "We'll see."

Meanwhile, Jools was ignoring his own food and randomly picking at everyone else's.

"How did you and Jools meet, Rose?" Gabriel asked.

"We met at the carwash. Jools works there."

"And how long have you worked there, Jools?"

Jools shrugged. "I don't know."

Then he reached across the table and picked up something off my plate.

Annie then changed topics, but only a little. "So Rose, what did you ever see in this guy?" She pointed at me.

"He looked lost, you know? Like a puppy. I felt sorry for him. He asked me out and he was so nervous, he was sweating through his clothes—and his leg was shaking, you know, like Elvis?"

Rose stood up and did her best Elvis impression, then sat back down. "So, if you put that all together, I guess I kinda pitied the fool.

"Oh, come on," I said. "There had to be other reasons. Surely you found me attractive in some way?"

"Nope."

"What about charming?"

"Nope."

"Well mannered?"

"Nope."

"You must have thought that I was funny."

"Nope."

I threw my hands in the air. "I give up. Guess I'm not a chick magnet."

Rose and Annie tried not to spit out whatever it was they were drinking.

Then I saw Mr. Swiper reaching across the table, heading for my plate again, and I snapped. I reached out and slapped his hand, just hard enough to send a message.

I pointed at Jools and asked Rose, "What the hell do you see in this guy?"

Before Rose could answer, Annie grabbed my arm and told me to shush.

"Oh, let him go, Annie," Gabriel said. "Michael's got a right to speak his mind. Why don't we let him share his thoughts on our new friend here?"

For once, I didn't need encouragement to tell the world my unfiltered feelings. "He's obviously an asshole."

"Tell us how you really feel," Gabriel said, wearing a smile big enough to hold all the water in the Naples reservoir.

Looking at Jools, I realized he was now eating something off Annie's plate. Rose saw my anger building and told Jools it was time they hit the road so we could finish our meals in peace.

"What's left for us to finish?" I said. "Your boy toy has eaten everything on the table, including polishing off all the wine."

Jools stood up, opened his mouth, looked from face to face, then let out a burp that seemed to last a millennium.

Take Me, I'm Yours

The four of us went back to my place for a nightcap. Upon our arrival, Daphne got frisky with old Gabriel, and I couldn't help but wonder how he was going to handle it. Meanwhile, Annie was acting strangely since our encounter with Rose and Dickhead.

Gabriel opened a bottle of Chimney Rock Cabernet and poured us each a generous amount. I tried it and was surprised how much I liked it. Actually, each time Gabriel uncorked a new bottle, I found myself looking forward to tasting it, wondering what kind of aromatic adventure awaited in the glass. Would it be fruity or more on the vanilla side? A hint of chocolate or a small bit of tobacco flavoring? My favorites were mostly turning out to be fruity.

Gabriel put his leather book and hourglass on my dining room table. The digital display now read 86 even. Daphne went over and whispered something into Annie's ear, which made Annie smile. Annie whispered something back, which made Daphne smile. Daphne then went over and whispered something in Gabriel's ear, which in turn made him smile. I seemed to be the only one out of the smile loop.

Daphne, pulling Gabriel by the shirt sleeve, announced to the room, "We're going for a walk. Be back soon." Then came the famous Daphne giggle. Gabriel shrugged, grabbed his glass of wine, and before you could say Jimmy Buffett, they were gone.

Alone with Annie at last, I went straight over and kissed her—hard and passionately. After a minute, I stopped, took a breath, then started kissing her again, only this time I did it slowly, with more purpose and heart.

Annie was on the same wavelength, kissing me right back in

the same way. We found our way to the couch, where we basically fell down onto it. Somehow I ended up on the bottom, which was fine with me.

Annie went from my lips to my neck, then back to my lips again, a total pro at getting me excited. She paused long enough to pull off her shirt, which she thew on the floor. Then back to the kissing and what I would describe as trying to have sex with our clothes on. We were grinding into each other in a good way, a very good way.

"Take your shirt off, Michael," she said. "In fact, take everything off."

She nibbled my ear, and when her mouth found mine again, her tongue taught mine the tango, I hit a plateau brought on by a series of things: add one part kissing, one-part dry humping, and a woman's voice saying to take off all your clothes—well, that was enough for me. I exploded like Fourth of July fireworks. Little Michael, as I sometimes refer to him, erupted like Mount Vesuvius.

I had to say something because Annie was still grinding away, and I needed to let her know that the party was over, at least for me. I needed the right word to let her know what had happened, so I went with, "Oops." Then, "I am so sorry, Annie. I just couldn't control it."

It took her a couple of seconds to catch on, but when she did, the look on her face almost made me cry.

Annie got up and sipped her wine, then quickly put her shirt back on. I went over and put my arms around her, then apologized for ending things before they actually got started. Annie turned, took me into her arms, and smiled.

"No worries, Michael. It happens to every guy sooner or later. And sometimes more than once." She kissed me softly on the lips. "Has anyone ever told you that you are a really good kisser?"

"Just my mom," I said.

She pulled away, shaking her head, then picked up her wine again. "Can I ask you a question?"

"Sure, but can I ask you one first? What did I miss before with Gabriel and Daphne? All that whispering and smiling, what was that all about?"

"Oh, I almost forgot. I think Gabriel is going to get lucky tonight. Daphne took him to my place. She planned to tell him, 'Take me, I'm yours.'"

Is It Too Late?

Five minutes later, I burst through the door of Annie's place. Why I felt the need to stop Gabriel from doing something that was none of my business, I don't know. What I did know was that I felt it was my responsibility to at least try and stop him. Annie trailed behind, bewildered about why I was in such a hurry to prevent them from curbing their urge to merge.

Then things got worse, or at least more confusing. I found myself in Annie's living room, staring at Daphne, who was lying on the couch, fully dressed, and crying her eyes out. Gabriel was sitting in a chair beside her, trying to comfort her. He was holding a box of tissues in his hands, peeling fresh ones off the top and handing them to Daphne as necessary. A large pile of used tissues sat on the floor.

My mouth did what it usually does and said the first thing that my mind told it to say. "What the hell is going on here?"

"Michael," Gabriel said, "I don't see where this is any of your business."

"I don't mind," Daphne said.

"Well, that's your decision, dear," Gabriel said, sipping from a nearly empty wine glass. "Did either of you think to bring another bottle of wine over?"

"Why are you crying?" Annie asked Daphne.

"Gabriel was kind enough to let me complain about something from my childhood. He's such a good listener. He has a way of getting people to open up. It's such a gift." She gazed at Gabriel. "Were you maybe a therapist in a past life?"

"Quite sure that I wasn't."

"Well, you certainly have the knack. I feel ten times better than I did an hour ago, and it's all thanks to you. If we could find the time to do this again before you leave on Sunday, I would really appreciate it."

"I will make the time, Daphne."

Gabriel pointed at my crotch area. "Michael, what's that stain there?" Then he leaned down closer to get a better look.

I tried to shield the evidence with my hand and told Gabriel it was nothing.

"But I'd love to know, wouldn't you, Daphne?"

"Definitely," she said, leaning down to get a closer look.

"It was just a small accident, nothing worth talking about. Let's open another bottle of wine, what do you guys say?"

"Maybe just tell them what it is," Annie said, "so we can all go to bed."

I looked from face to face, knowing I would regret this in the morning. "Annie and I were, you know, kissing and... and I had a small miscalculation and I..."

"Michael came in his pants while we were kissing, okay?" Annie said. "The gun went off early, no big deal. So, let's move on. He's embarrassed enough, aren't you Michael?"

I was now.

Bang Bang

Ten minutes later, Gabriel and I were back at my place. He popped a cork and was walking around in his angel jammies—white boxers and a tee-shirt that said: *Have you talked to your angel today?*

Falling onto my sofa, I figured now was as good as time as any to get some answers. "Spill it, Gabriel. What's going on with you and Daphne?"

"Daphne is a very pretty girl and I enjoy her company. And on Sunday I'm off, and that, as they say, is that."

"Can you offer anything else that might calm my nerves?"

"You'll have to calm your own nerves. Now tell me how things are going with Annie. Do you think there will be a second attempt at scoring or are you afraid of another offsides?" Gabriel laughed at his own joke. "You know, if Jimmy were here, he'd tell you that life is a journey that's not measured in miles or years, but in experiences. Does that resonate, Michael?"

"I'll think about it."

"Seriously, if you want to hit home runs, you have to expect to hit some foul balls. And I am sorry about the whole thing. Annie is a lovely girl, and she should not have had to suffer through your shortcomings."

"Ha-ha, ha-ha. You're so funny. Funniest angel I know."

Gabriel then produced his leather-bound book and hourglass, which read 84.0. "You've hit the halfway point, Michael. Time sure flies when you're having fun."

"So this is what fun is like?"

"I'm willing to wager that you'll miss me when I'm gone."

"Hey, Gabriel, tell me again what heaven is like."

"It's Some Fantastic Place. Will that do for now?"

"That'll do, Gabriel, that'll do."

The Waiting Game

It was almost 1:00 a.m., and my cell hadn't rung yet. Was Annie mad about the rocket ship taking off early? Maybe she was just tired and fell asleep? Or maybe she came to her senses and wondered what the hell she was doing with this schmuck. Fuck it, I'm calling, and I don't care if I wake her up.

She answered on the first ring. "What took you so long?" she said.

"How come you didn't call?"

"You know the phone works both ways, right?"

"But it was tradition. You always called me."

"Okay, okay, I'll call you next time, all right?"

"Are you mad at me?"

"Not at all, not in the slightest bit."

"Will I get another chance at you-know-what?"

"If you play your cards right."

"Thanks."

"You don't have to thank me. But let me ask you a question. Are you a virgin?"

"Ask me anything but that."

"I think I'll stick with that."

"Why do you ask? Is there a sign flashing 'Virgin' above my head?"

"So you are one then?"

I sighed. "Yes, I am. I'm a virgin and I'm stupid."

"Ha, I told Daphne, but she didn't believe me."

"Hold on, hold on. You and Daphne discussed me being a virgin?"

"Not in a mean way, just a factual way. No disrespect meant. It's just that... well, it's hard to understand, is all. You're a good-looking guy in your early forties, and you have a great job. How have you not played Pin the Tail on the Donkey?"

"It's hard to explain, but now that the cat's out of the bag, where does this put us?"

"Is there an us?"

"I thought there starting to be an us, didn't you?"

After what seemed like an hour but was actually about ten seconds, Annie said, "Of course there is starting to be an us."

"Did I spoil it with little Michael jumping out of the plane too soon?"

"You did not."

"Does my lack of experience create an issue?"

"It's nothing we can't deal with."

"Where do we go from here?"

"According to Gabriel, we're all going to breakfast."

I Don't Want to Grow Up

In the morning, we were back at Joe's Diner on Tamiami, and we all had huge appetites, especially Daphne. She ordered Waffles and Chicken, which totally grossed me out. Picture, if you will, four big waffles topped with chicken tenders covered in an abundance of maple syrup, then top that off with a heap of whipped cream—and you have Daphne's breakfast.

Gabriel's hourglass and book were on the table, as usual. Although I'd seen him take out that book dozens of times now, I realized I'd never seen him actually open it. That would have to be a question for Gabriel during our alone time.

"What's on the agenda today, Gabriel?" Annie asked as we all turned to him.

"Why is everyone looking at me?" he said between bites of biscuits and gravy. "It's not like I'm in charge or anything." Then he laughed. "Okay, here's what I've got for us today. I call it a one-two-three punch. We are going to hit three things today, and we are going to hit them hard. We'll start with a manatee sightseeing tour, then a dolphin sightseeing tour, and last but not least, an electric moped tour around Naples. Then Michael will treat us to a filling, mouthwatering dinner."

He stood and took a bow as Daphne clapped.

"What's a manatee?" Annie asked.

"It's something that looks terribly like Michael. It lives in the ocean but very close to shore, and it usually weights 800 to 1,300 pounds. Too big for the bathtub, but they are most adorable. So, let's finish our breakfast and get on with it, shall we?"

The small sightseeing boat could hold forty-two people, but it was only half full. It had a canvas cover for blocking out the sun and open-air seating. Gabriel acted like a little boy, bursting with excitement, and I wondered what that was all about. I could only imagine what one might find if the layers of the onion that we call Gabriel were pulled back and the true angel exposed.

By the time the boat pushed off, Gabriel and Daphne were behaving like little kids taking off on an adventure for the first time, like Peter Pan in duplicate.

The boat took us down a river, the name of which I didn't

catch. Annie sat close to me, so I reached over and held her hand, but the moment our hands touched, Gabriel cleared his throat loudly. I turned to see him give me a thumbs-up.

Our guide, Roberto, was wonderful. He even slowed the boat to show us a twelve-foot gator swimming along the left bank. Mr. Gator then made his way onto shore and plopped down on the sand. Roberto told us that gators liked to sun themselves daily.

Annie announced that she was not a fan of alligators and had no intention of petting one.

"What makes you think you're supposed to pet the alligator?" I asked.

"Gabriel told me they were friendly, practically housebroken, and I should feel free to pet them unless the guide said not to. Because once in a blue moon, they might not be friendly."

I turned back around to see Gabriel and Daphne laughing their asses off.

"Anything else from wise old Gabriel?" I asked Annie.

"He said I could ride a manatee if I spotted the first one, and he said that if I got too hot, I could strip down to my bathing suit and take a dip in the river here."

I didn't have to turn around this time because I could hear the laughter behind me. Then Roberto leaned over and told Annie not to listen to Gabriel anymore on this trip. In fact, he suggested that Annie do the opposite of whatever Gabriel told her.

Hesitation

Annie was simply amazed at the size of the first manatee we came across. Roberto said it was well over a thousand pounds.

It came right up to our boat and acted like it wanted to be pet, which Roberto confirmed. It seemed this large and incredibly ugly mammal just wanted some love.

Not that I'm ever the brave one, but for some reason my hand reached out to touch the manatee. I felt its slippery skin, and with each stroke I gave it, I'd swear that its eyes blinked in appreciation. Even Gabriel had no sarcastic comments or jokes as we each took a turn petting and stroking the manatee, except, that is, for Annie. Let's just say that she was on the hesitant side of this encounter.

I could tell she secretly wanted to, but she couldn't take the plunge, so I figured encouragement might be in order. "Annie, you know you're a major wuss, right?"

"Sticks and stones, Michael."

"When we're all back home, you're going to kick yourself for not doing it."

"I don't care."

"But Annie, do you think for one single minute that I'd let you get hurt in any way?"

"Of course not."

"Here's the thing. These creatures are referred to as sea cows, and they are known for their extreme gentleness. And you've never heard of cows biting, right? So go ahead."

Annie looked at Roberto, who nodded his approval. Then, inch by inch, she reached toward the manatee before pulling her hand back.

"Annie, there's nothing to fear here, I promise you." Then I guided her hand to the manatee and placed it on the slippery skin.

"Wow, I've never felt anything like this. It's like a cool kind of wet rubber."

Later, on our dolphin tour, Annie was much easier to

convince to get into the water and play with the dolphins. I would have bet that it would have been Gabriel and Daphne with the biggest smiles on their faces when the boat brought us back to shore, but I'd have been wrong. It was Annie who was beaming from ear to ear and acting like a school kid back from a class trip.

I Can't Hold On

If you've never swum with dolphins before, then you have no idea what you're missing. None of us had ever done it before, although we'd all wanted to. Annie, who had been most reluctant on our last outing, was first in the water on this one.

If a manatee felt like wet rubber, then a dolphin was the same but on steroids. We were put in the equivalent of a large swimming pool, no deeper than waist high, and we had to wear life vests. Our host, a Miss Aimee Mann, said it was non-negotiable; no vest meant no dolphins.

Annie was first to ride a dolphin. Daphne was second and squealed with delight. Gabriel didn't exactly ride a dolphin; it was more like he played vigorously with two of them. If I didn't know better, I'd swear his dolphins somehow knew him or knew where he was from. He roared with amusement as they pushed and pulled him around the pool. Next up was yours truly, and I couldn't wait. My dolphin's name was Simon and not only was this little sucker smart but he was also intuitive. And may I add, horny.

He wanted a piece of me, no doubt about it. Not in a mean or aggressive way, no. He had something else on his mind, although Aimee assured me that what was happening between

Simon and me was indeed normal.

Normal, my ass.

Simon made it abundantly clear that he didn't want me to ride him; however, he also made it abundantly clear that he wanted to ride me. It started with where he put his nose, and once it was there, Simon wanted to show me what he could do with his nose.

The next thing I learned about dear Simon was that the word "no" was not part of his vocabulary. Aimee then conceded that Simon was acting a tad unusual, and she tried to calm him down after he mounted me from behind. I could hear laughter and shouting coming from my three comrades, and yes, Gabriel was the loudest.

"Don't get there too early like you did yesterday," Gabriel shouted. "Simon might not be as forgiving as Annie." This was followed by hooting and more laughter.

Then, suddenly, the SOB was gone—nowhere to be seen. And for some reason, this scared me even more. I looked around half expecting to see him charging me, but Simon had gone into stealth mode. Until out of nowhere, that big sucker came up underneath me and picked me up. Now I was on top of this horny beast, being transported across the pool at lightning speed. I was pretty sure I could hear cheers coming from all directions. I do remember yelling at the top of my lungs that I couldn't hang on, but no one seemed to care.

I held on as long as I could but finally lost my grip and went flying at great speed. I woke up later in the locker room with everyone looking down at me.

"Awesome ride, my friend," Aimee declared.

"Michael, you had us all so worried," Annie said. "You don't need to try and impress me with your childish ways. You could have gotten hurt out there."

Strong in Reason

It was soon time for our electric moped tour of Naples, but everyone agreed to a quick hot dog and soda at one of the roadside places first, the kind with a pretty girl in a bikini standing next to a hot dog cart.

I would have to say that riding mopeds is something that everyone needs to do at least once in their lives. I would go as far as saying, do it as often as possible. It's that much fun. I had no hesitation whatsoever. I jumped right on and encouraged the rest of the group.

Annie was beginning to make me smile with incredible ease. It was just something about her that made me feel so comfortable, and she put me at ease with myself. Every time I'd look at her, I'd catch her staring at me, although she was probably thinking the same thing about me. At this point, I'd seen her with and without make-up. I preferred without. She had a natural beauty, and I was dying to tell her that, among other things. When you're on a moped ripping around the streets, your mind wanders, and mine kept wandering to Annie. It was crazy. I had literally zero experience in the romance department, let alone the love department, yet here I was riding around downtown Naples with a beautiful woman who actually wanted to be in my company.

If somebody had told me a week ago that I'd be here today with Annie, I would have laughed my ass off. But on the other hand, I wasn't stupid. I couldn't help but wonder what it would be like to do things without Gabriel around. Would Annie find me boring and dull? Would the allure disappear when Gabriel returned to heaven?

And then a bigger question hit me: Did I want to keep

hanging around with Annie once this little charade was over? Was it Annie that I was enjoying or was it the thrill of the four of us having crazy fun?

Wait one minute! Stomp on the brakes! How the hell could I have forgotten? This whole damn thing is about God answering *my* prayers. At the end of the week, Gabriel was going to reward me with the love of my life. Damn, I needed to keep things in perspective.

I wondered who the love of my life would be. What did she look like? What kind of body did she have? Would we have a lot in common? When would we meet? As soon as the hourglass ran out? Maybe the next day? And what about Annie? Should I keep her around in case the new thing doesn't work out? No, that wouldn't be fair to her. So, am I supposed to break it off with her on Sunday? Then again, is there something to break off with Annie? Maybe she's just here having fun for the week. Once Gabriel was gone, the big-time money spending would be gone also. So how could I find out if Annie was interested in me—the real me? Because once Gabriel was gone, I'd need a second mortgage on my house and a second job to pay off all this debt.

Before I knew it, we were at the Naples Pier. I parked and followed the gang out, walking beside the girl that made me smile.

Funny How It Goes

Funny how it goes sometimes, I thought as I took Annie's hand in mine and strolled down the pier. At the end, we stopped and enjoyed the view. Gabriel seemed content talking up Daphne, which still worried me, but I'd been told to mind my own business, so that was what I intended to do. Annie, on the other hand, was my business, and I wanted nothing more than to tend to her.

Then I got lost in my thoughts again and didn't hear Annie trying to ask me a question. She pretended to knock on my head. "Hello, anybody home?"

"Sorry, you caught me daydreaming."

"Anything to do with me?"

"Sort of, but not important enough to talk about. What's your thoughts on dinner?"

"No, no, no, mister. I'm not letting you off that easy. You admit you were thinking about me but you're not willing to share these thoughts?"

"I'm embarrassed. Can we leave it at that?"

"No. Spill it or I'll throw you off the pier. How does that sound, buddy?"

"Okay, but remember, you wanted to know. I was thinking about last night and wondering if tonight I was going to get another chance."

She smiled. "I'd say the odds are in your favor." Then she kissed me. A nice, tender, long kiss. Then she asked me if I wanted another chance.

"Yes," I whispered in her ear. "More than anything."

"Then let's make it happen."

Hers lips were back on mine when I heard Gabriel's voice. "Okay, you two. Enough. Why don't you go find a room already? There's more to life than kissing, and I'm about to show you one of those things right now." He summoned us all closer, as if about to share a secret. "People aren't supposed to do this, which means that technically it's not allowed, but sometimes rules are meant to be bent, and I'm about to bend one."

Here we were at the end of the famous Naples Pier, which has been around since 1888, and we were surrounded by about a hundred other folks. But Gabriel, it appeared, was now climbing onto a bench and up to a wide railing, where he made a speech.

"My friends and fellow pier walkers, I am here to demonstrate the thrill of living. By this simple act of courage, I will demonstrate how to take life by the balls and show it who's boss. I, Gabriel Angel, will dive with enough style and form to impress any Olympic judge. Behold, the dive of all dives. But to any kiddies here today, please don't try this at home."

He turned and faced the water, counted to three, and off he went.

Just as he predicted, it was the perfect dive. The crowd cheered, but the newly arrived police did not. They fought through the crowd so they could get down to the beach and get to Gabriel, probably to arrest his ass. I ushered the girls off the pier and back to our mopeds. Miraculously, Gabriel was already there, dripping wet and in a hurry.

"Police seem to want to speak with me about something. Heaven only knows what it could be, so I suggest we skedaddle."

Then he started his moped and took off. We followed suit, and as we turned the corner, I looked back to see the police approaching the spot we'd just vacated.

A mile later, Gabriel insisted we stop in for a celebratory round in honor of escaping the Five-0. We stopped in a bar, ordered some apps and drinks, and recounted the day. Gabriel was so proud of himself that he wanted to talk of nothing but his glorious swan dive. Annie, who was playing with her phone, interrupted with a moan of disappointment. "Darn, it's not here," she said.

"What's not there, dear Annie?" Gabriel said.

"I filmed you jumping from the pier, but it's the craziest thing. It's like you just disappeared."

"Well, I did actually. You must have started filming after I jumped."

"Darn, I really thought I'd captured it. That would have been so cool to see again."

"Maybe Gabe can do it again," Daphne said.

"Oh no, once is enough."

"Was it scary?" I asked.

"Not for a man like me, Michael."

"What's that supposed to mean?"

"I'm the strong, adventurous type. It just goes with the territory."

"If you say so," I said with more than a hint of sarcasm.

"What was the reasoning behind your dive, Gabriel? Why'd you do it?"

"Sheer delight, my pretty one, sheer delight."

"But you could have killed yourself."

"Thought never entered my mind . As I said earlier, I just wanted that feeling of being alive. Don't you ever want to feel alive?"

"Yes, but I'm not jumping off a pier to feel it. I'd like to think that love and companionship is enough to make me feel alive. What do you think, Michael?"

"I'm with you," I said. "It's the simple day-to-day things that make a person feel alive the most, if you let them, that is. No one should just walk through life with blinders on. Everyone should stop and smell the roses. Because if you go through life with your eyes and heart open, you'll have enough to get through each day without having to find other thrills."

"Bravo, Michael, bravo!" Annie said as she put her around me and planted a big wet one on my cheek.

Hope Fell Down

We limited ourselves to two drinks each because we still had the mopeds and didn't want to take any chances. But Gabriel and Daphne were as giddy as ever, and sweet Annie was hanging on my every word. It doesn't get any better than this, I thought. Then I looked at my watch and saw it was almost time to return the mopeds, so I signaled for the check.

"Michael, how incredibly sweet you are to pick up the tab," Gabriel said between sips of wine.

"Why don't you let me get a bill once in a while?" Annie whispered. "It's not fair that you always get the short end of the stick. I see what Gabriel does by sticking it to you just about every time."

"Trust me, it's every time. But frankly, Annie, I doubt the man even owns a wallet, let alone has cash."

"Stand up to him, Michael. Show him you are a grown-ass man. Take that bill and stick it in his hand and say with a firm voice, 'This belongs to you, and as a matter of fact, so does the next one and the one after that. Do it."

But I merely waved the check in front of Annie. "You know what I'm going to do with this? I'm going to pay it." And off I went with my tail between my legs and a frown on my face.

Annie, Get Your Gun

Soon enough, we were back on the mopeds, laughing our

collective asses off. Until we heard gunfire, that is. Gunfire has its own distinctive sound, similar to firecrackers but with more snap and pow. When you hear it, even if it's for the first time, your brain knows what it's hearing. But even armed with that information, reaction times vary from person to person. I was out front, so, I was probably the first to hear the crack-crack sound. Describing what took place over the next minute or so is hard to do, but if you've ever seen *Heat*, the Michael Mann film, there is a scene where a group of bank robbers exit a bank they've just robbed, and the cops are already there, so chaos ensues.

That is pretty much what happened here. We had stumbled into a bank robbery gone bad, very bad. I saw four men with ski masks on running out onto the street and firing big, loud guns, the type that can keep firing for a long time. The police were across the street firing smaller guns back at the bad guys, and even though the police had small guns, they were just as loud as the big guns.

As my mind absorbed the situation, my body had not yet had time to respond. It was probably the bullet that struck my moped that finally got my mind and body on the same wavelength—or maybe it was the second bullet to hit the moped. Either way, fear took over and I hit the brakes so hard that the moped turned on its side and began sliding towards the bad guys.

Instead of worrying about myself, my mind went straight to Annie, who had been just a few yards behind me. As I came to a stop, Gabriel screamed, "Duck, Michael! Keep your head down!"

I turned back to the sound of his voice just in time to see and feel Annie running over me with her moped, which then toppled over and sent her into the air.

Somehow I managed to crawl over to Annie, who was lying on her side a few feet away. I had no idea what kind of condition she was in. She could have been shot off her moped, for all I knew. When I reached her, she had the biggest smile on her face and was trying to tell me something. I took her into my arms, noticing the gunfire and everything else came to a sudden stop.

"Michael, you came for me," she said, sounding tired and hazy.

I returned her smile and squeezed her tightly. "Are you hurt?"

"I don't think so, just feel woozy, like the wind's been knocked out of me. How about you?"

"Well, I've been shot at by bank robbers twice and run over by my girlfriend while lying in the street, but sure, I'm pretty good."

"What did you just say?"

"I said that you ran—"

"No, about me being your girlfriend?"

"Oh, that. Yeah…"

"So I'm your girlfriend?"

"You two okay?" said Daphne, standing nearby.

Gabriel came jogging over a second later. "What in God's name has happened? You two are like trouble magnets. This is unbelievable."

Once Annie and I were up and had our senses back, we went and sat on the curb. Gabriel was talking to a police officer, then came back over to us. "Police said to stick around because they're going to need a statement from you both." He turned to Annie. "So why didn't you shoot at the bad guys?"

"I didn't have a gun."

"Maybe you should think about getting one. You know what Jimmy says, don't you? Never forget to duck."

Loving You Tonight

The girls were told to meet us at my place for pre-dinner drinks at six sharp. On my table, Gabriel had laid out a gorgeous charcuterie board, two bottles of Quilceda Creek Cabernet, four wine glasses and, last but not least, his leather-bound book and the hourglass.

The girls arrived at six on the button, and Gabriel fixed us all up with wine.

"Cheers," Gabriel said as we all raised our glasses.

Then Gabriel raised his glass and stated that he had a more poignant toast to make, which made a knot form in my throat and stomach. I felt sure that whatever he was going to say, it wouldn't be good.

"Ladies and Michael, in the immortal words of the great Jimmy Buffett, I'd like to say that in my experience walking around this great world, Jimmy and I have noticed something peculiar. It's very simple. Men have many faults, and women have only two: all that they say and all that they do. Then he started to laugh and laugh, with no sign of stopping in sight.

Annie booed, and Daphne gave a courtesy chuckle.

When Gabriel finally caught his breath, he raised his glass back into the air. "Just a bit of humor to lighten up the evening. Here's my real toast. It's people who make the world go round, and it's people who make life worth living for other people. The camaraderie that we all share, the love that we pass to each other, and the friendships that endure are what keep us from being alone and afraid. Which in turn produces happiness that flows through us all, reminding us that we are alive, that we are not just another number or another stranger walking around without purpose or love or direction. We are all loved, and we all love each other back.

"And because of you three, I was not alone this week, I was not afraid this week, and I did not feel unloved this week. So, I thank you for what you've given me. I'm loving each and every one of you tonight. Cheers again."

Annie and Daphne welled up, and even I might have had a slightly wet eye. Then Gabriel came over and gave each one of us a big kiss on the lips, followed by a hug, Gabriel style. Which meant that each hug lasted about five minutes.

There's No Tomorrow

Mediterano was a Mediterranean restaurant in the North Section of Naples. It was loved by all who had been lucky enough to eat there. For the rest of us, we had to just wonder what it was like. Reservations were six months out, and even celebrities who showed up without one were turned away at the door. Legend has it that Madonna showed up one night with no reservation. It was somewhere around nine pm, the rain was falling hard, and the wind was ripping around like juice in a blender. A large white limo stopped in front of the main entrance, and out comes Madonna with her retinue of friends and hangers-on. She walks straight in and tells the maître d' she has a group of six and would like a table because she is starved. And she mentioned that she would be very displeased if she were made to wait more than five minutes. She was told on the spot that the restaurant was at capacity and that there would be no seating that evening. Taking off her sunglasses, she looked the man in the eye and asked if he had any idea who she was. Before he could answer, she filled him in.

He looked at her and replied, "Such a pleasure to meet you, and if you come back in six months, your name will be on our list and I will be happy to seat you then. But not before."

Cursing ensued along with threats of social media devastation for the restaurant. So the maître d' said, "You're right. What was I thinking? I'll get you a table right away."

Two minutes later he returned carrying a small table meant to hold nothing more than a vase, and a second gentleman held a stool no more than two feet in height. As they passed her, they went straight out the front door and placed the items on the sidewalk, in the pouring rain. "Madame, your table is ready. One thousand apologies for having made you wait so long. Bon Appetit!"

After Gabriel announced that Mediterano was our destination, even I had doubts. Daphne, on the other hand, gave Gabriel a kiss on the cheek and told him that he was indeed the man.

After we had finished as much as we could at my place, we hopped into my car and off we went to the place that Gabriel referred to as a small drop of heaven on earth.

The one cool thing that I forgot to mention: Gabriel requested we all wear white this evening. Dressy white, no less. So here we were, four grownups dressed all in white, walking into the hottest restaurant in all of Naples. Definitely a sight.

A large crowd was gathered outside, though I've no idea why. Tapping Gabriel on the shoulder, I suggested we come back another time. "But Michael," he said. "you know as well as I that tomorrow is not promised."

" Jimmy?"

"No." He pointed up. "The big man."

Then he led us through the door. A sharp-dressed man

approached. "Mr. Angel, you're right on time, as usual. Please follow me." At our table was a bottle of Opus One. The man, who hadn't given us his name yet, pointed at the wine and said, "With our compliments, Mr. Angel."

There at the Top

We were barely seated when food arrived at the table. I recognized the first thing that was placed down in front of me, it was hummus, and it looked magical. The second thing was Pulpo A La Gallega, which we learned was Spanish octopus. In the center of our table, a large dish of Lamb Keftedes was placed, otherwise known as meatballs. To my relief, I soon found out that the entrées would be left up to us. Annie and I ordered Paella Valenciano for two. Daphne went with Beef Tagine, and good old Gabriel went with Orange-Glazed Moroccan Salmon, which he later boasted was the best he'd ever encountered. We were just finishing our entrées when something started bothering Annie.

She kept staring at a patron on the other side of the room, and it was beginning to get uncomfortable, at least for me. Gabriel was the one that finally brought it out into the open. Pointing at the man, Gabriel simply asked, "Is he a friend of yours?"

"That would be a definite no. He's my ex-husband."

I almost choked on my last bite of dinner. Annie tried not to keep staring at him, but she was failing miserably.

"So here we are at the best restaurant in town, and who in the hell do we bump into but my asshole of an ex?"

Gabriel smiled. "Do you know what ex-husbands have in common with tattoos? They're both permanent reminders of temporary feelings." Immediately, Gabriel chuckled.

"Jimmy?" Annie asked, smiling.

"But of course."

Then we all heard a clearing of a throat and looked up to see Annie's ex standing at our table.

"Hi, Annie," he said shyly. "Never would have expected to see you here."

"What's the matter, Gilson? You don't you think I belong here?"

"I didn't say that. I just—"

"Please leave. Your presence is not welcome at our table."

"I just came over to say I was sorry. I never got the chance to do so." Then he turned to Gabriel. "Haven't I seen you somewhere before?"

"Buzz off, Gilson," Annie said. "Peddle your bullshit somewhere else."

"Annie," Gabriel said, "aren't you going to introduce us to your friend?"

"Everyone, meet shithead. Shithead, meet everyone. There. Now get the hell out of here before I tell everyone all the shit you put me through."

"I just said I was sorry."

"How wonderful! You're sorry. Well, that makes all the difference in the world. I'll tell you what, why don't you pull up a chair and join us for dinner now that I know you're sorry for beating me to a pulp dozens of times?"

Gilson seemed to be caught off guard by that one, and the look on his face changed to pure evil. "You're a lying little bitch, just like I told the judge, and one day you'll get yours, I fucking promise you that." Gilson had spoken in a very low voice. We could hear it at the table, but probably no one else in the restaurant could.

I stood up like a bolt of lightning, but my arm was grabbed by Gabriel. "Sit down, Michael, it's all okay."

"But this schmuck is—"

"I know, just relax. As I said, it will be okay."

Gilson's companion approached. "What's going on, sweetheart?" she said. "Is someone at this table being rude? I mean, I could probably guess who it is."

"I'm fine, baby, just a little misunderstanding, that's all. Annie, this is my wife, Pauline. We were married last year."

"I didn't ask and I don't care," Annie said. "Now please go."

"We'll go when we're good and ready," Pauline exclaimed.

"Let's all take a step back and examine what's happening here, okay?" Daphne said.

"Mind your own business, bitch," Pauline shot back.

"Listen," Gilson said, "I thought I'd be the bigger person and come over here and apologize for my old misgivings, but I can see that you're not adult enough to forgive and forget. I feel sorry for you. I pity you, in fact."

"I told you it was a waste of time coming over to this bitch's table, Gilson."

Annie stood, and the look on her face said that something bad was coming. But before she said a single word, Pauline grabbed a glass of water and threw it on Annie.

Which brought us all to our feet. Annie reached for a glass of water, but before her hand touched it, Gabriel pushed it away and replaced it with his wine glass. Annie, not knowing about the switch, tossed the contents on Pauline and looked as surprised as Pauline did when everything turned red.

"Oh now, that is a shame," Gabriel said. "What a waste of Opus One."

Gilson stepped toward Annie, so I put up my arm to block the way. Gilson struck it down and stepped around me. Daphne leaned over and whispered something in Gabriel's ear that made them both laugh. Annie was trying to back away from Gilson, who was about to grab her, but I reached out and grabbed him instead. I twisted him around and threw him to the floor, but before I could check on Annie, I felt Pauline jump on my back. She pounded with both fists on top of my head while riding my back and wrapping her legs around my waist to keep her balance.

No matter what I tried, she wouldn't let go, and I couldn't free myself from her. Meanwhile, Gilson had gotten back up and was going after Annie. It seemed to happen very fast, but I'd swear I saw Daphne put out her foot and trip Gilson. He went flying into the next table, which had four people dining at it. The table flipped, spilling everything, and knocking over half its occupants.

I decided to spin to get Pauline off my back, and after three twirls she finally let go. But just like her husband, into a table she went, tipping it over and spilling everything on it. Gabriel, who had remained silent and non-confrontational throughout the ordeal, backed away and found a spot ten yards away to watch the chaos unfold.

Daphne went and stood beside Gabriel, and the two of them were laughing and giggling like high school kids. Waiters were everywhere trying to put a stop to the shenanigans, and then I heard police sirens in the far distance. A bill was stuffed into my hand, and an angry voice said, "Pay it now." I produced a credit card and shoved it into the waiting hand, then I went over to Annie and asked if she was okay.

She nodded slowly before giving me a small smile. "Thank you for your help, Michael. I'm so sorry for all this. I should have seen it coming and left the restaurant earlier."

"You did nothing wrong, trust me."

"Where did the rest of the troops go?"

I pointed at Daphne and Gabriel across the room.

"Can we get the hell out of here?" Annie said.

"Let's go." I reached for her hand, but we didn't even get one step before I was grabbed from behind. I raised my fist and got ready to swing, but it was just our waiter.

"Sir, your credit card has been declined."

Can of Worms

I could see Annie from my prison cell. She had her own cell a few feet away from mine. Her smeared make-up was all over her face, partially from what had transpired at the restaurant and partially from crying in the back of the police car.

I tried to be funny as we were driven over here, but it was a fail. In good news, I had seen Gilson and Pauline being put into a separate police car, although there was no trace of them here. And speaking of people who were nowhere to be seen, Gabriel and Daphne must have made a clean getaway from the scene of the crime.

What was bothering me the most, if truth be told, was that I had to go to the bathroom: number one and number two. There was a toilet in my cell for just that purpose, but it was visible to the whole world. No fucking privacy at all!

Not that there were any other criminals in here with me, but the guard would have a perfect view, and so would Annie. Under ordinary circumstances, I find that it's hard to pee if someone else is nearby, but if you add number two, fuhgeddaboudit! So I was holding everything in. I figured all I needed to do was hold it until we got out of this jam. Sooner or later, Gabriel or Daphne would surely show up here and bail us out. I just hoped that I didn't have an accident in the meantime, like in my pants. Annie would see it—and smell it—for sure. Damn, now sweat was running down my forehead, and my hands were shaking. Was I on the verge of pissing and shitting myself? I squeezed and paced to beat the band. *Come on, Michael, come on!*

"Hey, you in there," the guard said, "are you okay?" He was staring through the bars at me. "You're turning blue, mister."

Annie must have heard him and came as close as she could. "What's the matter, Michael? Are you all right?"

Then my stomach grumbled, a sure sign that something was coming—soon.

"I think I'm going to be sick," I said.

"That's what the toilet's for," the guard said, "and if you know what's good for you, you won't get any on the floor."

"You don't understand," I said quietly. "I, uh, I also need to use the toilet for other reasons."

He pointed. "Like I said, it's right there."

"But—"

"But nothing!"

Annie looked puzzled. "Can I help, Michael?"

"Nope, nope. All good." My voice was cracking.

"Michael, what is wrong?"

"I have to go to the bathroom," I finally said.

"Then just go." She pointed at the same damn toilet.

"I can't."

"Why?"

"Because you're here."

The guard laughed. "Sounds like you boyfriend's got stage

fright."

"Michael, just go," Annie said.

"There's no way."

"Then what are you going to do? Stand there until it comes out?"

A door opened down the hall, drawing everyone's attention, and another officer came into view. He went to Annie's cell first and unlocked it. "You've both been bailed out by Miss Daphne Sunshine. You're free to go."

"Please, Mr. Policeman, could you hurry? I really need to use the men's room."

"You've got one right there," he said, pointing.

"Not that one. Please, just let me…"

Oh no.

Heartbreaking World

Everyone was still wearing white, except for me. I was dressed in a prison jumpsuit, courtesy of the Naples Police Department. If I had to wager, that was the reason Daphne, Annie, and Gabriel were on the floor of my townhouse laughing. Or was it crying? Most likely both.

I was not laughing. If anything, I was trying to shut them up, but that only made them laugh more.

"Annie, tell us one more time how Michael waddled down the hall in search of a nonexistent bathroom," Daphne said.

"I'll have you three know that I did find a bathroom in time, but the door was locked. That cannot be placed on me."

"Did they make you help with the cleanup?" Daphne said through her laughter.

Finally, Gabriel waved his hands in the air and tried to catch his breath. "Okay, everyone, let's stop. Please. This isn't right or fair. Poor Michael has been through a very harrowing experience. We've all been in situations we'd like to forget about, so let's move on, okay?"

Gabriel had done what I didn't think was possible. He had gotten everyone to stop laughing. Amen to that. But then, thirty seconds later, he said. "Though I am curious. What did you do with the clothes?"

Once again, they erupted like an audience at a comedy show.

"Sorry, Michael," Gabriel said, "but it's a heartbreaking world out there and we all need a laugh every now and then."

Then Annie got up and grabbed a baseball cap from the kitchen counter. She brought it to Daphne and held it upside down.

"What are you doing?" I asked.

"Taking up a collection for you to buy some new clothes and to maybe persuade you to take a shower—sooner rather than later."

I'm So Dirty

"You know what?" I said. "There's no shower in my future! I'm going to stay just like this. It will be a reminder to all of you to keep your hurtful comments to yourselves. Now pour me a glass of wine, Gabriel, and make sure it's the good stuff because I'm getting picky. And you know what else? I might even enjoy that glass of wine naked. How does that sound? A naked, smelly, wine-sipping, broke fool?"

"You're broke?" Annie said. "But you have a job."

And that's when my cell phone rang.

"Who calls after midnight, Michael?" Daphne said. "You got a girlfriend you've been keeping from us?"

I glanced at the Caller ID. It was my boss, Chris Tilbrook. Something had to be wrong.

"Hey, Chris, what can I do for you?"

"I need a favor, Michael, and it's one you can't say no to. I know you're on vacation, but I've got to get you down to Miami for a show that needs reviewing. Stephen Large, our other critic, got in a car accident. He's going to be okay, but he'll be in the hospital for a few days, and he was going to cover a new play in Miami tomorrow night."

"What show?"

"*Up the Junction* with what's-his-name, Glenn Difford, the shoot-'em-up guy."

"You gotta be kidding."

Gabriel and the girls were staring at me, mouths agape, apparently able to hear everything Chris was saying.

"I'm sorry, Chris, but I'm with friends, and I can't just abandon them and run off to Miami."

"Bring them," he said. "I'll have four seats in the front row reserved for you, and I'll throw in dinner for everyone. And as long as you're in Miami, there's a big fashion show going on. Lots of pretty faces and celebs running around. You'll love it. I'll get you tickets for that also, and I'll owe you big time."

"It's a deal."

"I'll send the info. Check your e-mail in a few minutes."

And before I could say another word, he was gone.

"Looks like we're all going to Miami tomorrow. That is, if you don't mind being seen with a jailhouse shitter."

They all smiled and gave nods of approval, but I realized that

I felt twice as dirty now that I was expected to go to Miami and review that damn show.

Here Comes That Feeling

Half an hour later, showered and wide awake, I sipped on an ice-cold bottle of water. Staring at my ceiling, I asked no one in particular, "What am I going to do?"

"You're going to go to Miami and review a play tomorrow," Gabriel said. "You must go. Your job's at stake here, and the last thing you need right now is to lose your job."

"Especially since most of your credit cards aren't being accepted anywhere," Daphne said. "Add in the fact that you just spent a night in jail and you're now awaiting your day in court."

"And last but not least," Gabriel said, "you shit yourself in front of your girlfriend. I'd say you'd better get on down there because if your job goes bye-bye, what's left?"

"But do I need to remind any of you what happened a few nights ago with Mr. Glenn Difford or what happened when I reviewed his last play?" I looked around and noticed that Gabriel's hourglass was losing more of its sand from the top, and the bottom clearly had more than the top did. I couldn't decide if was a good thing or a bad thing, which made me consider again where I would I be when this whole fiasco was over. Would I be in a better or worse place? Would Annie still be here or had I put the final nail in our budding relationship?

"I want to go to the fashion show," Gabriel said out of nowhere. "I just Googled it and, wow, it's going to be doozy. For celebrity spotting, tomorrow's the day!"

Daphne waved her hand and said that she was in. Then all

three of us turned to look at Annie. She took her sweet Annie time, but after a few moments, she raised her hand and said she was in. She smiled too, but not in my direction—or was that just my imagination?

"Then it's settled. We're off to Miami. I'll drive if that's okay with everyone. And Chris is putting us up at The Ritz Carlton in South Beach, but only two rooms. I'm thinking boys in one, girls in the other?"

"Michael, you're no fun. Where's your joie de vivre?" said Gabriel. "Let's have the girls give their two cents before we—"

"I'll share a room with Daphne," Annie said quickly. "What time are we heading out tomorrow?"

"We'll pick you up at eight, get breakfast on the road, then head south."

"Then I need to sleep," Annie said. "Come on, Daphne. Time to go."

Annie did not look in my direction as she went to the front door, but she didn't look at Gabriel either, so I called it a wash. Then again, she had jumped on the opportunity to share a room with Daphne rather than me. I got that strange feeling in my gut again. Was Annie going to call my cell in a little while, or would tonight be a silent night?

Sound Asleep

After the girls left, I looked over at Gabriel. "What would Jimmy Buffett say about this? Did I throw it all away tonight or do I still have a chance?"

"Jimmy would say that only time will tell."

Off to bed I went, dreading the thoughts that would haunt me given all that had transpired and the pressure of the forthcoming trip to Miami. Then I fell asleep, but ten minutes later I was awakened by my cell. It was Annie.

"Did I wake you?" she asked.

"Did I shit myself in front of a dozen people?"

"Sorry."

"What for?"

"For waking you."

"Oh, thanks. Can I go back to sleep now?"

"Don't you want to talk?"

"Of course, but I didn't think you would want to talk to me after everything."

"Well, that's not the case. And I wanted to hear your voice before I fell asleep. I guess I like the sound of your voice."

"Are you sure it's not a pity call? Because I would understand if it was."

"Let me ask you this. If the situation were reversed, would you drop me like a hot potato?"

Shit, I didn't see that one coming, and I couldn't lie.

"Michael, I'm waiting. It's a simple question."

"Hey, I've got an idea. Let's talk about Miami. Sounds like a lot of fun, right?"

"Michael! Sop it and tell me your answer."

"Okay, I'd have reservations, all right? I mean, it's hard when you see something like that. Even harder to un-see it. Women are beautiful. They're something to behold, to be admired and looked at through eyes that only see unflawed perfection. And I truly believe that every single woman has a certain beauty in their own special way. They have the ability to make each man they encounter a better man. You've heard the expression 'my better half'? Well, it's true. I see you like I would see a gorgeous statue sitting on a pedestal. Something so wonderful and at the same time so fragile. I immediately want to be with you, take care of you, shelter you, and protect you from all harm. And all because of who you are and what you represent. But I don't want to see the underbelly of things because somehow that just spoils it. I know that it's hard to understand, but I'm doing my best to be honest."

"Wow, that was a mouthful. You been holding that in for a while?"

"It sort of just came spilling out, but it's true. If I find myself in a museum, I tend to be attracted to the prettier pictures or paintings, not the ones that show something grotesque. And if there is an accident on the road, I turn away. I don't want to see blood and guts. And if a pretty girl walks by on the beach, damn, I'm going to look. See what I'm getting at?"

"Oh yes, you've done a great job of making yourself perfectly clear. But aren't you going to ask me how I see you?"

"No."

"Aren't you a wee bit curious?"

"Well, I'd love to know what you think if it's something good, but I don't want to know if it's something bad."

"I think you're hot."

"Care to elaborate?"

"I find you original and sweet. You bring smiles to my face effortlessly. For the last few days, you're the reason I get out of bed in the morning. You're the first thing I think about when I wake up and the last thing I think of before I fall to sleep. You're in the shower with me. I take you to work and I bring you back home. I wonder what you're doing, what you're thinking when we are not together, and I wonder if you're thinking about me. I've thanked God for him letting you come into my life and, last but not least, I pray for you. For your well-being, your happiness and that you'll like me for who I am, not because I'm another pretty face."

I remained silent, stunned by the words I was sure I'd remember forever. To hear someone, profess words like that is overwhelming, and I tried desperately to find something to say in return.

"Did I say too much, Michael? Too little? Or just the right amount?"

"Just right, Annie, just right."

Crying in My Sleep

As I lay there in my bed, I felt whole. I had hung up with Annie over an hour ago and was only a few hours away from having to get up and set out for Miami, but sleep evaded me. My brain was pinging with endless questions, like how, in such a short time, could someone have feelings for me that ran deeper than I could have ever imagined? I had prayed for this almost my entire adult life, but now, like this? So out of the blue and with someone as pretty and smart as Annie? I couldn't believe this was happening to me. Add in the fact that this woman had seen me at my lowest points and still wanted to stick around. Damn!

A part of me wanted to quit this Gabriel thing and concentrate on the thing at hand, which was Annie. I'd even be willing to tell her all about Gabriel, including what he had been doing here and why.

But the deal with Annie hadn't been sealed yet, not even close. No "I love you" spoken between us, and I hadn't sealed the deal where performance counted. Not only does that count, but it's what we are occasionally judged on. Performance, endurance, and stamina. The three amigos of sex, and three things with which I don't have any experience, let alone talent. Reading up on sex and researching it with the occasional solo performance, which I now know does not make you go blind, wouldn't help me with the real deal. What if I blew it in the sex department? Would I get a second chance? A third? But then again, maybe, just maybe, I have a hidden talent? And since I've never had the opportunity to find out, I might be great, spectacular even.

Nah, I'm gonna suck.

Should I go to a hooker and tell her my dilemma? Have her teach me the ways of the force, so to speak, and the tricks of the trade? That could work, but it would suck. Who wants to lose their virginity to a hooker? Not to mention if Annie ever found out, I'd be up shit's creek without a paddle. Plus, I probably couldn't even afford a hooker at this point.

I needed to talk to Gabriel in the morning. Maybe he could help or teach me a few things—or at least I could get him to call off this whole bet thing.

As I drifted off to sleep, an image of a smiling Annie filled my brain. Then my phone dinged with a text alert. Uh oh, it was from Annie: *I know it's late, but there was one more important thing to say, something that should have been said earlier on the phone. I LOVE YOU! Sorry if I woke you again, but I can't sleep. PS: Don't forget about our appointment—the one we were supposed to have had a few hours ago. Hoping we can take care of business in Miami.*

Oh boy, the plot thickens! It was like I was in a stew that kept getting thicker and hotter by the minute. My brain went into overdrive. Should I call her? Should I text her back? Should I wait until morning? And then the big question snuck in around the back corner of my mind: Do I love her? Do I truly love her? If a person has never been in love before, how does that person know when they are in love? This went on for God knows how long before I eventually fell asleep. So, thank God for that.

Albatross

My sleep was fitful, to say the least. Normally I wake up a few times a night to pee, and while I'm doing that, I can usually remember what dream I was having. For the most part, my dreams are on the brighter side of things. In fact, I look forward to my dreams because they're fun and highly realistic. Tonight, was no exception, and in the morning, the final dream of the evening stayed with me. It went something like this: I was in high school, standing in front of my locker in my senior year. The bell was only moments away, but I was fumbling with my lock. I'd forgotten the combination and no matter how hard I tried; it wouldn't come to me. With my heart beating faster, I realized that I wouldn't make my next class.

Then, before I knew it, I was in a full classroom. Everyone had books on their desks, plus a pen and a pencil. My desk, however, was empty. A barren wasteland screaming out for a book or writing implement. But it wasn't to be, and my heart raced. Other students started to stare at my empty desk.

Suddenly, the teacher called my name and asked where my books were.

Then, in a flash, I was at the senior prom, alone and dateless. My hair was unkempt, my suit was wrinkled, and my face was a pimple farm. I stood alone in a corner, listening to a song that I liked. I was bopping to the beat, like really moving and grooving, and then I noticed that everyone was staring at me. The looks on the other kids' faces were enough to bring the panic of a fast-beating heart right smack to the forefront of my well-being.

Immediately, I found myself at the auditions for the senior play, *Macbeth*. I was on stage, determined to secure a role, any role, so I could look back and say I did it. But a nervous feeling in my gut grew into a full-fledged tornado. Why? Because I realized that I'd never memorized the script, and I didn't know a single line of dialogue. Then I heard that thunderous sound of my name being called, which added to my anxiety.

Suddenly, I was at my high school graduation. It was the point in the ceremony when everyone threw their caps into the air, followed by cheering and celebrating. I was the only one not celebrating. But then a tap on my shoulder made me spin around, and this is where the dream went into slow motion. Tapping my shoulder was a gorgeous girl I'd never seen before. Her smile was more radiant than a sunrise on a tropical island. She placed her hands on my cheeks and, ever so slowly, leaned in and gave me a congratulatory kiss on the lips. In response, I stuck my tongue straight down her throat as far as I could and began to wiggle it around.

She pulled away immediately with an expression of pure horror. Then she slapped me right across the face. Silence overtook the ceremony—for a full minute—before the crowd's laughter roared into my ears.

Slowly, the view pulled back on my fading dream to show me that everyone was laughing at me.

Images of love

"Time to wake up, Michael."

Clearing last night's eye crust away, I focused on the angel waking my ass up.

"The girls are already here. Let's go!" He stood over me dressed in white boxers with "God Rules" written on the back in pink.

"Okay," I said. "I just need a quick shower, and I haven't packed yet either, so I'll need more than a few minutes."

I did a fast shave and hopped into the shower as last night's dreams played on a never-ending reel in my brain. Add in that Annie professed her love for me last night, and I had one hell of a need for some Aleve. As I soaped up, a breeze blew over me, so I turned to find the source. Almost jumping out of my skin, I realized I was not alone. Annie was standing inches away, letting the water soak her naked body. Was I still dreaming?

Annie was smiling that beautiful warm smile of hers. *Damn.*

"What are—"

That's all I managed to get out before my mouth was covered with hers. The kiss lasted just short of forever and made a dear old friend of mine come around and salute her. She must have realized that there were now three of us in the shower because the kiss ended and the sightseeing began. She seemed genuinely interested in the arrival of my friend, and her expression was not one of disappointment, at least not yet. Meanwhile, I stole a long-overdue look at all that Annie had to offer.

At first, I was shocked because I never imagined someone looking this good without their clothes on. Her body wasn't like the ones you see in magazines. It was actually better! It shined! She was stunning—perfect in every sense of the word.

She performed a slow spin, stopping halfway to show me the view that, until now, had been hidden. Then she did a little shake and began to wiggle and gyrate ever so gently in a circular fashion. My temperature and blood pressure climbed as memories of the other night popped into my mind. I did *not* want a repeat performance, but she was making it difficult. I needed to turn away. I needed to pay my bills, do my taxes, weed the garden—anything to get my mind off of what I was seeing. Then she took my head in her hands and put her lips back on mine.

I jumped. Not because I was startled, but because all the townhouse's smoke detectors blared at once.

Damn, they were loud! The longer they went on, the louder they seemed to get. Annie suggested we go have a look at the rest of the place. Without waiting for a reply, she hopped out of the shower and grabbed a towel.

I peeked my head out. "Annie?"

"Yes?"

"I love you!"

She dropped her towel to the floor, took two steps forward, and was right back in my arms, dripping wet and planting her sweet Annie kisses on my wet lips.

If I Didn't Love You

Breakfast had been served. The girls must have brought it over with them. There was everything you could think of, especially things that were unhealthy: donuts, bagels, croissants, and breakfast sandwiches that had God-knew-what inside, plus three bottles of orange juice.

Gabriel passed a steaming cup of coffee to me.

"How was your shower, Michael?" Daphne asked with a grin.

"Just fine, just fine, thank you."

"Those smoke detectors have a habit of going off at exactly the wrong moment, don't they, Michael?" Gabriel said.

Wait a minute. Could he have had something to do with them going off and then suddenly stopping? He did have a mischievous look about him this morning.

"Any idea what caused them to go off?" I asked, not expecting a real answer.

"No, none at all," he said with his tongue planted firmly in his cheek.

"Hey, Annie," Gabriel said, "why is your hair wet? It wasn't wet when you came over this morning."

Annie smacked him on the back of the head. Not too hard but not too soft either, just the right amount.

Amidst the breakfast fare sat Gabriel's book and hourglass. I was tempted to pick up Gabriel's book and peek inside it, but I noticed that the hourglass's digital display now read 52.5, and for some reason, that number scared me.

"Well," Gabriel said, "let's turn up the heat and chill the rosé."

"Jimmy Buffett?" we all said together.

"But of course," he said.

The girls started packing things up in the kitchen, and Gabriel got up and did whatever it is that Gabriel does before heading out on a trip. My guess was he was packing nothing yet bringing everything.

Annie then came over and whispered in my ear. "So you love me, do you? Took you long enough to say it."

"I fell asleep last night after getting your text," I whispered back.

"Wait a minute, mister. A woman spills her guts to you, tells you that she loves you, and you... fall asleep?"

"Pretty much," I answered. Then I went into my room to get some more things.

Annie followed close behind. "You're not getting off that easy."

I took her in my arms and kissed her. This went on until Daphne came in. "Why don't you two get a room?"

"We have one," I said, breaking my lips off from Annie's.

Satisfied

It was a mostly quiet ride to Miami. The thing I remember most was the floaty feeling I had. I thought hard about how to describe the feeling that was keeping me floating high above everyone else in the world, and then it came to me: SATISFIED.

I had never felt more satisfied in my whole life. I wanted to tell Annie, but I didn't because in my brain, not my heart, I knew it would scare her and she might fly the coop.

Gabriel played Jimmy Buffett all the way there, but not loudly, just the right amount of volume. However, his singing definitely needed to be toned down. Most of the time, his eyes were closed as he sang along. Other times they'd be wide open, which was when he'd sing louder. Occasionally he'd beg us to join in, so we all sang along.

I was fairly sure that once this trip was over and Gabriel was gone from my life, there was a good chance I'd never play Jimmy Buffett again.

Daphne sat in the back with Gabriel. Through the rearview mirror I could see her occasionally give his leg a rub. Just a friendly rub? Who knew? Regardless, Annie was up front with me, rubbing my leg. And I knew exactly why: because the lady loved me.

Pulling into The Ritz Carlton in South Beach gave my heart a quick bump. "Magnificent" was too lowly a word to describe the beauty and majesty of this place. And the look on Annie's face told me her reaction. Daphne and Gabriel, though, acted as if they'd been here before—no biggie at all.

The lobby was something to behold. One could spend an entire day there just taking in its grandeur and elegance. It reminded me of a time and place from long ago, as if I were on a movie set. I kept waiting for some young couple to start kissing and declaring their love for one another. Then I imagined hearing, "Cut! Let's do another take please."

I feared that we were checking in too early and would be told that our rooms weren't ready, but to my surprise, both rooms were ready and we were quickly transported into unadulterated opulence. The hallways were fabulous. The elevators were spectacular. And when we were shown to the girls' room, I almost fainted. I could only imagine what was going through their minds. Even Gabriel was smiling, though he did seem to be off a bit. Maybe he was so used to planning everything that he was saddened by the fact that this adventure had nothing to do with him.

The girls' suite was better than any room I'd ever stayed in. The living room, which was bigger than the one in my townhouse, had sprawling ceilings and led to a balcony shaped like the letter L. One side showed the view of Miami's skyline, and the other provided a view of the Atlantic Ocean, which stopped my heart and made me gasp for breath.

The girls ran from room to room, giggling and chuckling as

they took in what I referred to as "the satisfaction guaranteed hotel room of all hotel rooms."

"Bathing suits, anyone?" Daphne asked, holding hers in the air.

"God," Annie said, "I don't know what to do first. A part of me wants to just sit here on the couch staring at this place until it's time to go home tomorrow."

"I repeat," Daphne said. "Does anyone want to put on a bathing suit and join me on the beach?"

Gabriel raised his hand. "I most certainly do, my dear."

We all agreed to meet at the pool and then hit the beach.

"But remember," I said, "the fashion show starts at 4:00 p.m. sharp. And I don't want to miss a minute." Then I grinned. "Just kidding. I don't care if we go or not."

"Oh no," Gabriel said, "we're not missing a minute of that show."

The girls nodded in agreement.

Patchouli

Gabriel's and my room was just like the girls' room, only times two. Enough said. After giving the bellhop a generous tip, we took a gander around and gave each other a look that said, Well done!

Immediately I detected an aroma that tickled my nose. In a good way. As I went from room to room, I couldn't figure out where it was coming from. It seemed to be coming from everywhere, all at once.

I turned to Gabriel, who was putting his book on the table beside the couch. "What is that odor? It's driving me crazy, but in a happy way."

"Patchouli."

"Patch what?"

"Patchouli. Don't tell me you've never heard of it."

"Never, and furthermore, I think you're making it up."

"Patchouli comes from a species of flowering plant. It grows as a bushy flowering herb mostly in southeast Asia. It's also currently being cultivated in the Caribbean and South America. Noted for its fragrant essential oils, it has many commercial uses, such as in perfumes and incense. And that, Michael, is what your nostrils are currently enjoying. Compliments of The Ritz Carlton."

"How come I didn't detect it in the other room?"

"Each room has a different scent. Their room had a subtle fragrance of lavender, not too strong, mind you, but just enough to enliven your senses."

"And you know all this why?"

"I keep my eyes and ears open. I pay attention when people speak. When something new comes along, I inquire about it and try to learn. Knowledge is the key, they say. I refer to it as feeding my brain. You should try it sometime."

Twenty minutes later we were at the pool awaiting the arrival of the girls. The pool area was just as astounding as everything else.

Gabriel tapped me and said he needed a minute and would be right back. No sooner did he leave than the girls arrived. It wasn't just my head that turned to watch this show of beauty make its poolside debut; every head, including those of the women, turned and stared.

The girls were dressed to kill in one-piece swimsuits. Annie's was eggshell white and Daphne's was a vibrant blue. Annie looked around and announced that she'd be fine grabbing a table with chairs and some loungers and hanging poolside for a few hours. Daphne shrugged and pointed to an empty spot a couple of yards away. As we set up camp, Daphne asked where Gabriel had gotten off to. As if on cue, Gabriel returned.

"Here I am, one and all. Ah, I see that you've chosen to be poolside. Wonderful choice." Then he placed a large tray on the table. It contained four bottles of sparkling water and a glass for each, filled to the top with ice. Also on the tray were four wine glasses that were of a shape I'd never seen before. They were fat in the center and slim on the bottom and the top. Last but not least were two bottles of Crown Point Cabernet.

"A little early for wine, isn't it?" I said.

"It's never too early for wine, Michael. I'd have thought you'd know that by now."

"How thoughtful, Gabriel," Daphne said. "Thank you."

"Thank Michael's boss, my dear. He's paying for it."

"You can't do that," I said. "You can't just charge things to the room."

"Oh, that's funny, because I just did."

Touching Me, Touching You

Gabriel and Daphne seemed to be having a hell of a time while Annie and I lounged and sipped on the water. At one point, Annie pulled out a bottle of sunscreen. I watched as she began applying it generously to her body. I could tell that she knew I was watching, and I could also tell that she was enjoying me watching.

"Why aren't you putting on any lotion, Michael? Are you one

of those guys who never wears any because it's unmanly?"

"No, I just forgot mine. I was kind of running late this morning, and my shower ran longer than planned."

"How interesting. Well, I'll tell you what. If you put some on my back, I'll let you borrow mine. And I'll even throw in a two-handed rub of lotion on your back and any other hard-to-reach spots. Deal?"

"Yes, ma'am," I said, starting to feel a little something-something down below.

Annie covered my back side with lotion, taking her sweet time. When it was time for me to return the favor, I had to do it without standing up. Which wasn't easy.

"Why don't you come around to this side?" Annie said. "It would be a lot easier for you."

Not knowing how to say no without looking like an ass, I relented and went around to her side, trying my best not to let her catch wind of little Michael.

"Oh, who do we have here?" she said. "I see our little friend is back. If your bathing suit wasn't from the nineties and so tight, I might not have noticed your friend. Something to think about next time you pick out a suit." Then she laughed the laugh that I found sexy and contagious. Soon I was giggling along, which helped send little Michael back to his room, where he belonged.

"Are we interrupting you two?" Gabriel said. "Because that would be the last thing we would ever want to do. But I wanted to alert you that your friend is here, and she's making her way over."

"What friend?"

And then I heard the voice and the words I'd come to dread. "Son of a bitch, Michael, what on earth are you doing here? This can't be another coincidence, can it?"

148

"Hello, Rose, and yes, it's just a coincidence."

But I've been here a dozen times, and I've never seen you here. You're with your three amigos, I see. Are they on your payroll? Because I can't think of any other reason people would want to spend this much time with you."

Rose was not in a bathing suit. In fact, she was wearing a lovely sundress with a matching hat and some serious heels.

"They're here to keep me company," I replied with a lazy smile. "And what are you doing here, Rose, if you don't mind me asking?"

"Not that I'd expect you to remember, Michael, but I've told you many times that I work in fashion. And this happens to be fashion week. Or are you now going to tell me that you've never heard of fashion week?"

"Rose, I am also here for fashion week."

She harrumphed. "I don't believe you for a minute."

"Well, I'm actually here to review a new play that's opening tonight at The Gary Nader Art Centre. It's called *Up the Junction*, starring Glenn Difford. And my boss thanked me for doing this review on short notice by throwing in some tickets for the fashion show."

"Well, well, aren't you the lucky ones." She pointed to the wine bottles on the table. "Do you always drink this early, Michael, on the days when you're working? When you're writing a review that has far-reaching effects on other people's livelihoods?"

"Touché, Rose, touché. But the wine belongs to my friends, and I'm here just sipping on water. What is it that you do in fashion again? It's slipped my memory."

"I'm a buyer. I'm here to try and find things for our next line. By the way, nice suit you've got there. Did you use your time machine to shop for it?"

Then she walked away, laughing at her own joke.

"Damn," I said, "she always gets to me, and I don't understand why."

"Really?" Daphne said. "Should we go over again what you did to the poor woman?"

Cool for Cats

We arrived at the fashion show without any difficulties or fanfare, which was surprising given how things had been going lately. The lobby was bigger than a football field, and the people walking about were, to say the least, beautiful. Champagne was being delivered to all by gorgeous women dressed as cats in a cool, sexy way. But then I noticed they weren't all women. Very surprising indeed.

I'm not a champagne drinker, and I do try my best not to drink on review days, but Annie and the gang accepted a glass and told me that I didn't know what I was missing. We mingled about and waited for the call to go in and find our seats. I had literally no idea where or how good our seats were, plus I'd never been to a fashion show and had no idea what to expect.

Someone called my name from across the crowd. I glanced over and didn't recognize the face, but I did notice right off the bat that the owner of the voice was hot—like supermodel hot—and she had a slight accent, one I couldn't quite pinpoint.

"Michael, I can't believe I've found you," she said as she planted a kiss on each of my cheeks. "It's so crazy. Are you here in search of me?"

This woman was every bit as tall as Gabriel and dressed to

150

the hilt. Holding both my shoulders, she said, "You do know who I am, don't you? I'm Domino. We were supposed to have a date last Sunday, but I lost my purse. It was just so crazy. My phone and my wallet were also inside, and I was simply frantic. I had no way of getting in touch with you, and I couldn't remember where or when we were supposed to meet except that it was Sunday. A thousand apologies, Michael. Please tell me you'll find it in your heart to forgive me? I was so looking forward to meeting you. Your sister had shown me a picture of you, and from that second on, all I could think of was my sweet Michael. Please tell me you forgive me and that you'll let me make it up to you."

I'd forgotten for a second that I was not alone. I glanced at my friends. Before I could introduce anyone, Domino took my hands in hers. "Please enjoy me when I'm onstage. I'll be thinking about you while I strut, do you like that?"

Before I could reply, she kissed me on both cheeks again. "I'll see you after the show. Until then, my dear." And poof! She was gone.

I stared, transfixed on her back side as she walked away in her heels.

"Any other surprises in store for us?" Annie asked sarcastically.

"Cat got your tongue there, Michael?" Daphne added.

Gabriel shook his head and stated that he was not getting involved with this one, no way, no how.

"Michael, oh my God, it is you?" It was another voice calling my name. Only I knew this voice very well.

Haywire

My face was grabbed and kissed, followed by a giant bear hug, then fingers running through my hair. "I can't believe you're here, and you didn't even call me. By the way, you are in desperate need of a haircut. No wonder you can't get a date."

As fast as I could, I introduced the new arrival. "Everyone, I'm proud to introduce——"

"Oh wow, we're actually getting introduced this time," Daphne said. "I'm flattered."

"I'd like you all to meet my sister, Lucy Shaw. She's a photographer, who I assume is here covering fashion week?"

"What else would I be doing here? The question is, What are you doing here?"

"First, I'd like you to meet the more-than-wonderful Annie."

Lucy started jumping up and down. "You have a girlfriend? You have a girlfriend? I can't believe my baby brother has a girlfriend!"

"Stop. Just stop! Besides, what makes you think we're boyfriend and girlfriend?"

"My baby brother has a girlfriend! This is the best news in the world. I've prayed for this, you know." She took Annie's hand. "He's a wonderful guy, trust me. And you won't find a kinder or more honest and loving guy than him, I swear."

Letting go of Annie's hand, she looked over at Daphne and Gabriel. "I'm sorry, you must think I'm so rude. I'm Lucy, Michael's older sister, but not by much. We're closer in age than you'd think." She shook their hands as I introduced them. And then I informed Lucy that she had just missed her friend Domino by a matter of seconds.

"Did she tell you about losing her purse and all that?"

"Yes, she was very nice. Thanks for trying to introduce us."

"It was very thoughtful of you," Gabriel said, jumping in. "I've heard so much about you from Michael, and I must say that it is ever so rare to find such a fine and close-knit relationship between brother and sister."

"I think I'm falling in love with your friend, Michael," Lucy said, catching her breath.

"Tell us about fashion week," Daphne said. "Is it all it's cracked up to be?"

"It is and it's not. The brochure actually gives the best description, and I memorized it. 'Miami Fashion Week takes place in Miami, a city that has evolved into the main bridge between the US and Latin America. This event goes beyond the runway, generating a mix of fashion, beauty, music, art, charity, latest trends, gastronomy, luxury, and lifestyle.' In essence, I always call it haywire week. If something can go wrong, it will." She leaned into the group. "Do you know who's here? Okay, I'll tell you. We always get our fair share of celebs, but today we've hit the jackpot. Ready? It's Glenn Difford! And his supermodel fiancée, Gloria Delmont. Can you believe it?" She turned to me. "And Michael, if you do bump into someone famous, don't embarrass yourself, you know, like staring or gawking, okay?"

Domino

Our seats were in the front row, but big deal. Fashion shows just mean pretty girls walking around in crazy-ass outfits, the kind a normal person would never wear, like a space suit gone astray. And let's not forget about the hats, which usually looked like they were made from old garbage can lids. So, my expectations were not very high.

Gabriel, though, seemed focused. Maybe he was planning to add a little color to his wardrobe?

My seat abutted two empty chairs on my right, which made a stomach-turning thought pop into my head. What if the empty seats were for Glenn and his fiancée? Nah, my luck wasn't that bad. I needed to stop worrying and concentrate on the show, which was about to start.

Annie tugged on my arm. "When were you going to tell me about your look-at-me, I'm-a-model friend?"

"There's nothing to tell, seriously."

"She picked you out of a crowd of thousands and kissed you a hundred times."

"Yeah, but I never met her before. My sister Lucy was—"

"Michael!" Domino said, reaching down to pull me from my seat. "Please come, I have a pass for you."

"Oh, that's—"

"A backstage pass for you, my Michael. Come!"

"What about my friends?" I said as I was led away.

"No, they will stay here. They have good seats; they'll be happy."

"Go ahead, Michael," Annie said from somewhere behind me. "Have fun with your new friend."

As I was pulled backstage, the last thing I heard was Gabriel shouting, "What kind of man leaves his friends to hang around with a beautiful woman? I never!"

Once I was backstage, I broke free of Domino's grasp. I was about to demur and return to my seat when I noticed that I was surrounded by fifty drop-dead gorgeous women. And many were in various degrees of undress, including a solid 25 percent who were topless. I repeat, topless.

The crazy thing was that none of them seemed to care that I was there with my jaw agape and eyes bugged out. A little voice inside my head whispered, "Life is good, dude, very good."

"Come, come," Domino demanded as she escorted me through the throng of models, dressing assistants, and photographers.

"How did you get back here?" Lucy called out to me between snapping photos of a statuesque woman. Before I could answer, she seemed to notice Domino, but the look on her face was not a pleasant one.

"Hey, Domino, I see you finally met my brother."

"Yes. He is nothing but wonderful. I'm taking him back to Italy with me when this is through."

"You're kidding, right?" Lucy said.

"Depends on how today and tonight go, right, my Michael?"

I mouthed the words HELP ME to Lucy, who mouthed back the word NO. "Well then," Lucy said, "have a great time!"

Domino nearly pulled my arm from its socket as she dragged me away.

"Where are we going?" I asked.

"Don't worry, you will love what you have to do for me."

"Which is?"

She answered with a devilish look.

Going Crazy

The outfits from the designers were not what I expected at all. In fact, they were kind of sexy. Many had a Caribbean flair to them. They were bright and colorful and swayed easily. Plus, no hats to be seen anywhere. Instead, some of the girls had their hair held back with silky fabric ties, which highlighted their faces and brought color and light to their appearance.

Each model came out onto the stage slowly, then stopped and did a turn, walked a few steps more, then stopped and turned again. They repeated this for the length of the runway, at which point they'd walk straight back and disappear behind the curtains. Two to three models occupied the runway at the same time. Some wore flat shoes, some heels, and some even had on flip-flops.

As the show progressed, the outfits became skimpier, until they were no longer dresses but island swimwear. I'd never been this close to such beautiful women; it was almost frightening. I'd never even been this close to *one* beautiful woman before. But again, none of them seemed concerned about my presence. In fact, no one looked my way or gave me a smile or even a how-do-you-do. I didn't know whether to laugh or cry.

But the good news was that it got my mind off my costume. That's right, my "greeter" costume, the one Domino made me put on. You see, the runway was decorated like the entrance to a tropical island, with torches everywhere, all lit up and glowing. Apparently, there was supposed to be a greeter welcoming the models to the island, putting a lei over their heads, and kissing them on the cheek. Domino had assigned me the role because the original guy had called in sick, so here I was! To be honest, a month ago, I would have killed for this job, but today I was sweating bullets and worrying about Annie's reaction, not to mention the reactions of the thousands of strangers in attendance. Because I guarantee that a bunch of people were hoping I'd screw up, maybe drop a lei or something. Because that's human nature. People like to see other people fuck things up.

When Domino came out, she kissed me on both cheeks before planting a quick one on my lips. Then she turned, walked a few steps, and looked back at me during a special type of swirl. None of the other girls had swirled like that, so I knew it was a Domino thing meant just for me. Another flourish, then she was off doing what the others had done before her.

My eyes darted to the front row and caught the fire in Annie's eyes. I didn't need a class in lip reading to tell what word was forming on Annie's lips: ASSHOLE. It was followed by a low flip of the finger, down by her waist, meant just for me.

That's when I noticed that the two empty chairs next to mine were now occupied by Glenn Difford and his fiancée. Glenn was leaning over to say something to Annie, who suddenly looked less angry. Because she was too busy laughing.

Then Glenn leaned in again to share another whisper, which resulted in another bout of laughter from Annie, who had seemed to forget I existed.

The lei in my hand was starting to shake, and as I looked up, I saw the next model was waiting for me to do my thing. To make matters worse, the girl behind her was waiting too. How long had I been staring? Damn, I could feel the eyes of the crowd burning through me, judging me for not even having enough talent to place a lei over a woman's head and give her a kiss. Pathetic. Just pathetic.

So I decided to speed things up. I'd get the show back on track in no time, then all would be well in the fashion universe. Of course, I fucked up royally.

Placing the lei over the next model's head, I got the ring I was wearing on my right hand caught on her outfit. I gave a small tug, but nope, still stuck. She then tried to help by pulling away, but we both pulled hard at the same time and off came her top.

It went flying two rows back, and out of the corner of my eye, I saw Gabriel try to catch it. But it went over his head and landed on some rich-looking lady's face.

The procession of girls behind me came to an awkward stop. The two girls already on the runway couldn't get back in because the area was clogged up with waiting models. A quagmire, to say the least.

The topless girl seemed to be the least surprised and didn't even try to cover up her newly revealed assets. In fact, she looked as though she wanted to know what all the fuss was about.

I started by trying to apologize to her but quickly discovered that she spoke no English. Then I looked for something I could give her to cover up her chest, but I didn't see anything handy.

I heard both Annie and Lucy calling my name from opposite directions while Domino appeared at my side. "What has happened?"

"Her top came off," I said, pointing.

"Why doesn't she put it back on?"

"It's in the audience, couple rows back."

Domino nodded and looked like she was trying to decide what to do next. Someone turned the lights up, and the host who'd started the show came out to calm everyone down. Meanwhile, the girls from backstage were now out and milling about randomly. Guess they wanted to see what the hell was going on.

One of the models who'd wandered out began to point at the topless model and laugh, which didn't please the topless model, who reached out and pulled off the laughing girl's top. The crowd, probably wanting to get a better look, rose to its feet. Then the two topless girls began yelling at each other in another language. A third girl, who stepped in to separate them, quickly found herself on the floor. She joined in the shouting, and her foot knocked into a floor light on my right. As it fell, the light made a loud popping noise, which caused an audience member to yell, "Gun!"

People then started to run, making everything a tad more hectic as the crowd rushed for the exits. The host pleaded for everyone to take their seats, but no one paid him any attention.

As if magically transported, Gabriel suddenly appeared by my side. "What in the name of God have you done, Michael?"

"What makes you think I have anything to do with this?"

"Really?"

"Okay, I might have played a small part, but it wasn't intentional."

Domino, who was still standing nearby, pointed at Gabriel. "Who would this be?"

"He's a friend of mine."

"He sure does dress funny."

Walk Away

"What in God's name is going on?" said Lucy, who had just joined us on the stage.

"Your brother removed the tops of two women," Domino said. "Exposing their breasts to all of the people here."

Gabriel chuckled.

"What?" I said. "That's not true! I only exposed one woman's breasts."

At this point, there were so many people moving and rushing about, it was hard to see who was who and which way was out.

No one was sitting, and everyone from backstage was now out on the stage.

"Tell me what happened," Lucy demanded.

"Don't leave out any of the good parts," Annie said, startling me. Apparently, she and Daphne were now part of the stage show. The sweat had returned to my brow as Domino was giving Annie the evil eye, and Annie was giving it right back. And let's not forget about Daphne, who was standing next to Gabriel and sharing a glass of red wine with him.

Next to approach me was topless girl number one. "You!" she screamed. She blasted me for a minute straight in what sounded like Italian. I got the gist. She was blaming me for her being topless, which she still was, by the way. After all that had happened and was still happening, her breasts were still flapping in the breeze.

"What is she saying exactly?" I said to no one in particular.

"She says you're the big fuck-up who started this whole thing," Domino said.

"Can you tell her I'm sorry?"

"I don't think she cares, but I'll try."

After some back-and-forth between them, Domino turned to me and shrugged. "She said for you to fuck yourself and to go shit in a bucket."

A waiter walked by, not to take drink orders but to help calm everyone down. That, however, didn't stop Gabriel and Daphne from trying to order more wine.

"Why do things like this happen everywhere you go, Michael?" Annie asked.

"Just lucky, I guess."

With so many people around, I almost missed the face on my far left, just staring and grinning at me—the face of Glenn

Difford. He then pointed at me with his finger, using it in the shape of a gun. He pretended to fire, then his smile faded as he put his arm around his companion and left. The man definitely had me on his radar.

Cold Shoulder

Giving someone the cold shoulder can be an art form, depending on how it's done. In Annie's case, she took the simple route and went straight for the silent treatment. She acted as if I didn't exist. We were all in the car heading back to the hotel, and I was doing everything possible to apologize to her. Not that I could figure out what I needed to apologize for. Should a person have to say they're sorry because they're having bad luck? It's not like I got caught getting Domino's phone number.

From the co-pilot seat, a voice demanded that we take a short break on our way back to the hotel, a pit stop, so to speak. Gabriel said that he just remembered that an old friend of his was playing in a bar nearby and that he'd never forgive himself if he didn't pop in for a quick hello. Following Gabriel's directions, we ended up at The Board Room Tavern, another place I'd never heard of.

The parking lot was packed, so I parked a few streets away after dropping the crew out in front. I walked in alone a few minutes later and was surprised at how many people were inside this small and rowdy place. The main room had the biggest crowd, with a spillover group in the decent-looking outside area. A country band played, and people were up and dancing.

We were dressed for a highfalutin fashion show, unfortunately, not for a honky-tonk. To say we were being gawked at would be an understatement. Gabriel was waving me over to a table up front, right by the stage. I'd love to say I was surprised at how good our table was, but I wasn't because I knew Gabriel was up to his old tricks again.

"Michael, over here!" Gabriel said. "I want you to meet an old friend of mine, Paul the piano man." He gestured to the bald man standing next to him. "At least that's what we call him. He's one of the best session men in the business and he's even played with Jimmy Buffett!"

"Nice to meet you, Paul. How do you know Gabriel—if you don't mind me asking?"

"Well, that's a long story, and I'll leave it up to old Gabriel here to tell it when he's good and ready. But if the story doesn't start off with me savin' his ass, then he's lying!"

Gabriel got a big chuckle from that, then whispered something in Paul's ear, which made him give me a sideways look. A quick shrug of the shoulders from Paul, then he was off. I grabbed the seat closest to Annie, planted my butt down, and took a swig from the Stella they'd ordered me. Then I spun my chair around to face Annie.

"Hey, girl, I don't know what's pulling your chain, but if it's something I did, I'm sorry. I truly am."

Annie rolled her eyes, swigged her beer, and slammed it back down on the table. Then she waggled her finger an inch from my nose. "Don't give me that shit. You know damn well what you did."

"I don't, but if you tell me, maybe I can explain it or at least apologize for it."

"Okay, fine. You didn't treat me like I was your girlfriend at the fashion show."

Gabriel and Daphne were doing their best to pretend not to

162

be listening, but I knew they were catching every word.

"How can you say that?" I said.

"You know it's true. So, what do you have to say for yourself?"

"I'm sorry?"

"Not good enough, not even close."

Love Circles

We were still going tit for tat when Paul the piano man interrupted us from the stage. "Ladies and gentlemen, it is The Board Room Tavern's pleasure to introduce you all to someone special. With her unique voice, sexy good looks, and the great fortune of being a close friend of a close friend of mine, I'd like you all to give a warm welcome to Miss Daphne."

Well, this was a surprise. Daphne sings? If Paul had introduced Gabriel, that would have been easier to swallow, but Daphne?

Gabriel rose to his feet, hootin' and hollerin' for his gal pal. Annie and I followed suit, and soon the crowd joined us in cheering her on. Taking the mic, Daphne gave a warm country smile and friendly hello to the crowd, waving to each section of the room. It looked as though she'd just possibly done this before.

As we all took our seats, I stole a peek in Annie's direction, which she caught and returned with a sneer. Is this what love is all about? I couldn't believe this was what I'd been praying for my whole life. I should have read more books, watched more movies, maybe learned a thing or two about this love stuff. Because it seemed like one big circle. You're happy, you're kind of happy, you're not so happy, then you're just miserable. Then the misery starts to fade, and a little sunshine sneaks back in. Then you're back to happiness and bliss, but how long before not-so-happy comes back around? Helluva circle!

Daphne cradled the mic like it was second nature, twirled the attached cord, then let out a voice that was not only sweet, honest, and downright pretty but also made you feel like you were a hot knife slicing through butter.

I looked at Annie, and Annie looked at me, each of us sending the gift of a smile to the other, the circle starting to spin again. It only took a line or two for me to recognize that Daphne was singing "Margaritaville." When she sang the part about stepping on a pop-top, I looked over at Gabriel, who looked like a proud papa watching his child perform for the first time. He flashed his pearly whites at me, and I do mean pearly whites, then pointed up at Daphne, and I'd swear I saw a single tear on that angel's face.

The band that was backing up Daphne couldn't have been any more accommodating and gracious as they let her do a second number. Plus, the crowd seemed like they might riot if she didn't. She chose "Come Monday," also a Jimmy Buffett song and one that I actually liked, though I'd never admit that to Gabriel.

The crowd went crazy for Daphne, and she deserved every bit of it. Grabbing my cell phone, I stood up and took a great shot of Daphne performing, and as I sat back down, I realized that in the last five days, I hadn't taken a single picture. Which was really strange. How could I not have a single picture of Annie on my phone? I needed to remedy the situation immediately.

When Daphne rejoined us—after a standing ovation—she

looked radiant, like something mystical had transpired. Paul came over and told her if she ever needed a permanent gig, she had a home here. Then Paul and Gabriel whispered again. When they were finished, Paul bid us goodbye and went off to schmooze with other guests.

"Daphne," I said, "I didn't know you could sing like that. It was amazing."

Annie said something similar, then Gabriel bearhugged her off the ground. Holding her in the air for what seemed like forever, he finally returned her to earth. "I didn't know you had it in you," he said, "but on the other hand, I did." Then he kissed her once and quickly on the lips.

"Okay, everyone, enough already," Daphne said. "Don't we have a play to review tonight? We can't hang around here all night drinking and singing Jimmy Buffett, can we?"

"I wouldn't mind," Gabriel said.

"She's right," I said. "We need to get back to the hotel and change." Then Annie approached, I wrapped her in my arms, and gave her a hug, not as ferocious as Gabriel's but one that was tender and said *I love you* without a word being spoken. Annie got the message and returned the hug with what felt like the same emotion I was giving her.

"Fine, if we have to go, we have to go," Gabriel said, pointing to the check. "Michael, would you be a dear and take care of that, please? And leave a generous tip. Paul is an old friend, and I don't want him thinking I'm cheap."

Piling back inside my car one, we decided that once we were ready, we'd meet at the hotel bar for one quick drink. The bar was called Gumbo Limbo and was a big meeting place for the rich and powerful. And as it turned out, it was also for lonely, semi-talented critics.

Mumbo Jumbo

Gabriel chose Hunnicutt Cabernet at Gumbo Limbo, which faced the ocean. What a place—definitely one of my favorites of all time. It gave me the most pleasant of feelings and besides, the name was super catchy.

The ladies were running late, but I allowed the bartender to pour me a small glass of the wine, mostly to please Gabriel but also to calm my nerves before we saw *Up the Junction*. What a silly name for a play, I thought, but then again, who am I to judge? Oh, wait, I'm the critic. Maybe I needed a bit more wine.

Gabriel was dressed in yet another white suit, and when I asked him why he looked so nice, he merely said, "The theater, Michael. The theater."

I'd chosen a sports jacket with matching slacks. The girls sauntered in a few minutes later, hitting the wine faster than lightning striking a grease-covered road.

"Annie," I said, "you look wonderful tonight." I kissed her gently. This was done with my eyes never closing or leaving her eyes, which was new for me. Then I lifted her hand, kissed it, and placed it back down by her side.

Finally, raising my glass, I made a toast. "To Annie and her lovely red dress, both of which glow with the deep color of a beating heart, one filled with love and beauty. As I walk into that auditorium tonight and every head turns to see who is accompanying this gorgeous lady in red, I will be walking on air because it will be me. Miss Annie, you've stolen my heart and I hope you'll keep it forever. Oh, and to my friends—what are your names again?—oh, yes, Daphne and Gabriel. Salud!"

We all clinked glasses, but for some reason, Gabriel looked worried. Oh well, I'd have to ask him later if everything was all right.

The bartender brought a second bottle of Hunnicutt Cabernet. He placed it down and announced, "Compliments of the house. Enjoy!"

As if reading my mind, Gabriel waved his hand through the air and assured us we had plenty of time. So I indulged in perhaps a bit more wine than I should have. But what the hell, I thought, a drop more can't hurt.

The wine was amazing, and I wondered if my tastes were changing. Did it have anything to do with Annie? Meanwhile, her dress kept drawing my attention. The way it clung, front and back, made it hard for me to look away.

Daphne raised her glass to toast, but Annie's red dress was talking to me. I found it more and more interesting.

"Aren't you going to raise your glass, Michael?" Daphne said.

"Sorry. I was thinking about Annie's dress and how lovely it is."

"Well, I was making a toast to our host with the most: Gabriel. Without him, none of us would be here. And we wouldn't have all of this." She waved her arms around. "It's only been a matter of days, but Gabriel has brought us to so many wonderful places, shown us so many wonderful things, and taught us all how to love a fine glass of wine. His laughter and generosity have infected us all, and I truly believe that each of us is better off today than we were a few days ago, all because of him."

"Cheers," everyone said together.

Daphne had hit the nail pretty close to the head. I mean, sure, Gabriel was responsible for picking out where and when most of the time, but let's not forget who was footing the bill. Not only was I paying the price monetarily but also physically and mentally. It wasn't easy knowing you've spent four months' earnings in just one month, with no end in sight. So if a glass was to be raised, maybe, just maybe, that glass should be raised *pour moi*.

Lost again in my own thoughts, I bumped into someone trying to inch up to the bar. The collision happened at the same time I felt a strange wetness come down over me—a red wetness, as it turned out. Before I could look to see what had transpired, I heard four words that made a lump appear in my throat: "Son of a bitch."

Departure Lounge

"Hello, Rose," I said, "who's your clumsy friend?"

"You follow me like the plague, Michael. I need to find some kind of vaccine for you. And you're the clumsy one. Look what you did to Keith, my date." She dabbed at Keith's jacket.

"There's no saving it, Michael," Annie said after assessing the mess. "You need to change."

"But I don't have anything else."

"No worries, Michael, you can wear something of mine," Gabriel said. "In fact, there's an outfit already laid out on my bed. It was my second choice for this evening, a choice I think you'll be pleased with."

"We're hardly the same size, though, Gabriel."

"Show some trust in me, will you, Michael?"

"Yeah, Michael," Rose said, "show some trust in your friend and stop spilling wine on people while you're at it."

"May we offer you and your friend a drink?" Gabriel said to

Rose. "It's the least we can do after Michael's clumsiness."

"Sure," Rose said as Keith, still staring at his stained shirt, nodded.

"Are you two dining here?" Daphne asked.

"No, just stopping in for a drink. This is one of Keith's favorite bars."

"Isn't that a coincidence? It happens to be one of Michael's personal favorites too."

A third bottle of wine seemed to have appeared, and the bartender was already pouring two new glasses while topping off the originals.

"Where do you live, Keith?" Annie asked.

"New York, but I travel a lot. Miami is one of my favorite cities. I just love getting in a convertible and driving through the Keys to enjoy the ocean views."

"Have you ever met Jimmy?" Gabriel asked.

Annie explained the Jimmy Buffett obsession to Keith. "No, can't say that I have, although many of my clients have."

"What is it that you do?" Annie asked.

Rose put her arm around Keith. "He's an agent. Represents some of the biggest celebrities in the business."

"Oh? Like who?"

"I'm not comfortable saying," he said as he handed out his business card to everyone: *Keith Wilkinson, Agent To The Stars.* On it was a picture of a night sky filled with stars.

"He represents Glenn Difford, you know," Rose said, squeezing his arm.

"True," Keith said, "and Glenn knows Jimmy Buffett. They go way back, I'm told."

"You're lying," Gabriel said.

"Nope, they're old friends. Glenn even occasionally goes on

vacation with the Buffets."

"Are you in town for Glenn's debut tonight in *Up the Junction*?" I asked nervously.

"Yes, how did you know?"

"I just put two and two together. Shouldn't you be heading over to the theater soon?"

He glanced at his watch. "Yes, we probably should be going, Rose."

"Michael and his friends are also going to the play, Keith," Rose said. "Would you like to know why?" Then Rose answered her own question. "Michael works for the *Miami Herald*, and he'll be reviewing the play for the paper."

Keith's expression shifted. A frown appeared but disappeared just as quickly. "Splendid. Maybe we'll see you all there. I'm sure you'll love it. It's one of the funniest things I've ever seen, Broadway-bound for sure. And I always use this place as a departure lounge before perfect evenings."

"You know what's funny, Keith?" Gabriel asked. "The last time your client was in a play, Michael also did the review."

"Really? Small world. Now, admittedly, that show had its problems and needed some tinkering. Had it stayed open longer, I think they'd have worked out the bugs."

"Come on," I blurted, "it was a classic piece of shit."

Keith looked startled. "I don't think that's necessary, Michael. In fact, it was because of people like you—so quick to judge—that the play never got a chance to hit all its marks."

"Funny, I thought that's what out-of-town performances were for. To clean up and dispose of all the wrinkles before heading to Broadway. And if memory serves, your buddy's play had three months of pre–Manhattan shows."

"Some plays take longer to find their groove."

"Trust me, if it were playing today, it would be grooveless. A piece of Broadway shit that only floats in the city's sewers."

"Who the hell do you think you are?" Keith said, no longer trying to hide his anger.

"I'm Michael Holland, critic for the *Miami Herald* and damn proud of it."

"Hey, Keith," Gabriel said, "maybe Michael will like this one."

Annie grabbed my sleeve. "Michael, if you're going to change, you need to do it now."

"Always a pleasure, Rose," I said before departing to my room to change.

Annie came with me, and I heard Daphne say some parting words to Keith and Rose. "Hope to see you both at the show. That is, if it hasn't closed down already."

Then I saw Keith flip Daphne the bird behind his back, which only seemed to please her more.

Vanity Fair

As promised, a cleaned and pressed suit lay across Gabriel's bed. Of course, it was white and just my size. In fact, it was a duplicate of the one Gabriel was wearing. On the floor beside the bed was a pair of matching white shoes, also in my size. Go figure. I hoped that if I wore these clothes, Gabriel's style choices wouldn't rub off on me. I had my own vanity issues, after all, and I didn't need any of his.

Oddly, Annie didn't question any of this massive sartorial coincidence.

"Hurry, Michael, no dilly-dallying."

"Okay, but there's something I need to know. Are we good?"

"Yes, we are good, but I'm going to continue to make you work for me. I don't come easy, you know."

"Works for me. I'll do whatever it takes for me to be with you, Annie. I love you, and in my heart, I know that I'll love you till the day I die."

"You keep that up and you'll do just fine." Then she came over and kissed me. It lasted so long that I thought she might suggest skipping the play. But then it ended, like all kisses do, and I got dressed. Unbelievably, I found a red rose carnation on the bed next to the suit, and under the jacket were a pair of white socks with a picture of baby angels kissing and a pair of white boxers with red lettering across the rear: *Have you kissed an angel today?* These too were my size, so I figured, what the heck? As I put them on, my cell rang.

"It's your boss calling," Annie said.

"Go ahead and answer."

She entered a moment later and giggled when she saw my boxers. "Uh, your boss wants to talk to you."

"Hey, Chris," I said, "how's it going?"

"Are you on your way to the play?"

"Just about to leave."

"Great, but listen, I need a favor."

"Sure."

"Um, I need a good review, Michael. I need a Humphrey Bogart, if you know what I mean."

"Of course, I do. I've been in the business almost as long as you. But I've never been asked to do one before."

"I'm asking now."

"May I ask why?"

"Sure, but I'm not going to tell you. I don't want this coming

172

back to bite me in the ass. Let's just say some chips are being cashed in by someone who's been holding them for a long time—someone we don't say no to, okay? I mean, I've done you a solid, haven't I? I put you up at the best hotel in Miami. I hooked you up with fashion show. And I let you bring three friends, all on my dime. Didn't you think it was suspiciously generous on my part?"

"Now that you mention it."

"Great! So, I just need a good review, an old-fashioned Humphrey Bogart, and we're all good. Plus, I saved the best news for last. You're getting the front page of Sunday's Entertainment section."

"Wow."

"Thank me later because there's more. Madeline Star interviewed Glenn Difford this morning, and she got a ton of good stuff. It'll all be on the front page. Half for her interview, the other half for your review. And one more thing—you're finally getting your picture."

"Are you kidding me?"

"I kid you not. From now on, every review you do, no matter what it's on, your face will be printed right next to it. We're talking big-time here."

"I can't believe it."

"Just get me that review no later than 3:00 p.m. tomorrow, okay? No later. Are we on the same page here? I gotta know before I hang up this phone."

"Yes, yes, we're on the same page." And he clicked off the call.

"What's a Humphrey Bogart?" Annie asked immediately.

"As you probably know, Humphrey Bogart is a star from the golden age of cinema. He portrayed a lot of gangsters but also a lot of good guys. He could credibly play it both ways. And he was also the star of Casablanca, one of the biggest films in history."

"I know all that, but what does the saying mean?"

"In the review business, when you do a review that's bought and paid for in advance, it's called a Humphrey Bogart. I don't really know why, but it goes back forever."

"So a review can be bought? I never knew that."

"Sorry to break it to you, Annie, but anything can be bought."

"I guess you're right. I just never thought about it before."

"It's as old as prostitution and just as wrong, but there's nothing anyone can do about it. You can buy votes, political favors, and sex, so why would buying a good review surprise anyone?"

"I don't know, it just does." Then she looked up at me and asked point-blank, "Are you going to do it?"

"You heard what Chris said. It's non-negotiable. He even threatened my job in a roundabout way."

Walk A Straight Line

In the car ride over, I explained to the rest of my cast and crew about the phone call from my boss. Daphne was horrified and said I should stand up for truth and honesty and take a stand against the wrong in this world. She said I should do my job as I see fit, not at the whim of another seeking to prosper through deceit. "Walk a straight line, Michael. You'll like yourself better in the end."

"When is the review due?" Gabriel asked.

"Tomorrow afternoon."

"Problem solved, then. Wouldn't you agree?" He winked at me via the rearview mirror.

Immediately I got the gist. I couldn't fib until after lunch on Sunday or I'd nullify our agreement. I couldn't possibly write a positive review if the play was bad. Which meant I had to go against my boss, maybe lose my job, and suffer whatever else telling the truth might add to my already-confusing life.

As if reading my mind, Gabriel threw out this little nugget: "It gets worse, Michael, but I'll tell you later because we're here."

After we entered The Adrienne Arsht Center, I was flabbergasted. In a word, *wow!* It sat 2400 people in its five levels, which included ten private boxes on each side of the stage. We were in a private box on the right, number nine, to be precise. Pretty snazzy digs.

The place reminded me of the Kennedy Center in Washington, D.C. Opulently designed, with particular care and attention paid to all the tapestries. The colors and woodwork were a feast for the eyes, and the seats were plush and deep, letting us sink right in as if we were in our own living rooms. It was like going to a show in Paris at a theater that reeks of history, one that envelops your body and enlightens your senses.

The place was sold out, but that didn't mean the show would be good. Having a star of Glenn Difford's caliber usually did the trick of putting assess in seats. From what I could tell, the parking lot had been filled with his shoot-'em-up fans, although he'd made comedies too, one out of four of which were actually funny. And on time, he played the bad guy you love to hate, which may have been his best role. It was interesting that he had a dark side to draw from, and I'd always hoped he find another role like that so I could see if his performance had been a fluke or a reflection of actual talent.

Our private luxury box came with waiter services. The drinks weren't free, but at least we didn't have to schlep to the bar and get the drinks ourselves. To no one's surprise, a minute after our asses hit those soft velvety seats, Gabriel gave our waiter an order for two bottles of the Leonetti Cabernet and four bottles of Pellegrino with lime. He then pretended to check his pockets for his wallet before asking me to take care of the young man. After digging for my last credit card, I dropped it on the waiter's tray.

Before the girls headed to the ladies' room, Annie gave me a quick kiss on the cheek, which Gabriel reacted to with a slightly raised brow. Once they were out of earshot, he leaned toward me and said, "We need to talk about that, Michael."

Long Face

"Does this have something to do with the evil eye you were giving me in the car?" I asked.

"Yes, it does. You have a bigger problem on your hands than that review."

"I do?"

"The problem is Annie. You have to break up with her."

"What? Why?"

"I blame myself for letting it get this far, but who knew it would go so well?"

"You're nuts, my friend. You've had too much to drink today."

"Michael, we made a pact, a serious pact. Those are taken very seriously by you-know-who." He pointed upward. "You prayed for a soul mate—every day—to God. Then you made a deal. If all goes well, and I have a feeling it will, you're going to meet the girl of your dreams, compliments of the big guy upstairs."

"What if I don't want this girl of my dreams anymore?"

"Too late for that. Can't go changing your mind in the last inning."

"Why not?"

"It's just not done."

Annie returned with Daphne. "What's not done?" Annie said.

"Ask loverboy over there," Gabriel said. "He can fill you in. And Annie, as we all know, is a woman who likes to hear every detail of a story, right, Annie?"

The lights blinked twice, telling the audience that the show was about to begin.

"We'll talk later, okay?" I said.

Annie nodded and started flipping through her playbill, so I did the same, immediately opening it to see the big bright smiling face of Glenn Difford, asshole extraordinaire.

Annie tapped me on the arm and whispered in my ear, "Your friend is waving to you." She pointed straight across the theater to another luxury box.

I had to squint to make out who my friend actually was, but by way she was waving, I figured it out: Rose was giving me the finger and waving it from side to side.

Before I could come up with an appropriate response, the lights went down and the curtain went up.

I grabbed my wine glass and took a long pull. It felt good and needed. I hoped it would cool down the furnace running on full blast in my gut, the one that cranks up when I'm stressed. It was hot and getting hotter. Did Gabriel really mean that I had to call it off with Annie? I glanced over to find him staring at me. Was it an angry stare or a sad stare? I wasn't sure, but either way, it wasn't a good stare.

Babylon and On

During intermission, Gabriel noticed the empty wine bottles. He wanted them replaced, but our waiter was nowhere in sight. Getting agitated, he said we should stretch our legs and look for a bar. The girls didn't need to be asked twice; they were already on their feet. I didn't want to go, but go I did because the girls each grabbed an arm and pulled me up.

The lobby area was packed shoulder-to-shoulder, but somehow I heard a familiar voice. "Son of a bitch, there you are again. Stalker."

"Hello, Rose. Enjoying the show?" I asked, not really interested in her answer. She was with Keith, the annoying asshole.

"What's not to like?" Rose said.

"Glenn's got a major hit on his hands," Keith said. "Broadway-bound in less than a month."

I mentally added "douchebag" to his list of nicknames.

"Nice outfit there, Michael," Keith said. "I see you and your friend must shop at the same store, Mark Twain R Us?"

Finding his own joke hilarious, Keith laughed with abandon. Then, taking Rose's elbow, he led her away rather aggressively. For a moment, I thought I detected sadness in Rose's eyes—or was it sympathy for me?

When I turned around, Gabriel and gang were gone. I followed the sound of a cork being popped and knew it would lead me to the man himself, drinker of fine wines, knower of all things worth knowing, and finder of trouble. They were all giggling and drinking red wine in the corner, and I wondered how a man who wears only white and drinks red wine by the gallon never spills a drop on himself. As I pondered, Annie came over and led me to a small empty table.

Two couples on our left were discussing the play. They were older than us, maybe early sixties. They were dressed well and spoke eloquently, which meant they probably knew a thing or two about plays, so I eavesdropped.

"How long can they just babble on about nothing?" the heavier woman said. "I mean, enough already. Give us something to think about, something to care about, something to sink our teeth into, for Pete's sake."

The man closest to her said, "Of course, dear, but we knew this going in, didn't we? Should we be surprised by the lack of quality and substance from this sham? But we all wanted to get a peek at Difford and his supermodel arm candy, no?"

They all nodded in agreement.

"Furthermore," the man continued, "I think half of our ticket prices should be refunded because the girlfriend is a no-show."

"At least," said the heavier woman.

Daphne and Gabriel joined Annie and I before we'd had much chance to speak.

"I don't know about you three," Daphne said, "but this show is gone to the dogs."

"Meaning?" Annie said.

"It's garbage," Daphne said.

"Oh, then I agree," Annie said. "I've seen better shows on a cruise ship. In fact, I wish I was on a cruise ship right now and not here listening to this garbage."

"It makes my ears ache," Daphne said.

"I'm not so sure it's as bad as all that," Gabriel said.

"Then tell us what the show's about," Annie said. "Give it your best shot."

"Well, it's about people."

"So you have no clue?" Annie said.

"Not a one," Gabriel admitted.

"Michael," Daphne said, "what do you think?"

"It's too soon to judge, Daphne," I said. "It's only half over."

"I knew in the first five minutes that we had a crash-and-burn on our hands," she said. "The tickets should have come with a disclaimer that stated, 'This show may be stupid and dangerous to your health. Previous performances have been known to cause vomiting and suicidal thoughts among audience members."

The lights blinked, calling us back to our seats. In truth, I had many thoughts about the play, but none that I wanted to share. Plus, Gabriel's words right before the show were making it hard for me to concentrate on anything. As fast as this week had been going, it had now grinded to a slow and painful crawl. What was I going to do?

Wicked and Cruel

After the curtain closed, there was practically a stampede for the door. I knew that I was in a hurry to get out, but I hadn't realized everyone else was too. It was like the audience was on a collective mission to put this piece of shit in the past and move on.

Given how much we'd had to drink, Gabriel hailed us a cab. "It's time we let someone else do our driving," he said.

We all agreed and climbed into the cab.

Gabriel chose our next destination: The Gabriel Miami on Biscayne Boulevard. It was not your average bar; it was downright exquisite. How did he find these places that always seemed to have his name in them or something to do with angels?

Of course, we got the one and only empty table in the joint. Gabriel ordered wine, then put his book and hourglass on the table. The hourglass read 38, meaning I had only 38 hours to go on my deal before I was a free man. Thinking back, it hadn't been that hard for me to tell the truth all week. It even felt like it had set me free in a weird kind of way. But what would happen when the time ran out? How would my life be changed? Did I want it to change? I started to feel lightheaded. What had Gabriel meant that Annie had to go? Had I misunderstood somehow?

My brain began to feel fuzzy. First thing in the morning, I had to have a sit-down with Gabriel and get everything out in the open. How many hours would be left on the hourglass then? Hm, I couldn't do the math. My brain seemed to be on a coffee break. Then I heard my name being called from somewhere, but I wasn't sure by whom.

"Michael, Michael, are you okay?"

It was Gabriel.

"Looked like you were nodding off there for a minute," he continued. "Is everything okay?"

"Oh, yes, all is well in Michael-land," I said, although I noticed Annie looking at me sort of funny.

"Maybe too much to drink?" Daphne said.

"I think it's that damn play that's eating away at him," Gabriel said. "Write that review and then wash your hands of it. You'll feel like a brand-new man."

"Have you decided what direction you're going to take with

the review?" Annie inquired.

"He should write something wicked and cruel as payback for making us waste two-and-a-half hours of our lives," Daphne said. "I'd love to write it for you, how about that? I'd do it justice and then some."

"Why don't we all write it together?" Annie said. "Right now. It'll be fun."

"I've already given you my review," Daphne said. "Feel free to quote me, but make sure you spell my name correctly: Daphne, with a D. Oh, and my review: crud. Just the one word, if you please: crud."

"Gabriel," I said, "you're being unusually quiet. What's your review?"

"It had its good points. For example, the venue couldn't have been better."

"So you go to a place to review a play and you end up reviewing the auditorium instead?"

"It was just a start, Michael. As I was saying, the show had many positive and rewarding attributes to its credit."

"Such as?"

"I'm getting there, I'm getting there. Again, as I was saying, *Up the Junction* might not have been the very worst play of the year, and here's why. Because it gave each and every one of us—"

"A headache!" Daphne yelled.

"No, no, I wasn't exactly going to say that, my dear Daphne. What I was going to say was that it reminded me of how good other plays have been. Which may not sound flattering, but think on it, if you would. Here's a play that has the power to bring you back to the other plays you've seen throughout your life and remind you of how good they were compared to this one.

182

Doesn't that say something of this play's power? I ask you again, my dearest and closest friends, doesn't it?"

Looking over at the hourglass, I noticed it now read 37. Could that be right? Another hour gone? Another hour closer to the finish line? Damn, it was crazy, but I wasn't sure it was a finish line I wanted to cross.

"I'm waiting," Gabriel said. "Tell me that wasn't one heck of a positive review."

"Oh, it was positive, all right," Annie said. "Positively shit." Annie laughed hard, and Daphne added a chuckle or two.

"Women do not understand me, do they, Michael? It's hard being me."

Out of Control

When the wine was gone, we needed food. The choices were to find an all-night diner or go back to the hotel and order late-night room service. The decision was made by the lovely ladies, who agreed that greasy was good—and a necessity to soak up the alcohol. So, after I paid the bill, we headed to Jimmy's East Side Diner on the upper east side. It had been a staple in Miami for years and was featured in the Oscar-winning film *Moonlight*. It's packed twenty-four seven and has an old-fashioned feel with red pleather seats and pleasant waitresses. I wish I could have taken credit for choosing the destination, but it was another Gabriel suggestion. In fact, I was half expecting to see his picture on the wall when we arrived or to have the owner run over and embrace him, but neither happened.

Did I mention that Annie has an ever-expanding appetite? Well, she does, and Daphne isn't far behind. Gabriel eats like a normal angel-person, and I, well, let's just say that a few hours at the gym each week wouldn't be a bad thing for me.

Annie ordered everything on the left side of the menu and Daphne everything on the right. Gabriel and I said we'd pick off their plates. The waitress laughed, then took off like the roadrunner from the Wile E. Coyote cartoon. Gabriel looked like his heart had been broken when he learned they didn't serve wine, so coffee and diet sodas were the drinks of the evening. They ended up going well with the biscuits and gravy, which are three words taken very seriously in the South—and for good reason: they are simply amazing. They are comfort food at its finest, and the texture is something of legend—creamy and hot and chunky and yum!

The trouble started when the door to the diner opened and in walked Glenn Difford with his entourage, including Keith and his date, the lovely Rose. Of course, as fate would have it, they were seated within earshot of our table. It took no longer than five seconds before the dirty looks shot back and forth between the two tables.

I'm not sure which table was producing the nastier looks, but trouble was brewing. It was only a matter of time before someone popped. We were still getting our fill of grease, and due to our earlier alcohol intake, the biscuits and gravy were beginning to take on the appearance of vomit. I know, quite the contradiction to my earlier description, but welcome to the South.

Trying to be the better man, I sent up a white flag by way of a friendly wave to Glenn's table, adding a smile and nod to Rose.

Rose managed half a smile, then turned abruptly away. The other women at their table started shooting the women at our table looks that could kill. Finally, Gabriel stood and addressed everyone at their table. "Hello, dear friends, so good seeing you all again. It would be our honor and pleasure to send you over a round of drinks, with your permission, of course." Then he did his best bow and sat down, only to rise up again with the widest of smiles to do an incredibly loud burp.

Plopping back into his seat, he began to pick at the food on the table.

Glenn shouted over that they could afford their own drinks.

"Not for long," Daphne said. "Not after that lousy performance of yours."

"How dare you!" Glenn practically screamed.

"I'm just stating the obvious."

Glenn glared at me. "So, shit-for-brains, are you going to make me wait for the review or are you man enough to tell me what you're planning?"

"If you want to read my review, it will be out Sunday morning. You'll have to pay to read it just like everyone else."

"I'll be happy to review it," Annie said.

But before she could mutter another word, Daphne jumped up. "No, please, let me, please!"

"Take it away, girl," Annie said with a smile.

"*Up the Junction*, the new play starring Glenn Difford, is pure, unadulterated shit. And here's the backstory: Once upon a time there was an actor who truly believed that he could act. He made some bang-bang-shoot-'em-ups that were mildly entertaining, but then he decided to venture beyond his skill level and more or less—excuse the expression—blew his load, and not in a good way. Comedy proved to be his worst genre, followed closely by drama. Both proved beyond any doubt that this actor should stick to what he does best—pretending to act. But no, out of the blue, he wakes up one day and decides he is meant to perform on Broadway. He's certain that stage performance is his destiny. But sadly, it doesn't take long before he realizes that there are major differences between 'Stop or I'll shoot,' and 'Romeo, oh, Romeo, wherefore art thou, Romeo?' So off he went, back to the land of Hollywood, where he found himself a supermodel trophy girlfriend and lived happily ever after. The end."

Two Forks

Glenn had no expression on his face as he rose from his seat. Looking directly at me, he snarled—yes, he snarled. Then, with lightning-swift speed, he flipped over his table, sending dishes, glasses, silverware, and an assortment of food and beverages flying into the air. A woman from his entourage picked up a saltshaker and threw it, hitting Daphne in the nose. The saltshaker was followed by a fork, but it went wide and missed.

The noise from the flipped table garnered the attention of the other patrons, and word quickly spread that movie star Glenn Difford was in the joint and making a ruckus.

Glenn then walked the four short steps to our table and punched me right in the kisser. Down I went like a shrinking violet. Keith tried to pull Glenn away from me, but Glenn wasn't finished. He kicked me in the stomach and as he geared up for a second kick, Rose came over to help Keith in pulling Glenn away. Glenn was screaming out rather creative foul language phrases, and spectators filmed every moment of the fracas.

Management arrived and did their best to drag Glenn away, but he put up one hell of a fight and somehow continued whooping yours truly. He even managed to flip over our table before finally being subdued. Everyone but Rose followed Glenn and his controllers into the back of the diner, and even in my compromised state, I could see Keith doling out hundred-dollar bills to tighten up any loose lips. But it was too late; people had surely uploaded their videos to social media already. I made a mental note to check later. Plus, I wanted to see the whole thing again since it had happened so damn fast.

As Annie leaned over me and tried to help me to my feet, I'd swear I saw Gabriel hovering a few inches off the ground. But when I got to my feet, I looked over and he was back on solid ground. Weird!

"Why do these things only happen to you, Michael?" Rose said as she appeared at my side. "No matter where you go, one way or another, trouble follows." She stared at me with her arms crossed while Annie tended to my bleeding nose and steered me toward a seat. But as my butt hit the chair, I screamed. Jumping back up and reaching around my body, I pulled a fork from my ass. Could this night get any worse?

I tried sitting again so Annie could have a go at my nose, but now my butt was killing me. Daphne dropped into the seat beside me, and her nose didn't look much better than mine. The whole affair had lasted less than five minutes, and in those five minutes, Gabriel hadn't said a word.

Sleeping with A Friend

The cab dropped us off back at the hotel around 3:00 a.m. Annie decided to stay in my room in case I had a concussion, and I had no say in the matter.

The rooms were just across the hall from each other, so we

all said our goodnights and then Annie and I were alone at last. But we were still half-drunk and I had just gotten my ass kicked, so it was a safe bet that there wouldn't be any hanky-panky going on tonight.

Annie retrieved two waters from the mini-fridge and presented me with one. Then she asked how I was feeling. While I told her that it probably looked worse than it felt, she slipped off my shirt. Followed by my pants.

"Don't get any funny ideas, mister," she said. "Just think of me as your live-in nurse tonight and nothing more, okay?"

"No worries, Annie, I couldn't even if I wanted to."

"Was that the first time you were ever punched in the face?"

"First time since the second grade."

Annie frowned at my nose. "I think we need to ice that sucker up. It's so swollen, it's starting to scare me a little." She headed to the bathroom and returned with Aleve and a towel wrapped around some ice.

As she dabbed at my face with her makeshift ice pack, I decided to do a little probing. "So Annie, if I wasn't all banged up and we were relatively sober—"

"Yes, I would," she said.

"But you didn't let me finish. How do you know where I was going with my thoughts?"

"A blind man could tell where you were heading."

"So… yes?"

"Yes. Do you want it in writing?"

"Would you mind terribly?"

"You do know there are other places I can stick this ice, don't you?"

I looked her in the eye and very slowly responded with, "Promises, promises."

"Oh, that's how you want to play this?" She leaned over and gave me the softest kiss imaginable—the best kiss in the history of kisses—at least in my history of kisses. After a minute, she slowly stripped down to her bra and underwear, then grabbed a chair, slid it over next to the bed, and sat down. "So, what do you want to talk about?" she said.

"Talk about?"

"Maybe you should just close your eyes and try to get some sleep."

"Are you nuts? How could I even think about falling asleep with you sitting there like that?"

"Pardon?"

"The way you're dressed."

"How am I dressed?"

"It's not how; it's what."

"What am I wearing?"

"You know what you're wearing. I don't need to tell you."

Annie pointed to what she currently had on. "You mean this?" Her voice turned to a whisper. "Come on now, get a hold of yourself. I wear less than this on the beach."

"Remind me to go to the beach with you sometime."

"We've already been to the beach together." She smiled seductively.

"Oh yeah. Lucky me!" Some kind of game was being played here, but I couldn't figure out the rules.

Then she stood and moved the chair closer to the bed before sitting back down.

"What was that all about, may I ask?"

"Just wanted to be able to see you better, that's all."

"That's all?! That's all bullshit!"

"Michael; I really do think you may have a minor concussion.

You're not making much sense right now." Again, up she went, slid the chair a few inches closer, and plopped back down.

"You did it again," I said, pointing at her.

"Did what?"

"Pulled your chair closer."

"No, I didn't. You must be imagining it."

"Okay, you win."

"What do I win?"

"Anything you want."

"What if it's you I want?" Then she leaned forward but instead of whispering, she gently kissed my ear. Not once, not twice, but continuously.

"I thought you wanted to whisper something in my ear."

"I forgot what I was going to say."

"So, what are you doing then?"

"Hanging out here until I remember what I was going to tell you. Is that a problem?"

"Not at all."

She continued kissing my ear and neck. When she finally stopped, I didn't know if I was relieved or disappointed. There's a fine line between starting and stopping. But then bam! Not stopping. She was just switching ears.

I Want You

Our foreplay should have been called all-play because that's all I was getting. After Annie's ever-so-brief interlude of kissing, she moved to the cuddling phase, climbing into my bed, and getting as close as one could get to another person. She swished around until she was comfortable, then settled in for the rest of the night. I could hear her heart beating and feel her warm breath on the back of my neck.

Before I fell to sleep, I felt a stir one final time, by my ear. It was Annie's last whispered words before falling off to sleep herself. "I love you, Michael, please don't hurt me."

All I could think of before I drifted off into never-never land was four words of my own: I want you, Annie.

I woke to the sound of someone pounding on the door. Jumping out of bed and heading toward the door, I suddenly stopped, turned, and noticed that Annie was gone.

The pounding started again, so I opened the door to find a very grumpy Gabriel, who was looking worse for wear.

"About time," he spit out at me. "Going to sleep all day, were we?" He made his way to the table, where he placed his book and hourglass. The hourglass was nearly empty! The digital display read a startling 26.

"What time is it?" I asked

"It's ten in the morning, Michael, and time is a-ticking, as they say. We've places to go, people to see, and things to do, not to mention a very short time to do it all in."

"But I'm not so sure I'm interested in doing it any longer."

Gabriel was at my side in a flash. "What did you say?"

I spun to face him. "I said that I'm not sure I want to do this anymore, Gabriel. In fact, I may tip that damn hourglass over and be done with whole damn business."

He looked horrified. "No. Oh, no, no, no. You can't do that. You mustn't."

Grouch of the Day

"This whole thing started out like a reality show," I said, "but I was the only contestant. And you said that if I made it to the end, I would meet my soul mate. Well, Gabriel, I don't feel like playing anymore."

"But it's not for you to decide anymore. You've already chosen. You chose to participate. You can't change your mind now because the road has gotten bumpy."

"Whoa! Slow down! This is not some game show for ratings. This is my life. Let's start at the very beginning, shall we? I was minding my own business, not hurting, or bothering a soul, when you came along and offered me a deal."

"But it wasn't just a deal."

"Sure, it was. I had been praying for someone for a very long time—I admit that, okay?—because it sucks being alone, it really does. Seeing other couples walking down the street holding hands. Watching two people stare into each other's eyes and then kissing. The list goes on and on. I wanted all those things and I still do. So when you said I could have all if I could go a week without lying, I thought easy peasy, lemon squeezy. But now, there are flies in the ointment. Annie, for one, and let's not forget about my job, which is at stake if I write an honest review. But then again, that means that I lose the deal with you, which has its benefits because then I still have Annie, and in the end, that's what I want no matter how this coin flip turns out. I want Annie."

"How do you know that you want Annie?"

"Because I love her."

"How do you know you love her? Do you have experience in the love department? Have you ever been in love before?"

"No, but—"

"Then how do you know that you're in love now?"

"I just know, okay? I mean, how does anyone know they're in love? It's not like you get an official email from the Department of Love certifying that you are officially in love. But when I wake up in the morning, my first thoughts are of Annie. Will I see her today? Is she thinking about me? When something happens to me, no matter how big or small, my first thought is to call and tell her about it. My last thoughts before I fall to sleep are of Annie, always Annie."

Gabriel pshawed and waved away my concerns. "Michael, you sound like a Nicholas Sparks novel. That kind of love is very rare and quite magical. Are you sure you and Annie have that?"

"I can't speak for Annie, but my gut says yes, she feels the same." I stepped close to him. "Why can't I just cash in my chips now, Gabriel? Say thanks for the opportunity but I'm bowing out. Isn't that an option?"

"Michael, you prayed for something for a long time, and God heard you. He is willing to answer your payers. You can't just dismiss that."

"Why not?"

"Because He's the big guy, that's why. It would be a slap in the face to Him, like, 'Hey, God, thanks for taking time out of your busy day for little old me, Michael Holland, but I'm good to go. I don't really need your help anymore, but thanks anyway.'"

"Sounds good to me."

Gabriel sighed. "Will you please slow down and think about this? Let's suppose for one minute that there is a wonderful woman out there who has also been praying for a man she could love, and be loved by, for the rest of her life. Now let's suppose

193

that when your prayers are answered, hers are too. And imagine that the plan *from the start* was to hook you two up, and now she is waiting for you. She has been told that God, in his almighty wisdom and graciousness, has answered her prayers and is going to bring her together with a certain individual—and that individual happens to be you. You see? Things are in motion, and it's all happening tomorrow—*if* you are willing to keep your end of the bargain. But what if, at the very last minute, this young lady awaits her introduction to her soul mate and he changes his mind? Just up and leaves her in the shit. She's left holding the bag, don't you see? A bag of shit! And you, Michael, are trying to sell me a bag of shit. So, what do you think will happen if you simply walk away?"

"Don't you see, Gabriel? In all of your scenarios, you never include Annie. How come? She's real. She's a person with feelings and a heart of her own. A heart that can break just like anybody else's. It seems to me that in your version, it's actually Annie left carrying the bag of shit. So let me ask you this. In the end, is it ultimately my decision to make?"

After what seemed like an eternity, Gabriel nodded, then plopped down onto the couch. He rubbed his temples and stayed silent. When he finally spoke, it was in a smooth, calm voice. "You are indeed in charge of your own life, Michael. It's your life and your life only. I wish you clarity of mind, and I pray that God looks after you and blesses you, no matter which direction you choose. Furthermore, I'd like to add that it's been a pleasure knowing you and sharing time with you here on earth. You're not someone I'll soon forget."

The hotel door was being pounded on again.

"Open up in there," Daphne shouted.

I opened the door, surprised to see both girls looking as

194

hungover as we felt.

I Won't Ever Go Drinking Again

"I won't ever go drinking again." Daphne exclaimed as she walked through the door. Annie gave me a quick kiss hello as she entered, which both Gabriel and Daphne noticed. Daphne dropped down next to Gabriel on the couch and gave him the once-over. "You look like something the cat dragged in."

"Right back at you, dear Daphne."

"How much wine did we consume last night? And why did we do such a stupid thing?"

"Gabriel made us do it." I said, only half-jokingly.

"Now, children, let's not bicker about things in the past, shall we?" Gabriel said. "We have the present to plan, and time is of the essence." He glanced at the hourglass. A

Annie stood, went over to the hourglass, and then looked at me with a strange expression.

Gabriel rose and took the hourglass from her. "Let's not drop that, Annie. It's a family heirloom." He gently placed it back down on the table.

Annie then picked up his book. "Are you ever going to tell us what's in this book you've been carrying around for a week now?"

Gabriel reached over and took it from her hands before she could open it. "All in good time, Annie, all in good time."

"Time, huh? She looked from the hourglass to the book. "All in time."

"I need donuts and I need them now," Daphne said. "Who knows the closest place?"

"The closest or the best?" I asked.

"Both." She got up from the couch. "Let's you and I go, Michael. Let these two stay here and chitchat about hourglasses."

In the car I asked Daphne how she was truly feeling, and she admitted that she was not as bad as she had been letting on. "How did you know?" she said.

"I'm a reviewer, I can tell acting a mile away, whether it's good or bad."

"How was mine?"

I shrugged. "For non-pros like Gabriel and Annie, you pulled it off, but the question is why?"

"I just wanted to rub it in a little with Gabriel, to show him that drinking so much is not always a good thing."

"Hm, I didn't see that coming. Are you starting to care for old Gabriel?"

"I'd say that old Gabe is a pushover, and he has a certain charm about him. And that's all I'm going to say for now. The rest of my review will follow later."

"Holy shit! I forgot to write my review for last night's play. Damn, it's got to be sent in this afternoon."

"Plenty of time, Michael. First, we need donuts, and fast."

I drove Daphne to my favorite Miami donut shop, Peace Love & Little Donuts. People flocked there because of their world-famous variety of unimaginably flavored toppings. I was addicted to the donuts that had Fruity Pebbles cereal on them. Sounds disgusting but once I tried them, I never tried another kind.

I bought a dozen, including four of the Fruity Pebbles, and Daphne chose the rest. The one that excited her most was topped with hot crushed bacon.

"Gabriel is going to love these," she said.

When we returned, we were greeted with the smell of aromatic coffee wafting through the air. Orange juice sat on the table next to four empty glasses and a bowl of assorted fruit. It seemed our beavers were busy while we were gone.

Annie took one look at the donuts and declared she'd stick with the fruit.

"You're making a large mistake," Daphne said as she grabbed a bacon-topped one.

"What on earth is all over these four?" Annie asked, pointing to my selections

"Fruity Pebbles," I said. "My favorite."

"I've never seen something so disgusting in my life. How can you eat that?" she said as she watched me put one in my mouth.

Gabriel took his time choosing, eventually going with one covered with white coconut flakes.

"I need some time this morning to write my review."

"The morning is almost over," Gabriel said, "so stop dilly-dallying and get to it, but be sure to think before you do." He cast an eye toward Annie.

"Why did you look at me when you said that to Michael?" she said.

"That's something you should take up with Michael."

"No, I'm taking it up with you."

I leaned back in the desk chair and looked at Gabriel. "Yes, why don't you tell her, Gabe?"

"My name is Gabriel, Michael, and I will not be put to the test. Be careful with your words and actions; both have repercussions, as you are well aware. Now I think a shower is in my near future, so please excuse me." And off he went, almost as if sulking.

Tempted

I was tempted to tell Annie everything and let the pieces fall where they may. But if I told her Gabriel was an archangel, she'd run as far away from me as possible because she'd think I was certifiable. So, I stayed quiet.

Once we were packed and ready to go, we piled into my car and headed west. We were four cranky, hungover, sleep-deprived individuals desperate to return home and put Miami in the rearview mirror. As soon as I got back, I had to write that review. And I still didn't know what I planned to say or how I would handle my angel/God situation. Here I was, being told by an angel that my private prayers were about to be answered and that I'd never be lonely again. But then there was sweet Annie, the first girl I ever had feelings for, and I might lose her if my prayers were indeed answered. Was it love I felt for Annie? As far as I knew, it was, even if Cupid hadn't handed me a diploma or affidavit or anything. I mean, does anyone know for sure when they're *in love*? And even if they do know, does it come with any type of guarantee? Or a warranty perhaps? How long would this thing between Annie and me last? Some people say love is fleeting; others say it's eternal. Go figure.

From the start, I had some type of chemical reaction to Annie's presence, and I couldn't stop thinking about her, nor did I want to. Thinking of her makes me feel good. It puts me in a pleasant place, one that I can't remember having been to before. But there was also confusion, doubt, indecision, and a host of other unwanted feelings, like hurt, anger, and regret. But maybe whoever said that you have to take the good with the bad was talking about love.

My thoughts spun for the entire two-hour drive. For every

question I answered, two more burst onto the scene like bubbles filling the air. But there was one big issue that I'd been ignoring and pushing to the back of my mind. Intentionally? Probably. But I needed to put it front and center: God.

Points of View

Where was God in all of this? He's how this all started. He was the reason I was in this car driving west with an angel, a girlfriend, and Daphne. I'd prayed to Him for a companion, a friend, a lover—a three-for-one deal, basically. I'd wanted someone to share the good times and the bad times and all the times in between. And honestly, I hadn't been expecting him to answer. I mean, I'd prayed for other things too, and I was still waiting. But on the other hand, I'm just a microdot in the big picture, and God does not have time to sit around and parse my wish list every day. Do we all really want or need the things we pray for? Could they just be passing whims? More importantly, do we deserve these things? And for those whose prayers are answered, does it end there? Or do they put their greedy little hands out again the very next day?

We are all given freedom of choice at birth. We are products of our own choices and actions. Life takes us in directions we have chosen directly or indirectly, through actions or inactions, spoken words or muted thoughts.

How would it be if every time we found ourselves in trouble, we just prayed to the Big Man and *poof*—all good now, go back and see what other kind of trouble you can get into.

I remember as a child being taught that praying was for *thanking* God or just talking to Him about random topics. I wasn't raised to believe that praying was like filling out a Christmas list for Santa.

To me, the funniest are sports prayers. You go to a football game and the guy on your right is praying for the Giants to win while the guy on your left is praying for the Cowboys to win. So how does it work? Whoever prays harder or longer gets the victory?

Or how about when you hear on the news that a plane has crashed? Sometimes it has hit a mountain and all on board have perished. But until then, the family members are praying that their loved ones are alive. And they keep praying until word comes back that no one has survived. So, their prayers can't be answered. But does that mean God wasn't listening or doesn't care? No, it just means that some prayers can't be answered or weren't meant to be answered.

Sometimes I think that what we are really doing when we pray is asking for direction. So maybe when I was praying for a companion, I was merely asking for some direction and guidance to help me choose the right path.

If I were alone with Gabriel, I'd ask him about praying and what's right and what's not so right. But from now on, I'll keep my requests to a minimum and use my open dialogue with God as a way to say thank you for His generosity, love, and understanding—and most of all for His forgiveness when I make mistakes, my many, many mistakes.

We all have our own points of view, and I don't claim mine are correct, but they're right for me.

Robert Remail

True Colors

Here I am in a car with an angel sent from God as a gift to me, and I'm contemplating returning the gift because I no longer want it! Actually, that's only half true. I do want it, but I kind of already have it—and I definitely don't need to have it twice. It's something I asked for hundreds of times, and now I can't use it.

Does God get offended if you return a gift? Is that a slap in the face to Him? Do the doors of heaven close on someone who does that? The last thing I want to do is offend Him, although He must know my true colors. And if He does, that means He knows that I have not a single ounce of disrespect toward Him, and He must know that love is driving me forward.

My life felt like it had become a roulette wheel and I was just waiting to see if the ball would land on red or black. I could handle either one, I supposed. My only true fear was that the ball would land on green, and if that were the case, I was well and truly fucked.

Until then I had a review to write and a romance to nurture—and I only had a few hours left of my week with an angel. I had to let the roulette ball drop where it may.

And with that decision, a weight suddenly lifted from my shoulders. I felt cleared of an overburdened conscience, and my worries floated away to where they couldn't trouble me any longer. Was this enlightenment? Did a little contemplation and deep searching of my soul bring me enlightenment?

As I pulled into my complex, I announced to my dozing passengers that we had arrived. The girls got out of the car, but Gabriel didn't move. In fact, he was snoring louder than ever. Looking at the girls, I whispered, "Let's leave him here until he wakes up. We could all use a little Gabriel-free time, no?"

They nodded their acceptance and off we went to Chez Michael.

It was good to be home. I loved the feeling of coming home from a trip, of being back in my own castle. But this time it was different—a bad kind different—so bad, in fact, that a tear dripped down my cheek, followed by many more.

Every single thing in my home was gone. It was as if I'd walked into an apartment that was awaiting a new occupant. As the realization set in that I had been robbed, I sank to the floor.

The Day I Get Home

"Who did you piss off?" Daphne said while her eyes danced around my empty place.

"Oh my God," Annie said as she went from room to room to see if they too were empty. When she came back, she knelt down beside me. "The whole place is empty, everything is gone."

"How?" was all I could muster.

Annie took my hand and gave it a gentle kiss. "I'm so sorry, Michael. I can't imagine who would do such a thing."

"Toilet paper and paper towels?" Daphne yelled from another room. Then she stuck her head into the living room. "They even took the toilet paper and the paper towels from their dispensers! Nasty little devils, they are!"

"Are my clothes—"

"Nope. They're gone too. From what I can tell, they didn't even leave a toothpick."

"My, my, what in God's name do we have here?" Gabriel said as he entered. "Did you forget to pay somebody, Michael? Or should I ask, Did you forget to pay everyone? Well, you know, fools and fortune tellers are always looking for fast cash."

"What does that mean?" I said

"Not a clue, but Jimmy says it all the time." He gestured to the capacious emptiness. "Thoughts?"

"Not now, Gabriel. My entire world is gone."

"Don't say that, Michael."

"Why not? Look around! I can't even change my underwear; they took those too."

"It's always darkest before the dawn," Gabriel said. "And that's not Jimmy Buffet, it's Thomas Fuller, by the way. It means—"

"I know what it means. I did go to college, you know, and I review books and films for a living. Wait! That could be it! Do you guys think Glenn Difford could be responsible for this?"

"He certainly would have the resources to pull it off," Gabriel said while scratching his chin. "But I don't think he would stoop this low. Hm, we were only gone a short time, so it had to be someone who knew your schedule in advance."

"My boss? You think he could be involved?"

"Newspaper editors don't empty out townhouses for fun," Annie said.

"I never would have thought I'd be asking for this today," I said, "but could you check the fridge, Annie? I need a beer."

"I can't," Annie said sadly. "They took the fridge too."

"Wait!" Gabriel screamed. "What about my wine?"

"Gone," Annie said.

Gabriel took a deep breath and scowled. "Now I'm pissed."

His House, Her Home

An hour later, the four off us were at Annie's townhouse. I'd called the police, but they seemed reluctant to believe it was a robbery because things like that so rarely happened in Naples. One of the officers even suggested that it must be a joke being played on me and that the joker would eventually reveal himself. But at least I'd filed a report.

So here we were sipping coffee at Annie's.

"Damn it," Gabriel said through gritted teeth. "Who steals a man's wine?"

"We only had one bottle left," I said to comfort him.

"Impossible! We couldn't have drunk all those bottles so quickly."

"*We* didn't. You did."

"What about the review, Michael?" Annie asked.

I glanced at my watch. "Oh shit, it's due in an hour, and I don't even have a computer."

"Use mine," she said. "And if you want, I'll even help you write it."

"Thanks, Annie."

"What does everyone feel like having for dinner?" Gabriel asked randomly.

Daphne must have read our minds because she took a pillow from the couch and hit Gabriel over the head with it twice. "Don't be a jerk, Gabriel."

The ringing of my cell phone startled me. It was the police, so I answered immediately. When the call ended, I couldn't have felt worse.

"What did they say?" Annie asked impatiently.

"They spoke to six of my neighbors. Not a single one saw

204

anything. Furthermore, they did the math and calculated that the robbers would have needed ten hours and a big moving truck, plus a half a dozen guys, to pull it off. And with not one person on my street seeing anything, they think maybe I was in on it."

"That's ridiculous," Annie said. "Go down there and file a complaint against these officers."

"My head is spinning right now, but I've got to write that review. I can't believe my life has turned upside down so quickly."

"This may be my house," Annie said, "but consider it your home for as long as you need to."

"Can I ask one of you for a lift back to my place?" Daphne said.

Gabriel agreed to do it, probably with the ulterior motive of stopping at Total Wine on the way back. And my suspicions were confirmed when he asked to borrow my credit card. But to his dismay, my third and final credit card had been declined at the diner last night.

"Do you have a debit card?"

"I do," I said hesitantly.

"Well, if you give me your pin number, I can stop and get us some cash before picking a little wine."

"Well, isn't that nice of you? Are you sure you have enough time?" I said as sarcastically as I could.

"Oh, I'm not worried about time, Michael, and it's no bother at all. I'm sure you'll need a nice glass of Merlot after writing your review. It's the least I can do. Oh, and can I borrow your car?"

House of Love

I loved everything about Annie's place. Her decorative style, similar to mine, made me feel at home, as did Annie herself. She went out of her way to make me feel welcome. I wasn't sure if it was because of her feelings for me or the fact that some asshole had robbed me of every possession I owned. Maybe a little of both?

"First things first," she said. "You need a shower. It will make you feel better, and I'll make you some strong coffee. The bathroom is fully stocked."

I nodded and headed off to the bathroom, where she'd laid out a pair of men's sweatpants and a matching sweatshirt. A razor and shaving cream lay atop the clothes. Hm, I wondered why she had such items.

When I was fully refreshed, I emerged to find hot coffee next to Annie's laptop, which she'd placed on her kitchen island.

As I sat down at the computer, I heard the shower turn back on. So that's where Annie was. Then I groaned. The last thing I felt like doing was writing that stupid review, so I procrastinated with the one thing I still owned: my cell phone. I checked the screen: seven missed calls, seven new emails, and eleven new texts. I went with the text messages first. One was from my sister Lucy, wondering how I was and asking me to reach out soon. The next nine were from my boss, all telling me that my review was long overdue. The last had come in from Annie while I was in the shower: *Check your voice mail.* So, I did.

I played the message from Annie. It was short, sweet, and to the point. "Michael, when I finish with my shower, I expect to find you waiting for me in my bedroom, and no, you will not be needing those silly-ass sweats, so take them off."

Oh boy! My mind began to race. Was this a good thing or a bad thing? Only time would tell, but I was terrified. This would be my first time! And also, *this would be my first time*! Damn, why now? But then again, why not now? No time like the present. Oh shit, what do I do? Then a little voice whispered inside my head: Get your damn ass in that bedroom now. Actually, it wasn't quite a whisper; it was more of a roaring command.

If we were at my place, maybe I wouldn't feel so nervous. Then I remembered I technically had no place at the moment.

The water from the shower shut off, and my ass was still sitting in the kitchen.

"Run to that bedroom!" said the voice.

So, I did, tripping over the coffee table on the way. Down I went, banging my head on the sofa. Then I jumped back up and checked to see if Annie had witnessed the fall. Nope! I was good to go. I entered her bedroom for the first time, and it was perfect. It wasn't overly feminine, and it wasn't drab in the sense of having no flair. It was just right. It said, *"Welcome home."* I might sound crazy, but every room of Annie's place seemed to speak to me that way, telling me that I, Michael Holland, belonged here.

"I thought I told you to nix those silly sweats."

I turned to see Annie standing in the bedroom doorway. My knees were shaking. My breath was running amok, and my sweat glands all opened at once. Because Annie was standing there naked as a jaybird.

Some Fantastic Place

Annie crossed the room and kissed me gently, then passionately, taking turns going back and forth between the two. She paused only long enough to pull off my clothes, then she pushed me down gently onto her bed.

"Annie, there's something that I need to tell you," I whispered.

"Tell me later."

"But what if it's important?"

"Won't it still be important when we're finished?"

"Yes."

"Then tell me later." Her mouth found my neck and that's all it took. There were no more questions and no more answers. No more delays and no interruptions from Gabriel. No second-guessing and most of all, no more waiting. The time was now, and the time was right. Our two bodies became one.

I liked the fact that Annie was wet and had just come from the shower. Plus, I always found wet hair on a woman to be sexy. As each second went by, my worries receded, and with them my fears. Even though I had no experience in this area, I could tell Annie was enjoying herself as much as I was. And you don't need to be an expert with hundreds of hours man-hours put in to know if someone is enjoying themselves.

At one point I realized my eyes were closed. I had gotten lost in the pleasure encapsulating me. So, I opened them to find Annie's eyes just an inch or two away, and they were staring directly into mine. There was an expression on her face, one I'd never seen before. It was an expression of urgency, of pure concentration and thrill, and lastly, of love.

Then her eyes closed and her body shook with convulsions,

and she let out a deep and undeniable sigh. When her eyes reopened, they brought with them a smile I'd never quite seen before. She let out a small giggle, then returned to kissing my neck, and I returned to a place I'd never been, one I didn't want to leave. It was some fantastic place that I'd wondered about all of my adult life, and now that I'd finally visited, I wanted to stay.

After we finally broke apart and took in each other's warmth and smiles, we cuddled. It felt as good as what we had just been doing, like two pieces of a puzzle coming together. I was her Frick and she was my Frack.

Labeled with Love

I wanted to say it first, but Annie beat me to it. I knew it wasn't a race but hearing it from the lips I'd just been kissing made me feel special. And I knew that I could never walk away from this, from Annie.

"I love you, Michael. I love you so much, it hurts."

"More than the previous owner of the sweats lying on the floor?"

"Definitely more."

Then I felt that wet kiss of hers touch me, and I really felt stupid having asked that stupid question. It must be a guy thing, being so territorial.

"I want you to stay here as long as you want," she said. "I can't imagine what you're going through right now with being robbed and all. So, my house is your house, and we can talk about rent later." Annie said that last part with a smile that led me to believe she was teasing.

Rolling on top of her, I put my arm behind her back and

brought my face within inches of hers. "Annie, I love you. You know I do. And I promise I'll never hurt you and that I will take care of you, and I will—"

"Slow down, mister. I'm not asking for a contract here or any promises. I just wanted you to know that I love you with all my heart, that's all."

"I didn't mean to put any kind of label on it. It's just that I've never been here before, and I was trying to express myself to the fullest. Too much?"

She kissed me again. "It was just right."

I started a series of my own kisses across her neck, cheeks, and lips.

"I think I feel our mutual friend getting ready for a repeat performance," she said.

"Encores, I'm told, are important."

She smiled. "I'm so glad you're no longer worried about the review."

Jumping out of bed, naked and standing at attention, I gasped. "Damn! I forgot! My boss called over a dozen times."

I fell over twice while trying to put on my loaner sweats. Annie found it hysterical.

Before I left the room, I paused and turned to her. "Just for the record, I love you more than my tongue can speak."

Then I was back in the kitchen, which is when the front door opened. Gabriel walked in with a boxful of wine bottles. Daphne followed a few steps behind Gabriel and seemed to being playing with a make-up case of some kind.

"They don't knock in heaven?" I asked as he put the box in front of me. "You sure you have enough?"

"If I don't, I'll simply go out and get more. You could say thank you, you know."

"Say thank you for giving you my card so you could buy more wine for yourself?"

"No, for giving you two lovebirds some time alone to get better acquainted. How about that?"

Book Three

Beautiful Game

The digital hourglass display read 20. It sat on Annie's kitchen table next to Gabriel's book. It was hard to miss, seeing that it was only inches from Annie's computer, the one I was currently sitting at trying to write a review that didn't seem to want to be written.

Words refused to come to me with the hourglass reminding me that my time with Gabriel—and possibly Annie—would soon end. I started thinking about where I'd be at this time tomorrow and who I'd be with. My life was riding on a dime, which worried me to my core. It was just after 4:00 p.m., and I hadn't written a single word yet! I did, however, return Lucy's call. After catching her up on everything, she insisted on coming over at once. I tried talking her out of it, but she wouldn't hear of it, so she was on her way.

Daphne and Gabriel were on Annie's patio enjoying the view with glasses of wine. Meanwhile, Annie was trying to remain unseen, hoping to give me the time and space I needed to write the review. Then, just as I had my first coherent thought and my finger was hovering above the keyboard, the doorbell rang, bringing Annie out from her hiding place. I recognized my sister's voice immediately.

Lucy and Annie hugged and said a quick hello, but then Lucy

took one hell of a long look at Annie.

"Something wrong?" Annie asked

"No. In fact, I must say, you're glowing. I'm trying to figure out why." Lucy then glanced my way and smiled. "You have anything to do with this glow, Michael?" Without waiting for an answer, she doubled the size of her smile and jumped up and down. "I don't believe it! I just don't believe it! I can't believe it's happened!"

Annie giggled and tried not to let Lucy see her.

"Well, just fucking believe it, okay?" I said. "And let's move on, shall we?"

"Okay, fine, I'm done, but I need to give Annie another hug." Which she did, but this time it was longer and more of a bear hug. She might have even had a tear in her eye.

"Lucy, sweet Lucy, we meet again," Gabriel said as he came in from the patio with Daphne. "Please tell me that you've come to join us for dinner this evening. It will be our last, for some of us anyway."

"Why do you say last?" Lucy asked.

"I'm heading back home tomorrow afternoon, and I'm afraid I won't return for some time."

"I'm sorry to hear that. You seem to have been a good thing in Michael's life. Is it work that's taking you away?"

"Yes, I must get back to work."

"What it is you do for a living again?" Annie said.

"Oh, Michael can tell you all about that. He has a better way with words than I do."

"But I'm not asking Michael. I'm asking you."

"I'm sure it would bore you silly if I tried to explain."

"Gabriel, you play a beautiful game of evasion of bullshit, you know that?"

"I'm sure I have no idea what you are talking about, Annie."

"I have a sneaking suspicion you know exactly what I'm talking about."

"Hey," I said, "I'm still trying to write a review here, one that was due hours ago. Could we all talk about this later perhaps?"

"Oh, Michael, I forgot to tell you. I felt so terrible about all that's happened and the pressure you're under that I took it upon myself to email your boss," Gabriel said. "I explained that you needed more time to write your review."

"What exactly did you tell him?"

"Just that you've had a tough last few days and needed more time to heal up from your medical condition."

"What medical condition?"

"I told him you were suffering from gonorrhea."

"Jesus! I don't have gonorrhea."

"Well, your boss doesn't need to know that, does he? Look at it this way—I bought you some time. You have until ten tonight to get the review to him."

I rolled my eyes and gave Gabriel a reluctant bit of gratitude.

"Now listen up, one and all," Gabriel said. "I'm taking us to one of the best restaurants in town, one that will have you fantasizing for months to come."

Last Time Forever

The formal name of the restaurant was The French Brasserie Rustique, but everyone in Naples just called it The French. It was easier to remember and besides, French fare filled eighty percent of their menu. I'd never been there before, and reservations were a must, of course, but Gabriel did his usual hocus-pocus and in we went. We were seated at a table that practically put us on display, and I could only wonder where this evening was headed. Gabriel ordered two bottles of Silver Oak cabernet as well as every appetizer on the menu for all to share.

When the corks were popped and the glasses filled, Gabriel rose from the table to make a toast. "There's a little toast that's a favorite of mine and no, it's not from Jimmy Buffett. It goes something like this: To the last time forever." With that, Gabriel raised his glass and drank. We followed suit despite our confusion over the toast.

"That was beautiful, Gabriel," Lucy said. "Where does it come from and what does it represent?"

"Well, dear Lucy, its origins are unfamiliar to me, but its meaning is not. 'The last time forever' is a metaphor for when a group of close friends get together for the last time during a given time together, such as a holiday. They know that even though it's their last time together for that particular event, they will always be together in spirit, in each other's hearts and thoughts, as if they were one unit, one body, one soul."

"I can't believe I've never heard it before," Annie said, "but that's what getting together with other people is all about. You can come away learning so much from others if you allow your mind to be open to it."

"I agree," Daphne said. "There's nothing I love more than good conversation with lovely people. I come away with a new regard for new things."

When the appetizers arrived, our collective breaths were taken away. If food could be an art form, then this was truly it. The smells alone were enough to ignite anyone's gastronomic passions.

Cradle to the Grave

After taking a sip of her wine, Daphne rose and made a toast. "To friends old and new. Some are old, some are young, some not even begun. They carry us through life, helping us over the bumps in the roads that we cross. They help us with the crazy turns that we don't see coming. And they're there when we cross the finish line to congratulate us and help us celebrate. Without friends, we are alone in a strange place in the darkness, waiting for the light to arrive. But together we help each other shine and bring brightness to the world. We lead the way for each other, and we hold each other when holding is needed. And we do this not because we're told to do this. We do it of our own free will, which means that we want to do it. In my own little way, I love each one of you here tonight, including you, Lucy, whom I've only known for a short while, but I truly do, in my way, love each and every one of you. So please, everyone, raise your glasses and take a good look around the table. Look into the eyes of your friends here tonight and be thankful for them. From the cradle to the grave, all we have is each other. To us all. Salud!"

And with that, we all took a good look around and toasted each other. Daphne's words were poignant and right on target. In fact, I wish they'd been mine.

Gabriel was wiping at his eyes with a napkin and not trying to hide it. I looked over at Lucy, our newcomer, and she too had a wet eye. Annie's hand found my knee under the table and gave it a reassuring rub. Then our eyes met and, almost reflexively, we simultaneously leaned close to each other and did the simplest of things that two people can do. We kissed. And if I had to give it a review, I'd say it was up there with the best.

In retrospect, I'm sure that neither of us meant to give our

216

tablemates a show of our feelings, but we did, and they applauded when our kiss ended.

"See? I told you all, and I was right!" Lucy exclaimed.

"True love," Gabriel said. "Is there anything better than gazing upon it? Watching it bloom and flower before your very eyes? I say, Absolutely no." He wiped away his flowing tears.

As our table was stripped and readied for our entrées, Lucy asked me which direction my review might be headed in.

"I will share this much," I said. "I've definitely decided in which direction my review will go. In fact, it's practically written up here already." I tapped my head. "But that's all I'm willing to share at the moment."

Annie pshawed. "If I wrote reviews, I'd share them with you before I submitted them, Michael."

"Good try," I said, "but you'll read it in the paper tomorrow like everyone else."

"Really? You're not going to let me read it before you send it to your boss?"

"Correct."

"But why?"

"It's just the way I want it, that's all."

Everyone else chimed in with their complaints, but I stayed strong. "Patience is a virtue," I argued. "You'll all see it tomorrow—if I get home in time to write the damn thing."

"I'll have you back in plenty of time," Gabriel said as he flagged down the waiter to order more wine.

Someone Else's Heart

The entrées looked like they were straight from a magazine,

complete with an aroma that floated in the air around us.

After tasting her food and declaring it the best thing ever, Annie looked over at Gabriel and said she had a monumental question for him.

Dabbing his lips with his napkin, Gabriel told her to ask away.

"Have you ever been in love?" she said. "And if so, please provide the detail."

"What if I was in love more than once?"

"Then just tell me about the one. *The* one."

"Very well. I'll start by saying this is the story of someone else's heart, a heart that belonged to a woman named Laurel. To tell you that she was beautiful would be an understatement of great magnitude. She was the daughter of my neighbor when I was a youth back in Greece. She was two years my junior and caught my eye early on. I couldn't have been older than twelve, and we were both inexperienced in the ways of the world." He sipped his wine as his expressions changed like passing clouds—smiling one moment, on the verge of tears the next.

"We played together throughout our childhood. We asked each other the questions that all children wonder about but never ask their parents. We shared our deepest and innermost thoughts and fears. As the years passed, we never strayed far from one another, and as far as I know, we never had thoughts of others. We were young, we were curious, and we had each other, which made things much easier as we grew up. Of course, it was too early for thoughts of anything intimate, but that would change with time.

"By our mid-teens, we began to question if we had more than a simple friendship. Could it be something that neither of us had ever experienced but had heard stories about for as long as we could remember?"

Gabriel seemed like someone else as he enthralled us with each detail, as if he were telling the story from someplace far away. I kept waiting for someone to overturn our table, start a fight, or kick us out for insufficient funds, but all was quiet. No chaos—and no Glenn Difford.

Love's Crashing Waves

"Laurel knew before I did what was happening between us," Gabriel continued, "and her parents had guessed. When our schooling was finished, it was time for decisions to be made. She was my best friend and the one I wanted to spend the rest of my life with. One day we took a walk through a beautiful meadow and Laurel asked me to marry her. Knowing her as I did, I didn't find it shocking that *she* had asked *me*. She was an independent spirit and a rare beauty. Fiery red hair, impressive height, and a face of pure porcelain. Cutest of all was her petite, button-shaped nose. It was a perfect match for the dimple on her chin.

"Her clothes seemed to have been made specifically for her, and she brought them to life with every step, swivel, and turn of her body. She was Laurel, and there was no one else like her in the world.

"According to her, she was all mine, and it goes without saying that I belonged only to her. So I spoke with her father, who'd been expecting my knock on his door. He answered with graciousness and a welcoming smile. I'd been part of their family for years, after all, and after I'd expounded upon my feelings for his daughter, he said he'd be pleased to make it official.

"We came from a small village, so everyone was invited to the wedding. Laurel's father insisted on paying for everything and decided to make it the greatest ceremony the village had ever experienced. Laurel looked stunning in all white, in a gown that had been passed down through generations of her family. It captured the breath of all in attendance.

"Because Laurel and I were old-fashioned, we waited until our wedding night to consummate the marriage. Anticipation doesn't come close to describing what we both experienced as we waited for that moment to arrive. Remember, we'd been together most of our lives, and passions can grow volatile when they burn for so long and aren't allowed to breathe.

"The wedding turned out to be everything her father had promised, straight out of a storybook. Afterward, Laurel and I walked hand-in-hand to our honeymoon suite. Rose petals covered the top of our bed, a fire burned in the fireplace, and there was wine to spare. I took my lovely wife into my arms and, well, I'll say this: Laurel and I shared a remarkable, unprecedented level of love and bonding in our collective hearts, something beyond magical that brought us to a place we'd never been before and, as it turned out, a place we'd never go again.

"You see, two days later, Laurel drowned. She was caught in an undertow and pulled out to sea while swimming with her family. We didn't know anything for certain for three long days, and words do not exist to describe the profundity of my grief and despair. Finally, the sea gave up its dead, and Laurel was brought back to me. We buried her not far from where we had been married only days before."

Robert Remail

Goodbye Girl

With tear-filled eyes, we took turns telling Gabriel how sorry we were about Laurel. I must have had two dozen questions bouncing around my head, but I didn't think it appropriate to ask them. Because before me, graciously accepting his friends' condolences, was a new Gabriel, one I hadn't been expecting or even knew was possible.

When the table went quiet again, I figured I could at least make a toast. "Gabriel, I want you to know that I am heartbroken for your loss, and at the same time, I'm beyond sad for Laurel. First, she didn't get to spend the rest of her life with you, and that's an unfathomable loss for anyone. And second, her life was cut too short, and the world lost out on the joy, love, and kindness she had yet to contribute. Although I never had the honor of meeting her, I raise my glass here today and I say goodbye to Laurel. Goodbye, girl."

Gabriel came around the table to clink his glass against mine and kiss me on the cheek. Everyone else raised their glasses and toasted to Laurel's memory.

Dessert was a little lighter in spirit, it was hard to recapture our earlier joviality. Then, in the end, Lucy reminded me that time was running out to complete my review. I looked over at Gabriel's hourglass sitting to his right. Fifteen hours left.

Gabriel asked for the check, and when it came, he took great pleasure in announcing that tonight's dinner was on him. Then he removed a wad of cash from his pocket and counted out a large sum, throwing it on the table with a flourish.

Outside the restaurant, he whispered in my ear, "Thanks for dinner tonight, Michael. Very generous of you."

"My cash, I assume?"

221

"Of course. And by the way, you might want to think about making a deposit. Your account is running on fumes."

Tough Love

Back at Annie's place, everyone enjoyed a drink out on the patio while I wrote the review. When I actually finished, I was surprised by how little time it had taken. With a huge smile, I stepped outside and announced that I'd sent the finished product to my boss. The patio revelers cheered, and Gabriel declared that we must go out and celebrate the completion of the dastardly review. The ladies agreed, so we all gathered our things.

Annie tried one last time to get me to let her read the review. But I stuck to my guns. "Sorry, Annie, but no one reads it until it hits the paper. I guess that's what we call tough love."

There was booing from Annie and Daphne, but that quickly subsided when Gabriel suggested we walk to the pool bar for our nightcap. There was a party going on, and it would be open for another hour or so.

Roughly fifty people were milling about, dancing, drinking, and gossiping. Gabriel called gossip "the devil's radio" and advised that people should avoid it because it only led one way: the bad way.

We found a table and made ourselves comfortable. Daphne then noticed that everyone had brought their own food and drinks—which meant no wait services.

"Never worry, never fear," Gabriel said. "Gabriel is always here, supplied and ready to go." He placed his book, hourglass, and two wine bottles on our table, taking them all from a bag that I'd swear he wasn't carrying when we had arrived. Next, reaching into the same bag, he brought out five beautiful wine glasses and a corkscrew.

A DJ on the far side of the pool played '80s dance music, and at least a dozen people were bopping around. Daphne jumped to her feet when he played "Wild, Wild West" by Escape Club. "Come on, we've got to dance!" she said, pulling Annie and Lucy to their feet. And off they went.

"How did the review go, Michael?" Gabriel said. "Did you follow your brain or your heart?"

"A little of both, I guess."

"Was it the right one or the wrong one?"

"As Jimmy Buffett would say, only time will tell."

"Touché, Michael, touché."

"After an entire week together, I guess you rubbed off on me."

"I'll miss you, Michael. I'm telling you that here and now because who knows what will happen tomorrow, especially given your pigheadedness."

"But after that story you told at dinner, I thought you'd relate."

"Losing loved ones is one of the hardest human conditions to endure, Michael."

"You know what I mean—making me give up Annie to keep my end of the deal—but none of that is sitting pretty with me. Not one damn bit, and I think there are still pieces of this puzzle waiting to drop."

"What is that supposed to mean?"

"I think you know, and I think you've known all along. You're just not willing to share yet, are you?"

He gave me an innocent look.

"Come on. Ever since we met, I've had a strange feeling

there's more here than meets the eye. I can't put my finger on it, but I'm still trying. I'll figure you out yet, Gabe."

"Good for you, Michael. I like a man who uses his head and doesn't give up at the first sign of trouble."

"Can you at least tell me how this is going to fan out tomorrow? The when, where, why, and how? It would be nice to know so I don't have to worry about what's coming round the bend."

You Can't Hurt the Girl

As Gabriel contemplated my question, I pointed to Annie on the dance floor, who was shaking what she'd been given. "That girl cannot be hurt," I said. "Do you understand me? Under no circumstances can she be hurt. I don't care about me so much, but I care about her. And speaking of caring, what's the deal with you and Daphne? She knows you're leaving tomorrow, right?"

"She is well informed."

"So... what then? Aren't you the least bit sorry you're leaving her this way? I mean, you've just spent a week with her laughing and doing whatever else you two do when I'm not around."

"Shame on you, Michael. Those kinds of thoughts will get you nowhere.

"So, you're just gonna say, Later, Daphne! It's been real and thanks for the memories?"

"Hm, I haven't quite thought that far ahead, but yes, something like that. With more finesse, of course."

"Gabe," Daphne called from the dance floor, "you promised you'd dance with me if the opportunity arose." She sashayed over. "It's arose! Now come dance!"

"I knew that promise would come back to hurt me," Gabriel said as he followed her onto the dance floor. The DJ was playing a tearjerker by Aerosmith. It was called "Angel," of course.

Before the first verse was over, Annie was pulling me out to the floor.

"Penny for your thoughts?" she said as I wrapped my arms around her.

"Sure, but I want the cash first."

"You don't trust me?"

"In God I trust. All others pay cash."

She pulled me closer and whispered, "I love you, Michael Holland. Now tell me, what's going to happen when this roller-coaster of a week comes to an end? What happens to us once Gabriel's gone and I'm back to work? Will things change between us?"

The song ended and "The Flame" by Cheap Trick—another slow one—started.

"Let me throw the question back at you," I said gently. "What if you want to move on once our lives return to normal? What if you figure out that you're really in love with the chaos and Gabriel's never-ending wine supply?"

Annie pulled back, then came in close, pressing her lips to mine. I guess that partially answered my question. When she finally broke free, she gazed into my eyes and asked a question. "Okay, now where is that wine you were talking about?"

I grinned. "Hey, I think my sister really likes you."

"And I like her. She also seems to adore her brother and want only the best for him."

"She's been like that since our parents died."

"You mentioned once that your parents were deceased, but

you didn't say much else."

"They were great. Generous, loving, all that good stuff. They were both big laughers, always laughing at something or someone, and occasionally each other. My childhood memories are fairly good, which I'm really thankful for."

"How did you lose them, if you don't mind me asking?"

"Mom died of pancreatic cancer but fought it hard. She was given a year from the get-go, but like I said, she fought it and hung on for almost two years. And my dad, well, he drank himself to death. Lucy and I thought it was just some phase after Mom passed, but it was a phase without an end. At Mom's funeral, he said he didn't want to live without her. Lucy and I thought that was just something someone says when they lose a spouse, but we were wrong. And the timing was bad. He'd just retired when she got sick, and after she was gone, he became a TV junkie and full-time drinker."

The music had already stopped, and we were the only ones left on the floor.

"Come on," Annie said, "I'm taking your tired ass to bed."

"And when you say bed, do you mean romance or sleep?"

She gave me a small whack on the head, so I assumed the latter. Then Lucy got up from the table and gave me a whack on the head too.

"What'd you do that for?"

"You let Annie do it, looked like fun, and it was."

I'm at Home Tonight

After a final nightcap, our troop of vagabonds made its way back to Annie's. A strange feeling floated through the air as we sat around her living room. At first it seemed that no one wanted to speak, and melancholy had overtaken us. Gabriel's hourglass had hardly any grains of sand left. The display read 11, which made wonder if I'd get any sleep tonight.

"What's up with this crowd?" Annie finally said. "It's not the end of the world. I mean, yes, Gabriel is heading back to wherever he resides. Lucy will return to her job but let me state for the record that life will go on. So why don't you all wipe away your sad puppy-dog eyes? We still have tomorrow and I, for one, plan to have fun until the fat lady sings."

Gabriel got up and gave her the hug of hugs. "This calls for a drink," he said.

"What doesn't call for a drink in your book, Gabe?" Daphne said.

"Careful, Daphne, I know where you live."

Daphne shot him a look I'd seen before, but I couldn't interpret it. My thoughts were interrupted by the ringing of my cell. It was Chris, my boss. I listened for a full minute as he read me the riot act. "And I'm not printing this review, so you'd better write another. Pronto! You agreed. Now keep up your end of the bargain."

"Uh, you know what, Chris? Go fuck yourself." Then I hung up.

"What the hell?" Annie exclaimed.

"Something tells me he didn't like Michael's review," Gabriel said as he uncorked and poured.

Daphne sprung from her seat. "That means your review was not positive, right?"

I shrugged my shoulders, and my cell rang again. "Yes, Chris?" I said. "No, I won't do it, and I'm not changing my mind... Yes, I absolutely appreciate everything you've done, but you did most of that stuff because, frankly, I fucking earned it. So, throwing it back in my face won't help your case... Yeah? Then go ahead and fire me. I don't give a rat's ass... I'm not caving on this, so move on... That's your choice, but you do know I can post it online myself, don't you?... That's right, tomorrow morning, along with a statement that I was fired for refusing to be blackmailed by my boss, who's clearly on the take. So, how's that for a shit sandwich, Chris? Hope you enjoy every bite as it goes down... Guess we'll find out tomorrow when I open the paper. If my review is not there word for word as I wrote it, then the real review goes online, capiche?... Yeah? Well, you can shove it up your junction then!"

As I set my phone down, I looked around to see a roomful of smiling faces showing nothing but approval.

Striking Matches

"Michael," Daphne said, "you may have just struck a match to your career, but I'm damn proud of you."

"Do you think he'll print it?" Annie asked.

"He'll go in the bathroom and sit on the toilet while he's thinking about it. That's his MO, never fails—big decision, big dump. Then he'll print it."

"Why?"

"Because he's got no guts, and he hates confrontation. I guarantee he'll print it."

My cell went off with a number I didn't recognize, and for some strange reason, I answered. Bad idea! The familiar voice on the other end let me have it. "Listen up, you fucking asswipe, we had a fucking deal, so you better put all that sanctimonious bullshit behind you and write one hell of a review for tomorrow's paper."

"Glenn, how do you know I'm not recording this call?"

"You're not recording it. You're too dumb to even think about recording it."

"What do you want, Glenn? I'm trying to get some sleep."

"I'm not hanging up until you tell me you're writing a new review."

"The review's already written and sent."

"Not that one, the new one!"

"There is no new one and there never will be."

"Remember, asshole, you fuck with me, I fuck with you."

"Glenn, I'm just doing my job, which is to watch something, then write a few words about it using solely my opinion. Did you get that, *my* opinion? That's not fucking with anyone. It's called work. *Your* work is to memorize lines and say them for an audience. Whether or not you do your job well is up to you, hence a review. Now if you would like to publicly review my review, that's your prerogative; have at it. And if you call my review a flaming piece of shit, here's what I can guarantee you: I won't call you, threaten you, or bribe you. Because I'm a big boy, and I'm wearing my big-boy pants. So, eat shit and bark at the moon, for all I care, you talentless waste of space." And with that, I ended the call.

My fan base stared at me with bewilderment.

"Michael," Annie said "I didn't know you had that in you. That was... brave!"

"Hear, hear," Daphne said, "I move to formally induct Michael into the hefty-balls club!"

Lucy simply came over and gave me that sisterly hug of hers, the one she does so well, while Gabriel stared into space, doing

229

his best to avoid eye contact.

Black Coffee In Bed

I've aways wondered what it would be like to wake up with three women in my bed. I've pictured it many times, but never did the scenario include my sister. Oh well, you can't have everything.

It was just after seven when Annie's bed began to bounce around. I awoke to the sight of Annie holding a copy of the morning paper. To my right, Daphne, still in her colorful PJs, sat on the bed, and Lucy, wearing borrowed sweats, sat on my left. All three were jiggling the bed and acting giddy as I rubbed my eyes.

Without warning, Annie dropped down on top of me. "It's here!" she shouted. "The Sunday morning paper! The front page of the entertainment section has two stories—an interview with dickhead and a review of *Up the Junction*, by, in my opinion, the cutest reviewer in town, my boyfriend Michael Holland!"

After the cheering died down, I had only one thing to say. "Could someone please get me a cup of black coffee?"

Lucy jumped up. "On it."

"Who gets the honor of reading aloud to the others?" Annie asked. "Me, right? Thanks, everyone, for choosing me. I promise to do it justice."

Lucy came back and handed me a cup of steaming black coffee. I sat up, took a delicious sip, and prepared myself for the reading. Lucy and Daphne were still on the bed, and I spotted the outline of Gabriel in the doorway.

"First," Annie said, "I would like to state for the record that the forthcoming review by Michael Holland, does indeed include a photo." Ooh's and aahhhs filled the room as Annie showed off the picture. "This is Mr. Holland's first portrait to accompany one of his reviews, which means Mr. Holland has hit the big-time, at least for a day." Then she read the review word for word:

Up the Junction

A Review by Michael Holland

Up the Junction is the new play at The Adrienne Arsht Center in downtown Miami. It's here on a limited run before it heads north to the Great White Way. Most Broadway shows open outside of New York City because the producers like to preview it with an audience so they can tinker with it and iron the kinks out. I'd wager that with the help of some time and rewrites, *Up the Junction* should be ready for NYC in a few short years. Three, tops.

If I were the producer, I'd begin my improvements by assessing the players. I would throw them all out and recast every single role. Next, I'd order a total rewrite of the script, followed by the hiring of a new director, composing a new score, and overhauling the costumes. The ones they wore at my showing appeared to be left over from an early-aughts high school play with a low budget and too much parental involvement.

Up the Junction is intended to be a comedy. The definition of "comedy" goes something like this: Com-e-dy: 1. A noun meaning professional entertainment consisting of jokes and satirical sketches, intended to make an audience laugh. 2. A movie, play, or broadcast program intended to make an audience laugh.

The chief problem with *Up the Junction* is that neither definition applies. In fact, this mishmash of a production doesn't even hint at being a comedy, not once in its short but too-long run time. *Up the River Without a Paddle* might have been a more apt title. The play runs for just under two hours, clocking in at 1:52, to be exact. I felt that it could be trimmed by at least 111 minutes. The only moment that brought a smile to my face was when this embarrassment ended and a stagehand mercifully closed the curtain.

To say that the problem was with the story would be an injustice to the concept of story because there simply wasn't one. This reviewer finds it baffling that someone could actually write something so unintelligible and incoherent and pass it off as a play. Even more baffling is that others bought and produced this jumbled disaster. It boggles the mind that no one piped up, called Houston, and declared a problem.

Perhaps the acoustics were not in tip-top shape, but the beautiful and stately theater, which holds 2500 people, remained silent for most of the play's duration. Not a laugh, chuckle, or chortle to be heard as they were replaced by the occasional cough, mumbled criticism, or groan. Usually in a situation like this, my heart goes out to those responsible. I feel for them and wish them well. Because no one sets out to make a bad play, star in a bad movie, or write a bad book. So how do I explain this play? I can't, and I don't think the people who made it can either. It is pure junk from the opening scene until the final curtain.

Usually there is a standing ovation or at least a long round of applause after a new show. Performers come back out for a curtain call, taking an extra bow, or simply waving at the audience to thank them for attending, but not last night. Instead, I witnessed something that surprised even me: dead silence. Audience members glanced at each other, unsure what to say or do. Was it over? Had the story ended, and if so, what story? Were the actors returning to take a bow? And then it happened. Out they came one by one, the look on their faces saying it all. No one in The Adrienne Arsht Center was happy, not the audience and certainly not the cast.

The actors quickly sought refuge backstage, scurrying behind the curtain from which they'd emerged, eager to escape the critical eyes eating through them. It wasn't a hostile crowd, but perhaps hostility would have been preferable to the subdued and nearly comatose reaction from the theatergoers as they exited their rows and ambled, shoulders slumped and heads hung low, toward the lobby.

The beautiful and talented Angela Rothchild, who still shines and exudes class and elegance with every pore, seemed lost in her role as Ellen, the matriarch. She tried her utmost with what little she'd been given, but even her charisma and charm couldn't get the horse out of the barn. The stage has rarely seen such a talented actress as Miss. Rothchild, an actress with vast experience and versatile skills, but why she chose to waste her valuable time with this piece of utter detritus is beyond this reviewer's comprehension. Maybe one day the truth will reveal itself, and the world will know what wickedness trapped her and forced her to take part in a play so below her usual standards. If you are one of her many fans, *Up the Junction* is not for you. It will dim your heart and sour your perception of this gifted artist.

As for the male lead, we have action hero/movie star Glenn Difford dipping his toe back into the Broadway waters that are usually reserved for the great thespians of our time. He once again attempts to prove to the world that he is not just a movie star but an actor as well.

In his first stage foray two years ago, Mr. Difford chose a project that did not highlight his attributes, thus sending critics and theatergoers rushing to get refunds, if not for their ticket prices, at least for their time. The play closed quickly, and Mr. Difford returned to making shoot-'em ups. As Mr. Difford has aged and his fan base has dwindled, he is once again trying to expand his range, but as before, he has chosen poorly in colossal fashion.

When faced with such utter atrocity, this critic is forced to wonder if money might explain why certain people accept certain projects, but Mr. Difford likely has all the money he needs from his film career, so what could be the possible motivation to star in this rot?

To say that Mr. Difford brings nothing to the table would be an understatement because there is no table to bring anything to. *Up the Junction* is the equivalent of last night's fish dinner sitting on the curb so that the stench won't irritate anyone in proximity. It is simply the worst play I've ever had the displeasure of seeing. The only comfort I take in having wasted part of my life watching it is that I was paid to sit through it. But what little comfort that brings still can't compensate for the pain inflicted on my senses last night, starting with my eyes and ending with my ears.

My first thought upon leaving the theater was that I needed to demand a raise from the *Miami Herald* after being subjected to such drivel. But then I recalled how lucky I am that I am often paid to enjoy lovely works of art, outstanding plays, inspirational films, and extraordinary books. If only such had been the case last night.

To be one of the first to experience great art and feel such pleasure when doing so is magical, and I experience magic on a regular basis. Thus, complaining about my wasted time at the premiere performance *Up the Junction* seems futile. Instead, I will continue to do my job and inform you, the public, about wondrous productions and utter stinkers so that you can best decide how to use your time. As for this *Up The Whatever*— after watching it, no one will care what it's called—consider staying home, saving your money, and streaming something worthwhile. I boldly predict you'll thank me later.

Bored almost to death by another Glenn Difford play,
~Michael Holland

Slap and Tickle

"Well, Michael," Daphne said, "that was one hell of a slap and tickle for old Mr. Difford!"

"Well done, bro!" Lucy said. "You covered all the bases and did it with tact and dignity. I wonder how long they'll keep the play open before closing the doors for good."

"You handled that review like a champ, Michael," Annie said, kissing me on the cheek. "An honest champ."

"And it was definitely on the professional side," Gabriel added as he stepped in. "I still can't believe your boss published it. In his defense, it took a lot of you-know-what for him to let it go to print."

"Not to change the subject, but is there anything that anyone would like to do before I head out this afternoon?" Gabriel asked, sounding a little tired.

"I'd like to start off with a great big breakfast," Daphne said.

"You know, get all my calories in at once. I call it front-loading."

"I just call it breakfast," Gabriel said, exiting the room.

"Hey, Daphne," Annie said, "what's a slap and tickle?"

"Oh, it's an old one, goes way back. It sort of means that Michael slapped him in the face but did it with a smile."

"Perfect," Annie said.

"Okay," I said, "let's get this final eating show on the road, and then decide what we're going to do afterward." I wanted people out of Annie's room so I could get dressed. As far as clothes went, I didn't have much except for what Gabriel had given me. And of course, that's when Gabriel came back in with an assortment of clothes in his outstretched hands. Before I could say thanks, he was off. The outfit, to my surprise, was not all white. The shorts were off-white, and the shirt was pure Jimmy Buffett, with a parrot perched on the branch of a tree that faced the ocean. A blue sky and big waves filled out the rest of the shirt. Last but not least, he'd supplied a pair of gray Crocs.

Once I'd dressed, I looked like a cross between a tourist and a K-mart shopper, but I liked what I saw—a lot! Maybe after Gabriel was gone and I found a new job to replenish my bank account, I might do a little wardrobe shopping.

When I headed to the kitchen to show off my outfit, I realized Gabriel and I were wearing the same exact outfit. Everyone hooted and hollered. But even more surprising was that for the first time in a week, Gabriel wasn't wearing white! All three ladies wore summer slipover dresses, each colorful in their own way, but none that screamed, "Look at me!" like Gabriel's and my matching outfits did.

Sitting in its usual spot was the hourglass. The sand was eerily low and somehow that made it frightening. I gave Annie a kiss on the cheek and asked if we had decided on where to

236

indulge our bellies for our last breakfast together. Lucy said she had the perfect spot. "It's close and affordable, and the portions are something to write home about. Plus, there are three chefs, each one bringing their own magic to their part of meal. Gentlemen, welcome to Chez Annie's, home of the really big breakfast!"

"Are you kidding me?" I said. "You're going to cook us all breakfast?"

"Not just me. Annie and Daphne will be joining me in the kitchen, so please keep out."

"But how?" I asked.

"Annie and I snuck out early this morning and rounded up supplies. Now go relax and we'll call you in when everything is ready."

Slaughtered, Gutted, and Heartbroken

A half-hour later, Gabriel and I were called into the aromatic kitchen. Steam radiated from numerous places, adding to the decadent smells that dove deep down to our souls. It reminded me of a childhood breakfast on Christmas morning.

The girls put the last of their creations on the table, then we all sat and gazed at the feast before us. All the usual beverages were there, plus toast, English muffins, butter, assorted jellies, and peanut butter. I saw bacon, sausage, ham, and a platter of pancakes. The eggs were scrambled perfectly in a bowl that was as pretty as the eggs themselves.

But the thing that caught my eye and wouldn't let go was the large plate covered with an assortment of donuts—too many to describe. It almost looked too good, too professional, like something that Gabriel had magically conjured. Best of all, the smiles on the faces of the ladies said it all: happiness, pure unadulterated happiness. And shockingly, there wasn't any wine to be found on the table.

The food reminded me of the TV show *Survivor*, when the two tribes merge and they share a terrific feast before playing the game again, against each other.

At one point, Lucy asked Gabriel for his number so they could keep in touch, and she also asked him if he was on Facebook. He said that Facebook was too complicated and messy for him but that he'd certainly leave his number.

Daphne rose from her seat holding a glass of juice. "Hear ye, hear ye, I officially dub this wonderful breakfast of ours The Slaughtered, Gutted, and Heartbroken of breakfasts. Please raise your beverages and join me in this hearty salute to the feast which we are about to receive. Amen, brother, Amen."

Annie leaned closer to me and said, "She certainly has a way with words."

I nodded and then started to think about the hourglass sitting a few inches away from me.

While we stuffed our bellies and our faces, we shared memories of the fun and craziness we'd all endured during the past week. Lucy couldn't stop laughing after hearing about some of our escapades, surely wishing she had been there to have experienced it with us. Annie kept catching me staring at her, but she accepted it with a smile and an occasional wink, which I found terribly sexy. Then Annie took things a wee bit farther and let her fingers do the walking under the table. Getting my full— and I do mean full—attention, I slowly slid my chair closer to her, hoping that no one noticed.

Just as I reached the perfect position, Annie abruptly got up to clear the leftovers. But before she was out of sight, she turned back and gave me that seductive Annie smile, followed by her bedtime wink.

Letting Go

Later, on Annie's deck, I found Gabriel, who was definitely not acting like himself. It had to be due to that damn hourglass, which kept announcing itself with every drop of sand that fell to its base. I was also feeling out of sorts with the realization that time and contracts were racing toward a speedy conclusion. But my letting go of Annie was not in the cards, no matter who they had lined up for me. I wanted no part of that scenario. I just wanted Gabriel to go back to doing what he did—but with someone other than me.

Sure, I understood the whole thing about offending God, but He gave me free will, and I'd opted to exercise it. It was literally a God-given right, after all. Would I feel guilty if another woman got hurt by my actions? Of course. But that was never my intention, and I would do whatever it took to comfort her and explain things, emphasizing that it had nothing to do with her and everything to do with me finding true love on my own—the very thing I'd been waiting for my entire life.

Tapping Gabriel on the back, I said that we needed to talk. He turned around and gave me a hug that penetrated my bones. It was calm, reassuring, soothing, and loving. Serenity filled my entire body and made me feel as if I were floating, not too high but at least a few inches above the ground. I loved it!

"I know what you want to speak about, Michael, and I've already given it much thought. I have the best solution for you, for Annie, and for us all."

"Great! What have you got?"

"Fib, Michael, fib away. Lie your ass off and you'll be free—free to have Annie and for Annie to have you. If you lie, this will all be over. One stinking lie, and you and Annie can move on and avoid offending the boss."

"That's your big idea? Lie? And then we all go on our merry way?"

"Yes. It's a win-win for us all because—trust me—you don't want to piss off the big guy, Ever."

"But then what? We live with ourselves based on a lie, a misconception in how we chose to move forward? It's deceitful, and I'm shocked you would even consider it."

"But it only need be a little white lie, one that would hardly be held against you. We angels call it a white audible, and this one would be for the greater good."

"Whose greater good?"

"All of ours."

"What about… her?"

"Who?"

"The one I'm supposed to meet later this afternoon, my soul mate extraordinaire."

He waved away my concerns. "Eh, don't let yourself get caught up in all that. It will work itself out."

"How, exactly?"

"I don't know, but it will."

"What's the old saying, Gabriel? The devil's in the details? Isn't that how it goes? Let me take it a step further and quote Jimmy, if you don't mind: 'Questions are the easy part, it's the answers that raise the doubt.'"

Gabriel looked like he'd been hit by a train. For the first time, he had nothing to say. He turned and looked out into the woods, keeping his thoughts to himself.

It's Over

I went back inside and found all traces of breakfast gone and shimmy-shined. Daphne was practically bouncing up and down with excitement.

"So, what's it gonna be? Where are we going and what are we doing for our last morning? I say we go out with a bang."

Gabriel cleared his throat as he entered through Annie's sliders. "Before we decide, Michael and I have some unfinished business to discuss."

"Do we? Thought our business had found its own conclusion," I said.

"Okay, Michael," Gabriel said, "but tell me, are you sure you want to deal with the repercussions of your decision?"

"Are you threatening me?"

"Of course not. It's just that for every action, there's a reaction, and there are no guarantees that the reaction will be pleasant."

I pondered for a tense moment as I envisioned an eternity of fire and brimstone. "Gabriel, isn't there another way that I could end you-know and walk away without a trace of responsibility?"

"If you're thinking what I'm thinking you're thinking, don't do it. You'll regret it."

"Why not? It solves all your problems, just like your other idea would have."

"No! Your way is different. Do not do it."

I grinned defiantly and turned away from him. "Everyone, I

think that proper introductions are in order. Let's all take off our masks, shall we?"

"Careful Michael, careful."

All eyes fell on Gabriel as the tension mounted. But then my cell rang, and damn if it wasn't my boss again. Or should I say ex-boss?

Picking Up the Pieces

"Yes, Chris, what can I do for you?" I said into the phone.

"First, you can stop with the fucking attitude. Let me tell you something. You're a king idiot, throwing your job away over something as insignificant as a Glenn Difford play review. These fucking actors aren't worth it, do you hear me? Now I've spent the whole night picking up the pieces, and it was not easy. All you had to do was tell a little white lie and everything would have been hunky-dory, but no, you had to go all Sir Galahad on me and take the high road. Can you at least be honest with me now and tell me *why* you couldn't throw me the Bogart that we'd agreed on."

"In a word, conscience."

"Conscience? What kind of fucking answer is that? It's not even a real thing."

"For some of us, it is."

"And that's it? That's all you got for me? Conscience?"

"It's all any of us have for guidance anymore, isn't it, Chris? Otherwise, we're left with anarchy."

"What the hell?"

"Let me explain. Conscience is the key to keeping us all on the right track. What if I walked into a store and saw something

242

I liked but didn't have the money to pay for it? What if I just took it and walked out? And than what if everyone started doing the same? Where would we be then? Up shit's creek, that's where. But a conscience stops the bulk of us from doing that."

"But a skewed review isn't exactly stealing, is it?"

"Okay, what if I decided one day that I wanted your wife or wanted to tarnish your reputation or just be a nasty piece of work to everyone I encountered. Anything can be accomplished if you put your mind to it, right? But it's that little voice in the back of my head that keeps me in line, that stops me from fucking up and helps me choose the right path. Keeps me safe from myself, in a way."

He sighed. "You hear that, Michael? It's the sound of me clapping over here. I'm touched, really I am, but I also don't give a flying fuck about your conscience. Let's go back. Like I said in the beginning, you showed some guts with this review, and that's what got me thinking last night. Aren't you the least bit curious why I published your review? You must have wondered when you opened the paper and saw your ugly mug staring back at you as you rang up the death knell for *Up the Junction*."

"I figured you had a sudden bout of guilt, you know, as if your conscience directed you."

"Ha, no way. It's because I like you. Bottom line, I just fuckin' like you and I'd miss your ugly mug around the office, so consider yourself rehired. I've even got a few things to give you to apologize for what I did, so come to my office tomorrow and we'll iron everything out. Are we cool?"

"Thanks, Chris, but I need a little time to think about it."

"Are you pulling my fucking chain?"

"Just give me one minute and I'll call you right back, okay?"

"I'll give you two. After that, don't bother calling back."

Tears for Attention

I was in shock when I hung up the phone, and my audience, who had overheard most of the conversation, was right there with me. Lucy jumped into my arms and gave me the big-sister hug. "I knew they'd never really fire you! I'm so happy for you."

Annie came over and rubbed my back. "Sounds like you can move out of Chez Annie now that you can afford to refurnish your place. But don't be in any rush. In fact, I'd love to help you redecorate because your place needed a woman's touch here and there."

Throughout, Gabriel stayed silent in the corner. I watched him watching me until he suddenly pointed to the hourglass on the table. The top half had run out of sand! Nothing left, not a single grain.

Gabriel then shook his head, and I had no idea what it meant.

"So, Michael," Annie said, "why did you tell Chris you needed time to think about keeping your job? Don't you want to go back to writing for the *Herald*?

"I do, but I don't want them to know that. Besides, I've got an idea."

"Oh boy," Lucy said, "here comes trouble."

"We'll see," I said. I slipped out to the patio and called Chris, who answered on the first ring.

"Well?" he spat out.

"I've got conditions, Chris."

"Oh shit, here we go."

Robert Remail

By Your Side

"I'd like to take a look inside my file, if you don't mind," I said to Gabriel as we strolled around the pool area. I had asked him to take a walk with me after my phone call with Chris.

"But I do mind, and so does the boss."

"Would you say it's a rule?"

"Yes."

"But aren't rules meant to be broken?"

"Not always, and I'm not doing it."

"Why?"

"I've already told you it's not happening. Not now, not later, never. Why do you want to see it anyway?"

"I'd like to know what kind of guy I actually am."

"Don't you know that already?"

"Maybe, but I want to see how I'm perceived by someone else, someone like, let's say, God."

"Oh, I see. Well, that's interesting, but I'm not showing you the file. That said, I can share that God likes you."

"Doesn't He like everybody?"

"Pretty much."

"Then where does that leave me?"

"Right where you should be."

"Can't you give me something? Something to hang on to?"

"Look at this way. God liked you enough to answer your prayer, and that's a rare honor."

"So, I don't have anything to worry about then?"

He shrugged. "What happens from here on out is up to you. I can't see your future, nor would I share it with you if I could."

"So, I guess this thing is going ahead then, huh? Since the hourglass ran out, and I kept my end of the bargain?"

245

"It would seem so."

"Will God be there?"

"God is always there, Michael."

"What will happen exactly? Where will we be?"

"Slow down, Sir Lancelot. I'll be by your side the whole time, and I'll see you through this mess that you plan to create for yourself. I just wish that I could talk some kind of sense into you before you make this humongous mistake."

"If you can't see the future, how can you be so sure it's a mistake?"

"Well, it's been my experience that decisions such as yours usually lead to problems, to say the least."

"I'm a grown man, Gabriel, and I plan to take my free will out for a spin."

"Do what you will. I've done my best."

"I know I'm going to hate myself for asking this, but what would Jimmy do if he were in my shoes?"

"Ah, I thought you might ask me that very question, so I came prepared. Jimmy would say, Pour me something tall and strong, make it a hurricane, for I go insane."

"Yep, I hate myself now."

Gabriel chuckled.

"Okay, one more thing," I said. "Any chance I could get a look at Annie's file, just for a couple minutes?"

Gabriel gave me a surprised look, then pulled a very solemn face. "You know what? Why not? You've put up with so much this past week, and my presence became quite a burden on you. So, I will let you take the quickest of glimpses into Annie's past so you can assess if she's up to your standards."

"Really? That's great!"

"Hell no! I can't believe you even asked such a stupid

question." He shook his head and strolled on.

Hard to Find

We got back to Annie's a few minutes later and found it empty. Gabriel wandered to the wine counter and examined a bottle as if he were some type of inspector.

"Something wrong?" I asked.

"Just wondering if it's too early for a small glass of the grapes?"

"Go for it. Why not?"

"I like your logic, Michael." He uncorked the bottle.

"Hey, how come you're not wearing white today? It's the first time I've seen you without head-to-toe white."

"What's your point?"

"I haven't got one. Just curious."

"Well, don't be."

I called Annie's cell, then Lucy's, but no luck. "Hm, that's strange."

"Maybe they're out doing girl stuff or buying me a farewell gift." He sipped his wine before continuing. "It's getting close now, Michael. Time for the all the chips to be cashed and all bets settled. Are you nervous? Because I am."

"Why are you nervous. You're about to say no thank you to God. Hey God, turns out I didn't need you as much as I thought, but have a great day and thanks for coming down! How does that sound?"

"Better to say nothing at all, perhaps."

"One more quick question. Does God hold grudges, and if so, for how long?"

"Let's see, last time He got ticked off, He stewed over it for two millennia, give or take a decade."

"Damn!"

"A question for you, my dear Michael. Will you miss me when I'm gone?"

"You know, I haven't had much chance to think about it, but—"

"Don't worry, I understand. I'm not offended in the slightest. I only bring it up because I will miss you. In fact, I will miss you terribly. I've met so many people here, but as I mentioned before, you are one of my favorites."

"Not number one, though?"

"Don't push it. There's a guy from Pittsburgh dying to move up on my list. And he's only one spot below you."

"Are you allowed to come back for a visit?" I asked hopefully.

"No, unfortunately, although I am allowed to check on you once in a while. For example, I can review your file and see what you've been up to. And occasionally I'm allowed to peek in at the live action."

"Uh oh. Like what?"

"Well, picture a crystal ball like when the Wicked Witch watches Dorothy in *The Wizard of Oz*."

"And what if you tune it in at an inappropriate moment?"

He clapped his hands together and grinned. "Then lucky me! Or if that bothers you, just don't do anything inappropriate ever again."

Nirvana

The hourglass still sat empty atop the leather-bound book on Annie's kitchen island. Without the sand traveling through it anymore, it just seemed like an artifact from the past—my past.

But the book still intrigued me. It almost seemed to be calling my name, drawing me in, and demanding that I open it to see what wonders it held. I stepped toward it, and when I was inches away, it called to me again, like a far-off voice whispering my name.

My fingers reached for it. I could see them as they made their way to the book, moving in slow motion. But then the voice grew louder.

I touched the book, grazing my fingertips against its smooth, worn leather, and that's when I felt a small electric current run through my hand. And it didn't stop there. It continued up my arm, then surged through my entire body. Not painfully—in fact, quite the opposite. It was a feeling I didn't want to end.

"Michael," Gabriel said from behind me, "it's time."

His voice broke my concentration and my physical contact with the book. But immediately, I wanted that feeling back. I wanted to grab hold of it, press it against my heart, and never let go. It had been pure Nirvana.

"Come, Michael. This is what you've been waiting for, and regardless of what happens in the next few minutes, know that I'm here for you, no matter how bad it gets."

"Stop already with the 'bad' stuff. Let's just pray that all goes well. But then again, that's how I got into this mess, isn't it? By praying." The thought stymied me for a moment, but then the doorbell rang and brought me immediately back to the present.

Gabriel and I glanced at each other, then we both turned our heads toward the door. I quickly wondered where Annie, Lucy, and Daphne could be, but then realized it was probably a good thing they weren't here.

The doorbell rang again.

"Aren't you going to get that, Michael?"

"Aren't you?"

"It's not for me, it tolls for thee."

"Thought you couldn't see the future."

"Are we going to start that again? Really? Now let's go. If you keep the boss waiting, it's a bad reflection on me."

The doorbell rang for the third time.

If It's Love

The door answered itself. Because whoever had been doing the ringing had grown impatient and decided to just come on in. My heart raced, and judging by Gabriel's perspiration and rapid breathing, he was suffering a similar malady.

I certainly never expected this scene to take place in Annie's living room. I'd pictured a beach, a garden, or a deep forest, someplace with a tropical theme, birds, flowers, you name it. But now it was showtime, and here I was in Annie's home. My legs began to shake, and my hands followed because, hell, it's not every day that God drops by to fulfill a prayer.

With that thought, my brain did the Indianapolis 500 at warp speed, and I thought I might faint—or vomit! Do people do that in the presence of God? Which was worse?

And then my brain came to a violent crashing stop, one that nearly knocked me out of my shoes. I'd been going full speed forward and now I'd hit a brick wall with such force that it propelled me instantly back to reality and the present moment. Because before me stood Annie. And Annie looked like an Angel.

She wore a beautiful formal white dress, not a wedding gown but just as perfect. It clung to her sides and had turned her into a flawless hourglass. On her feet were three-inch white heels and in her hair was a bow the color of white cream. She was followed by Daphne, also dressed in all white, but not nearly as stunningly as Annie. Daphne's smile was contagious and soon Gabriel also smiled like a proud father.

I couldn't make sense of any of it, but I'd never felt happier. Finally, I blurted out, "Is anyone going to tell me what's going on?"

Gabriel put his arm around me. "My boy, my boy, your time has come and not a moment too soon, I might add."

"I second that," Daphne said. "Not sure I could have gone through another day of all that tomfoolery. I was getting such a headache." Then she glanced toward Gabriel's half-empty wine glass. "No, no, no, Gabriel. You said you were done last night, vacation over, no more wine."

"Yes, dear Daphne, I do remember what I said, and I meant it at the time, but vacation isn't over if we're still here, is it?"

"Technically, that's true, Gabe, but come on, you're dragging it out worse than the last two times."

"Not true! Napoleon had just freed Paris and *everyone* was celebrating in the streets. Wine was free and plentiful, and I couldn't help it if someone handed me a bottle and said, à votre santé, monsieur!"

"Excuses, excuses, my dear old friend."

"Please, someone," I said, "please tell me what in the name of love is going on here."

"Precisely, Michael—love," Gabriel said. "If it is indeed love, but you two have to tell us to be sure."

"I'm so lost."

"Make up your mind, Michael. Love or hell?"

"What?" I shouted.

"Leave them alone, Gabriel," Daphne said, smiling. "They've had enough of us, don't you think? Or at least of you.

"So, you two know each other," I said. "Like really know each other."

Gabriel glanced at Daphne. "Catches on fast, doesn't he?"

I Learnt How To Pray

Annie came over and took my hand. "Michael, I'd like to introduce you to my friend, Daphne. She is my favorite lady angel."

"I'm a little surprised you didn't catch on," Daphne said, "seeing that you had one of your own for the past week."

I spun to Annie. "Wait, are you an angel too? Because honestly, you sure look like one."

"Nope, I'm just ordinary Annie."

"There's nothing ordinary about you," I said. "Nothing at all. In fact, I think you're the most special person I've ever had the privilege of knowing."

"Aw, shucks," she said, grabbing ahold of me.

"I'm still foggy on everything, though," I said.

"After I was divorced from my wicked ex, I prayed to God and asked him for the true love of one man—a fine and deserving man. Someone I could love without holding anything back. Someone I could look up to and respect, who would make me proud, comfort me, walk with me through thick and thin, care about what I had to say, and love me. And that's you, Michael. It's you."

"This is beyond my wildest dreams, truly. But I gotta know"—I lowered my voice—"is God here?"

Gabriel pointed up. "Upstairs."

"In Annie's bedroom?"

"No, Michael. In heaven. Be real, what would God be doing in Annie's bedroom?"

"I thought He was going to present me with my one true love." I gestured to Annie. "And here she is."

"Hm, I don't remember ever telling you that God Himself was taking time out of his chaotic day to hook you up with a chick."

Daphne looked over at Annie. "He's always had a way with words—and the ladies."

"Oh, don't listen to her," Gabriel said. "She's just jealous, always has been. It goes back to the Boston Tea Party. She wanted to join in and dress up like an Indian, like the rest of the Patriots, but I told her it wasn't the right thing to do. And at the time, I felt strongly that I was in the right. But then there was the day we were drinking in the streets of Paris after Napoleon set it free, and I confessed to Daphne that I'd been wrong and should have let her dress up and take part in the tea party thing. But I should have kept my angelic mouth shut because she's never let me forget it."

"Oh, please," Daphne said. "You bring it up more than I do."

"Rubbish! You bring it up every time you get the chance."

"Take that back, Gabriel, right now."

"I will not."

"Man," I said, "you two are like an old married couple. How

long have you known each other?"

"We go back at least, let me see here…" Gabriel said.

"You're asking him?" Daphne said. "That's like asking Don Juan how many girls he's kissed."

"Well, I'm impressed that you two went an entire week without pulling each other's hair out."

"That's because under all this bickering," Gabriel said, "we feel nothing but love for one another, right, Daphne?"

"I guess I'll second that. Seeing that we are an old married couple! Can't believe neither of you put two and three together to come up with the fact that Gabriel and I are one—in a married sense that is."

"Wait a minute," I said, "then you've been married more than once, Gabriel?"

"No just the one time."

"But what about Laurel?"

"Ah, yes, let me explain. In Greece, it's pronounced Laurel, but in other parts of the world, Laurel translates to Daphne." He gestured toward his angelic wife with a beaming smile. "Everyone, meet the missus—my darling wife and the best friend a man could ever have." Then, with a quick turn and a graceful swoop, he took Daphne in his arms and kissed her long and tenderly.

Every Story

We all sat down, although Daphne soon got up to pace as she explained things. "Michael, as you know, you prayed to God for true love, as did Annie. And here's the cool part: God listened and took action, answering both your prayers. Of course, the fact

254

that you two fit together perfectly helped."

"So you came to hook Annie up with me, and Gabriel came to hook me up with Annie?"

"Right on the money, Michael," Gabriel said while sipping his wine.

"In heaven, we like to say that every story has a happy ending, and this is your happy ending," Daphne said.

I turned to Annie. "What conditions did you have to meet so you could be introduced to me?"

Annie looked confused. "No conditions. I just had to wait. Daphne said that that she would need a week to get you and me on the same page."

Gabriel averted his eyes as I glared at him. "Really?" I said. "No conditions? No promises? Nothing like that?"

"Not a single thing. Why?"

"Because dear old Gabriel there said I had to go a week without lying in order to get my prayer answered."

"Michael," Gabriel said, "it was for your own good. It helped establish the ideal relationship between the two of you, don't you see that?"

My BS detector went off, but then again, maybe he was right.

"Gabriel does that all the time," Daphne said, sighing and shaking her head. "I would like to apologize on his behalf. He doesn't mean any harm; he just does it for fun. Now, if I may continue? It was Gabriel's job to tell you that your prayers were being answered and to then introduce you to Annie, after which he was supposed to split and go on vacation, which is what he is technically on now. I was to do the same because, let me tell you, angeling can be stressful!

"When angels go on leave, we can go wherever with whomever, so Gabriel and I decided to have a little fun with our assignments as we occasionally do, and you two were our assignments. Yes, sometimes we do just drop and go, but other times we stick around, like we did with you two. Seriously, take it as a compliment because we only do that with the interesting people we get assigned to."

Annie and I glanced at each other and smiled like the two interesting people we were.

"And now," Daphne continued, "we're at the end of our vacay, so we must say goodbye to you lovely people." She grimaced. "I do hope we haven't done any irreversible damage to either of you by perhaps overstaying our welcome."

"Not at all," Annie said, waving away Daphne's concern.

"I've still got a question," I said, turning to Annie. "Did you know that Gabriel was an angel—my angel, in fact?"

"Not a clue! I just figured he was some drunken friend of yours who'd be gone in a week."

"Okay, then," I said, shifting my attention to Gabriel, "your turn."

"Gosh, what can I add to this fine stew?" Gabriel said. "I thought Daphne summed it all up beautifully. Brava, Daphne, brava!"

"How about an apology or two—or three?" I said.

Gabriel pulled a blank face. "For what?"

"For lying, perpetrating a hoax, and numerous other offenses."

"I'm afraid you've lost me, Michael."

"Well, what about God?"

"Oh, He's just fine. I'm sure He'll be happy to hear you were asking about Him."

"What about when you said on day one that I couldn't tell a lie for one week?"

"Made it up."

"And what about my soul mate coming here—the one that was personally chosen by God?"

He pointed to Annie. "As promised."

"But you recently told me it was someone else!"

"Made that up too."

"And all the stuff about me offending God?"

"Made it up, made it up, made it up." He sipped his wine and let out a satisfied exhale.

Break My Heart

"You know, Gabriel," I said, pacing now, "I haven't slept in days because of you."

"Have you tried sleeping aids?"

"I was so worried about possibly breaking Annie's heart that I nearly went insane."

"You were worried about breaking my heart?" Annie said. "Oh, that is so sweet of you, but why were you worried about it?"

"Because this clown told me I needed to get rid of you because God was supplying me with someone else, and when I said no to that, he said it would be a slap in the face to God."

"I was just playing," Gabriel said. "I am on vacation, after all. Plus, no harm, no foul. Let's toast on, shall we?"

"No!" the girls and I said together.

"I think you're all acting cagey."

Annie took both of my hands and looked directly into my watery eyes. "The way I see this is simple. You loved me so much that you were willing to turn down a gift from God in order to keep me, is that right?"

"Yes," I said softly.

"Why? Why would you do that for me when we've only known each other a week?"

"I've known you my whole life, Annie. We just didn't meet physically until a week ago. I've been trying to find you since the day I was born, and now that I have, there is no way I'm letting you go."

"Told you he was one of a kind, didn't I?" Daphne said. "I only wish I could stick around long enough to go the wedding."

"What wedding?" I asked.

"Oh, don't you worry about that just yet, Michael," Daphne said. "Take some time to digest all that's happened. The wedding talk can come later."

My eyes doubled in size but I knew enough to keep my mouth shut.

"Our work is done here, my sweet Daphne," Gabriel said. "Another feather in our caps."

"We're the best, Gabe."

"Hey, how come she's allowed to call you Gabe and I'm not?" I said.

"Daphne has known me for ages, Michael. You've only known me for a week. And besides, she's the wife."

"Fair enough, fair enough. By the way, where is Lucy?"

"We have her running some errands," Daphne said. "We didn't want to have this talk in her presence. Rules are rules."

"Wait, you mean I can never tell Lucy about any of this?"

"Sorry, Michael, that's a definite no. I hope you understand."

Daphne grabbed Annie and asked her to help her get ready to leave. "We've got to go, Gabe. Time to gather your things." Then she headed to the spare room.

Heaven

Instead of gathering his things, Gabriel poured me a glass of red wine and made a toast. "To new friends!" We clinked. "Salud!" Then he polished off the remainder of his wine in one gulp.

"Is this it for us, then?" I asked.

"Afraid so, my dear friend."

"So I'll never see you again?"

"Correct. That would be a rulebreaker."

"Although you do seem to be one who enjoys breaking the rules."

"I've been known to have the occasional adventure or pick up a glass once in a while, but rulebreaker, no. I am an angel, after all. It's what I do—and sometimes I'm even good at it."

"Did you have to go to angel school or anything like that?"

"No such thing."

"Then how does it work."

"Like anything else. You start at the bottom and work your way up, though I sort of skipped to the front of the line." He winked, and it was delightful. "Let's just say I had a connection with management and got a little special attention."

"To answer your earlier question, Gabriel, I am definitely going to miss you. Life won't be the same."

"That's what they all say, but in a few weeks, you'll hardly have time to think about an old angel who occasionally over imbibed."

"You did say there's wine in heaven?"

"Most definitely, but I don't indulge like this unless I'm on vacation."

"I can't believe you chose to spend your vacation here with

me, causing trouble and mayhem."

"Believe it or not, it was tremendous fun."

"How hard was it to convince Daphne to join in?"

"Not too difficult. I've convinced her a few times to go along with my childish side. And she's always been one to—how do I put it?—acquiesce to my many charms."

"I have an idea. Can you hang out another minute?"

"As sure as Bob's your uncle."

I ran to the kitchen and grabbed the half-full bottle of red wine, then I hurried back to fill Gabriel's glass to the brim. "Here you go."

"That's a rather generous pour, but thank you."

As he went to take a sip, I stopped him. "Wait! Here's what I want. I want you to chug the whole glass as fast as you can."

"But wine is not meant to be chugged, Michael. It's meant to be savored and enjoyed."

"Yeah, keep telling yourself that. Now please, just do this one last thing for me. Chug!"

"Fine." He lifted the glass to his lips and drank it in one long sip. When he finished, he placed it on the table and burped.

"Okay, Gabriel, as fast as you can, close your eyes and tell me the answers to these questions. Is there food in heaven?

"Yes."

"Are we young or old in heaven?"

"Young."

"Does everyone get a pair of wings?"

"No."

"Is heaven the same or different for everyone?"

"Different."

"Do we get to meet God?"

"Yes."

"More than once?"

"Yes."

"Do we get to see old friends and loved ones?"

"Yes."

"Do we have jobs in heaven?"

"Yes. And No."

"Is heaven forever?"

"Yes."

"Does everyone get in?"

"No."

"Am I getting in?"

Gabriel opened one eye and looked at me. "Asshole." Then he shut the eye and waited for the next question.

"Is there also a bad place, located in, shall we say, the basement?"

"Yes."

"Do a lot of people end up there?"

"Yes."

"Will I end up there?"

Gabriel did the one-eye thing again, then closed it quickly.

"Okay, strike the last question. Does God love me?"

Gabriel opened both eyes, smiled widely, and stood to give me his angelic bear hug. "Yes, Michael, God loves you more than you'll ever know." He broke away and tilted his head. "Now it's about that time, I'm afraid."

He left my side and went to find Daphne.

Final Score

Annie had a very high ceiling in her living room, and when I reentered after tidying up the patio, I heard Daphne regaling the others with a typical Daphne story. "It was the second of December in 1804, and it was as cold as cold can be. Napoleon's damn coronation at Notre Dame lasted for three hours, and if it weren't for all the free wine flowing in the streets of Île de la Cite at the mouth of the Seine, I would have been bored out of my wits.

"Did I mention that it was colder than a witch's tit? But the wine kept everyone from heading home, plus they were handing out food like there was no tomorrow. And Napoleon's outfit—can we talk? It was so regal and stunning, and I saw it from only a few feet away. And then—Gabriel, who was that young couple we were with?"

"Sorry, Daph, can't remember. I have trouble remembering one hundred years ago, let alone two."

"Well, anyway, someone gets the great idea of firing off the small cannons in front of the cathedral, and before you know it, cannon fire is blasting over our heads like we were at the Battle of Waterloo. But you can't kill an angel, right, Gabe?"

Gabriel gave her a thumbs-up.

"But the couple we were with were our responsibility, just like you two are right now. And if they got killed by a stray cannon fire, it wouldn't look good on our weekly report, let alone our permanent records. So needless to say, we had to be careful with them."

"You know what I told that couple when the cannons began to fire?" Gabriel said, not waiting for a response. "Never forget to duck, which, in a weird twist of time, ended up being a Jimmy lyric!"

"Anyway," Daphne continued, "we got those two lovebirds away from that shindig as fast as we could. Gabriel wanted to fly them out, but I was like, 'No way, no how. Too many witnesses.' So, we led them out as quickly as we could. And you know what? They had a wonderful life together."

"Hold up!" I said. "Did you say you wanted to fly them out?"

"I thought it best," Gabriel said.

"But you could have?"

"Sure," Daphne said, shrugging her shoulders.

"Then you two must have wings."

"Told you he was a smart one, Daph," Gabriel said, pouring himself yet more wine.

"Please!" Annie said. "You've got to show us those wings!"

"Oh, I'm afraid not," Gabriel said. "I've got to put my foot down on that one, dear Annie."

"But why not?" I said.

"Yeah," Daphne said. "Why not? Let them see our wings." She smiled a glowing smile, and Gabriel sighed and shrugged in resignation.

"Okay, okay." He rose from the couch, placed his wine on the coffee table, and stepped a few feet away.

Daphne stood by his side and gave him a gentle but loving peck on the cheek. "Ready?"

"Play on, my dear, play on."

Suddenly, they both started growing tiny wings on their backs. A popping sound filled the room as their wings came through their clothing. And as their wings grew, so did their smiles. When their wings were finally done sprouting, I gaped and Annie gasped. The wings were stark white, each pair in perfect proportion to their owner. Gabriel's were thirty inches wide and at least four feet long. Daphne's were smaller but just as awe-inspiring.

And then the darn things started to flutter. At first, I thought it was my imagination, but Annie and I both witnessed two beautiful angels decked out with gorgeous fluttering white wings, who then lifted off the ground and began to fly!

They ascended to Annie's ceiling, the one I mentioned was so high, then they moved right and left and gracefully circled each other. It was beyond magical and well worth every minute of pain and suffering that Gabriel had inflicted upon me. It was payday, bonus day, and Christmas morning all rolled into one.

My jaw remained slack, Annie remained speechless, and Lucy, who had just entered unexpectedly through Annie's front door, screamed in a way I didn't know she was capable of. She dropped the bags in her hands and fell to the floor. Then she covered her eyes and tried to block the image of her two friends flying around the room. When she finally dared a peek, it was just in time to see Daphne and Gabriel landing on the floor.

"May I ask," she muttered, "why winged people are flying around Annie's living room?"

Annie rushed over to comfort her. "It's okay, Lucy. It's all good. It's just that Daphne and Gabriel are, well, angels."

I joined Annie and my sister.

"Like from heaven?" Lucy said. "Sent by God?"

"You got it," I said.

"But what does God want with me?"

"Nothing. They were here for Annie and me. To fix us up, you know, like Cupid."

"Oh, okay," She stood up, quickly regaining her composure. "So, God doesn't want anything to do with me? Just you guys?"

Daphne appeared and put an arm around Lucy. "God wants and loves everyone, and trust me, he definitely wants and loves you. But this week, we were here to help Annie and your brother. They're soul mates, meant to be together.'"

Lucy swallowed and turned immediately practical. "How come nobody told me? Why wasn't I informed about you angel people?"

"We'll let your brother fill you in after we leave," Daphne said, turning to Gabriel. "Which it's time to do. You ready, Gabriel?"

"As ready as I'll ever be."

The Very First Dance

"Not just yet!" I declared. "No one is going anywhere until I say so."

"Sorry, Michael," Gabriel said, "but it doesn't quite work that way."

"Tell me, Gabe, old buddy, when do you technically report back to work?"

"Eight tomorrow morning. Same as Daphne."

"And how long does it take you to get from here to there?"

Gabriel snapped his fingers. "Like that."

"Then we're off. Everyone, pack up and follow me."

"But we're done. It's time for us to go."

"That's where your wrong," I said, "because I'm not done with you and Annie isn't done with Daphne." I shot my sister a knowing look. "Lucy, you're coming too, of course, but remember, what happens on earth, stays on earth."

"Got it. I'm in." I turned to the angels. "Grab your angel gear and let's rock. My car, five minutes."

"Any chance of telling us your plans?" Gabriel said, seeming a tad grouchy.

"Let me see. How about… no! But here is your one and only

hint: Annie and I get the first dance—Annie with Gabriel, and me with Daphne. And that's all you get. To the car!"

Paradise Coast Sports Complex was an easy drive, considering the car had five people stuffed inside, four of whom had no idea where I was headed. Annie sat next to me, pretty as could be, and Gabriel seemed extra-grouchy, probably because he was the one who usually suggested our adventures.

It did cross my mind that I was stone-cold broke, but I shoved my financial concerns to the back of my mind and let them go. Then I turned into the stadium, feeling damn heroic because I wasn't doing any of this for me. I was doing it for someone else, someone who could not possibly see this coming.

But far better to give than to receive, right? In my opinion, truer words were never spoken.

Out on the Dance Floor

And there we were, third row center, dancing our asses off. We were moving and grooving to the sounds of the one and only Mr. Jimmy Buffett. And who knew that I knew so many of his songs? Apparently, I'd always been a fan, but I just hadn't realized it.

Our seats put us right in the middle of the action. Plus, it's one thing seeing Jimmy, but it's another seeing him from only a few feet away! Lucy, Annie, and Daphne danced like crazy to "Too Drunk to Karaoke," and Gabriel was happier than I'd ever seen him. He knew the words to every song and was more than happy to show off his vocal talents with each one.

To no one's surprise, it took minimal encouragement to get Gabriel dancing in the aisles. He had the crowd cheering as he danced his way into their hearts during "The Devil I Know." I'm not positive, but I think he was a few inches off the ground as he swayed and spun, waving his arms, and singing at the top of his lungs.

Daphne gave me multiple fist bumps and mouthed the words "thank you" more than once. Money well spent, I thought, but then I remembered that it was my boss who got us the tickets. It was my one condition for going back to work at the *Herald*. Thanks, Chris!

Gabriel was suddenly up and standing on his chair, hooting, and hollering with the best of them. I only wished he was wearing one of his white outfits. I'm not sure why, but they'd grown on me. Still, it was perfect that he was decked out in what I'd earlier thought of as a Jimmy-inspired outfit.

When Jimmy took his final bow, Gabriel started jumping up and down, telling anyone who would listen that he knew what the encores would be. I'll tell you what, that angel went three for three—and he got them in order.

Jimmy ended with "He Went To Paris," followed by "Fins," and closed the show with "Down at the Lah De Dah." I expected the lights to come on with an announcement that Jimmy had left the building, but then I remembered that that was impossible.

Discipline

Gabriel had no desire to leave the stadium, saying he wanted to savor every moment and get every inch out of the night. He just stood there and stared at the stage in awe, as if willing Jimmy back out for one more song. But it was not to be.

I finally told Gabriel that traffic was going to be a bitch, and we needed every available second to get the hell out of there or we'd be stuck for hours. But after he relented, the crowds had already swelled, and it appeared that everyone had the same idea.

"Don't worry," I told Annie as she grabbed my arm. "There's a door up on the right that lets you out to the parking lot in case of emergency. We're not supposed to use it, but if we don't get caught, we're good."

"How do you know about this door, Michael?" Gabriel said as we approached security door number 15.

"I'm a critic, a reviewer extraordinaire. I've been through a thousand doors, some secret, some not so secret, so have faith and I'll get you to the parking lot before you can say, Desdemona's Building a Rocketship."

Gabriel laughed aloud. "He's catching on. That's a Jimmy song."

I opened the door and immediately heard, "Stop right there!"

Standing in front of us were two burly security guards. "This area is off limits. Please turn around and head back in the direction you came from."

I reached into my back pocket and showed them a piece of paper that had an official stamp on it. The bigger guard looked closely at it, counted us, and nodded. "Okay, second door on the left. Enjoy."

I led the gang to the second door on the left, peeking behind me to see their stunned faces.

We passed through a long, dimly hit hallway that led to a door with bold letters across it: Backstage. I pulled on it and found it locked. A lump the size of NYC formed in my stomach, and the lump had a mind of its own. It wanted to rise up and out of my mouth. Then it occurred to me to bang on the door. So, I did—

twice and very hard.

It took only a second before the door opened with two more burly guards. I showed them my stamped paper and we were waved inside to a noisy, brightly lit room the size of a wedding hall. A hundred people milled about, and Jimmy Buffett music played in background. On the left was a royal food spread including everything from lobster tails to cheeseburgers. There were desserts and snacks from every part of the food spectrum, and along the opposite wall sat three bars. Heaven!

The attendees at this shindig seemed to run the gamut from hippies and politicians to grandparents, young adults, surfer dudes, and businessmen—not to mention movie stars. All were waiting for a chance to meet the short man in the center of the room, Jimmy Buffett himself. To say he was sweaty would be an understatement, but he had a jovial smile and eyes that stayed with whomever he spoke to. That said, he definitely drew the attention of everyone at once.

What would it possibly be like to hold that kind of power over people? Would it be a curse to be on 24/7 and never let your guard down? Would you feel like you owed these people something because they came to see you? Because they buy your records and keep you in margaritas?

The more I thought about it, the more I realized it might be a curse—a weight you could never put down. I pictured a young unknown with a dream to become the biggest and the best before realizing what that meant. I pictured Elvis on his bathroom floor at forty-two years old—same age as me now—alone and deceased at two o'clock on a Tuesday afternoon. If he could have seen that image of himself beforehand, would he have done something different? Lived a different life? Or would have shrugged and figured that's the price you pay for wanting it all—

and getting it.

At least Jimmy seemed to have it all figured out. He still made new music, performed, and smiled the whole time, despite being well into his seventies. But how? Why wasn't he on some bathroom floor or overdosed in some hotel room? What made him different? And then there were also the plane crashes or tour bus accidents that claimed so many performers, or cars that were driven too fast and recklessly by those who had made it.

Was discipline the answer? Or was it pure luck? Maybe a combo of both.

Happy Days

When Gabriel spotted Jimmy speaking to one of the Coral Reefers, he practically fainted. It took a full minute for him to regain his composure before he looked at me with shock and newfound respect. "Michael, how did you do this?"

"I learned a little magic from a friend of mine who's been staying with me the last few days."

"I can't believe this. It's like a miracle."

"Just a small one for you, Gabriel, just a small one. Let's call it your going-away present from Annie and me. It's our way of saying thanks for everything you and Daphne did for us." I gestured to Jimmy. "Now come on. Grow a pair and go say hello to your pal, Bubba."

"You know his nickname!"

I nodded, and a tear ran down Gabriel's cheek. Then, as he took his first step in Jimmy's direction, I grabbed him and pulled him back. "One more thing, Gabriel, how do I say thank you to the big guy for bestowing a gift to a lackey like me, who wasn't even worthy to receive it? Because there have got to be many people more deserving than me to receive God's attention and blessing. Any advice?"

"Of course. Just relax. You've already thanked him because he just heard everything you said."

"How?"

"Not your concern. Just know that he hears you and loves you. And as far as love not being important enough for God to lend a helping hand, what could be more important than love? It makes the world go round. It keeps us happy, makes us get out of bed in the morning, and spurs us to move forward. It drives each and every one of us as we either pursue it or strive to hold onto it once we have it. Not to sound sappy, but love is the breath of life. It's why humans help strangers and put others before themselves, even if it's just for a minute at a time. And what's greater than that? Without love, there's only chaos and confusion, crime, and injustice, evil and wickedness, all running amok. Love is not to be taken lightly."

"Okay, but still—"

"You want to know why you were singled out?" Gabriel shrugged. "That's for you to ask when your time comes to meet Him."

"Still can't believe I'll get to meet Him one day."

"You will, Michael, and it will be divine."

I reached out and hugged my angel. And my angel hugged me right back. I'd delayed Gabriel so long with my question that Annie and Daphne had made it to the front of the line and were chatting Jimmy up. I patted Gabriel on the back and gave him a gentle shove. "Now get over there and enjoy the moment!"

I would love to say Gabriel flew over, but it was more of a glide. Then he reached out and took Jimmy's hand while flashing that Gabriel smile, the one that lit up his face and charmed anyone lucky enough to see it.

"Son of a bitch!" a too-familiar voice said from a distance. I turned to my left and spotted Rose a few feet away. She was talking to a handsome member of Jimmy's band, The Coral Reefers.

I grinned and ambled over. "Hey, Rose, what on earth are you doing here?"

"Same as you, obviously, Michael. If I didn't know better, I'd say you've got a thing for me, always showing up in my shadow the way you do. Hard to believe it's all coincidence, isn't it?"

Then she suddenly seemed to remember that she'd been in a conversation with a Coral Reefer. She apologized to him and introduced him to me as Jimmy's drummer. We shook hands, and he promptly made an excuse to depart.

Rose turned to me with a playful scowl. "See that, Michael? You drove off another one. Subconsciously, you must want me single so I'm always available for you."

"I'll say this, Rose. If I didn't keep running into you, I think I'd be disappointed. You bring a smile to my face every time I see you."

Rose's smile erased any signs of her scowl. "Thank you, Michael. That's kind of you to say. So does that new girl of yours have any single male friends who might be looking for a special someone?"

I cocked my head and nodded. "You know what? That's a stunning idea. I'm sure that between Annie and me, we could come up with someone."

"You'd better," she said, stepping closer to me. "Otherwise, I'll haunt you forever."

"Forever is a long time, Rose."

272

She closed the distance between us, kissed me sweetly on the cheek, then spun and disappeared into the crowd. Before I could even peruse my mental list of single friends who might be a match for Rose, Lucy sidled up and interlaced her arm with mine. She rested her head on my shoulder and pointed to Gabriel, who was regaling Jimmy with his tales. I'd heard that Jimmy was a great raconteur himself, but he'd probably never met someone like Gabriel, who had thousands of years' worth of anecdotes to share.

"Is he really an angel or is this some kind of dream?" Lucy said.

"He's really an angel, and for the last week, he was my angel."

Later, after Gabriel had hogged Jimmy for a full hour—without Jimmy seeming to mind at all—the five of us stood alongside my car and relived Gabriel's encounter with Jimmy, amazed at how the angel had enraptured and entertained the man who had entertained him for so long. We laughed and hung out for so long that it seemed as if no one had anything else to do. But that wasn't true. In fact, for two of us, it was way past the time of departure.

No Place Like Home

"Are you sure you can't stay one more night? I can get my hands on one fine-ass cabernet—and I'll even pay."

"Sorry, Michael, but it's past time to go, unfortunately."

Daphne came up alongside Gabriel. "Michael, there's no place like home, and whenever I go back, I'm at my happiest. But leaving all of you here will tug at my heart like never before.

And you know that I say what I mean and mean what I say." She embraced me then with love that sizzled calmly through my bones. Then she turned to Annie. "Annie, I treasured every second we spent together. You are up there with the top one hundred people I've helped!"

Annie looked confused. "Is that a good thing?"

Gabriel stepped in. "Yes, sweet Annie, that's a very good thing." He then wrapped his arms around Annie too, and the two angels rocked her for what seemed like a small eternity.

After they both said goodbye to Lucy and thanked her for all she had done to make their stay a fun one, Lucy smiled and wiped away tears.

Gabriel grabbed both my shoulders and kissed me on both cheeks, slowly and with great affection. "I'll never forget you, Michael."

"Never is a long time, Gabriel."

"Don't I know it!" he said with a wink and a smile. "Take care of our sweet Annie, and don't give up on Jimmy. He will grow on you more each time you listen to him. And lastly, in case I bend a rule now and again, always keep a bottle of the good stuff tucked away in your home. You never know when an old friend with a heavenly thirst might stop by."

Gabriel and Daphne stepped back a few feet and sprouted their wings. Even though I'd seen it already, it still knocked my socks off watching their wings pop through their clothing and achieve perfection.

Gabriel and Daphne began a slow wave, then simply faded away, slowly becoming part of the air until they were no longer visible.

I glanced around. There were thousands of people still in the vicinity, but not a single one was staring in our direction. It was as if we weren't even there.

All's Well

Lucy informed us on our drive home that she really needed to get back to her life, so I dropped her off at her car, which was parked in front of Annie's. We said our goodbyes with both words and hugs, and when she was finally gone, I turned to Annie. "Now what, sweet Annie?"

"Who are you?" she asked with a puzzled look.

For the second time in the last few hours, my heart sank. Then I pulled Annie close and gave her a slight shake. "Annie, you okay? Annie!"

"Why are you touching me?"

"Annie, it's me, Michael."

"Michael who?"

"Michael Holland, your soul mate, that's who."

"Soulmate? Ha! There's no such thing. Next, you'll be telling me we were introduced by angels."

I leaned in close and looked at her hard in the eyes. "Damn you, girl."

"Gotcha, didn't I?" she said, roaring with laughter.

Oh man, what had I gotten myself into?

Then we got back in the car and I pulled up to my place. "Here is to the start of something beautiful," I said, leaning over to kiss her softly on her red lips.

"Now that was worth waiting for, Michael."

I repeated the process and then made my way down her neck, taking the long way and avoiding all shortcuts. Annie moved her body in a captivating rhythm and started breathing heavier before finally pulling away. "Why are we at your place? You don't have any furniture, and I think we kind of need some. Like right now."

I glanced at my place, a bit surprised. "Hm, habit, I guess. Let's head to yours."

I put the car in reverse but stopped suddenly as I noticed a huge white bow attached to my front door. It was the brightest white I'd ever seen.

Annie followed my gaze, and the two of us got out of the car. As we approached the door, I spotted a sparkling envelope attached to the bow. As I tore it open and wondered who it was from, a small voice called out in the back of my brain. "Gabriel, you idiot."

I read the card aloud. "Terribly sorry for the mess I made of your life during the past week. With love from your friend and favorite drinking buddy, Gabriel."

"No way," Annie said, reaching for the doorknob. As she opened it, I was hit with the scent of vanilla, an aroma I loved. And it was a creamy kind of French vanilla, my absolute favorite. Then we slowly entered.

"Wow!" I shouted. My place was completely restored, back to exactly how it was before Gabriel had ever stepped foot in it. On my kitchen counter sat a second card, but it was leaning against a bottle of Opus One. A few inches to its right sat the hourglass and the leather-bound book.

Annie reached for the book and I went for the hourglass, our hands touching on the way. But a quick jolt of electricity made us both stop. We looked at each other, shrugged, then proceeded to examine the gifts left by Gabriel.

The hourglass felt heavy, even though it was just a few inches in height, and surprisingly warm. I realized that during Gabriel's entire visit, I'd never held it before. I turned it upside down to watch the sand flow, then I returned it to its upright position. Meanwhile, Annie flipped through the pages of the book.

"You going to keep me in suspense?" I said.

Annie turned to me with wide eyes and spoke in a soft voice. "It's a Bible, Michael, his own personal Bible. There's an inscription inside for you."

"What does it say?"

"'To my dearest Michael, Thank you for being such a good friend to me this past week. I meant it when I said that I'll never forget you and Annie. She's a fine girl, and you're lucky to have her. If you always remember that and treat her the way you want her to treat you, then you will both be truly blessed and happy for all your days to come. Please cherish this book as I have; it's got some milage on it, but its message is not lost, nor shall it ever be. ~Gabe'"

Annie opened the card leaning against the Opus One and read it aloud. "'If you look around, I think you'll find everything in your home as it was before I—and my zaniness—arrived at your door. You'll also be delighted to find that your bank account is at the exact amount it was before our initial encounter at the marina. Your credit cards have been reactivated, and you may even find that nary a one of them currently carries a balance. Sorry again for the headaches and the angina. Your hungover angel, Gabriel.'"

The End

Acknowledgments

I'd like to thank my wife, Colleen, who has sportingly promised to buy a copy of this book. I'd also like to thank all of you who purchased a copy of my first two novels, *Better Days* and *The Diary of Dusty Fisher*. To my astonishment, both books were purchased by people who hailed from far and wide, including Australia, France, and England, to name a few. Some copies even traveled through time, reaching folks I hadn't spoken to since grade school. Imagine hearing the voice of someone you haven't spoken to in over forty years calling to congratulate you or simply wish you well. Last but certainly not least, thanks to a special friend who helped me out with this book. She remains nameless only because she prefers it that way, but without her there would be no *Once Upon a Drunken Angel*, so thank you from the bottom of my heart, my literary ANGEL!

About the Author

Robert Remail spent most of his life in Point Pleasant, New Jersey, After retiring from a career in construction, he and his wife moved to Southport, North Carolina, where he dabbles in film, swims till he turns blue, and attempts to stay out of the pickleball kitchen with his wonderful neighbors.

Robert is the author of *Better Days*, a dark romantic tale of second-chance love, and *The Diary of Dusty Fisher*, a country music story of reinvention and romance. Currently at work on his next novel, he loves to hear from readers. Feel free to connect with him on his Facebook Fan Page: Robert Remail Books

Made in the USA
Columbia, SC
10 October 2023

24218216R00171